M000207512

A WESTHAMPTON BEACH
Christmas

A TouchPoint Romance
An East Coast Love Series® Novel

ROBERT BABIRAD

A WESTHAMPTON BEACH CHRISTMAS
A TouchPoint Romance East Coast Love Series® Novel
By Robert Babirad
Published by TouchPoint Romance
a TouchPoint Press imprint
Brookland, AR 72417
www.touchpointpress.com

Copyright © 2021 Robert Babirad
All rights reserved.

ISBN: 978-1-956851-03-8

This book is a work of fiction. References to real people, events,
establishments, organizations, brands, or locales are intended only to provide a
sense of authenticity and are used fictitiously. All other characters, and all
incidents and dialogue, are drawn from the author's imagination and are not to
be construed as real.

Except for review purposes, the reproduction of this book, in whole or part,
electronically or mechanically, constitutes a copyright violation. Address
permissions and review inquiries to media@touchpointpress.com.

Editor: Paige Ripperger
Cover Design: ColbieMyles.com
Cover image: Sweet couple kissing in front of a Christmas tree by Merla (Shutterstock)

Connect with the author on Facebook @robertbabiradauthor

First Edition

Printed in the United States of America.

Dedication

For my sister, author and poetess Christie Leigh Babirad, who has always encouraged me to continue writing.

For my family who, in the words of Robin Leach, have always believed in my "champagne wishes and caviar dreams."

CHAPTER 1

There were secrets in every city and sometimes Christmas even helped with discovering them. Some of those secrets were known only to one person. Others were restricted to a select group of locals. However, some remained available to anyone who decided to seek them out. A single secret revealed could lead to something as significant as a change in destiny. Others might be as simple as the revealing of a quiet place in a crowded city.

The city of New York developed its own frenetic and rarified energy as the holiday season approached. Tourists arrived in great numbers to experience its distinct atmosphere at Christmas. It was a moment in the year unlike any other. It was also a unique time when having a secret place to get away from it all became even more special and significant to those in the know.

Marcos was in a secret place this afternoon. He walked through the double glass doors that led outside. There was a meeting approaching shortly. Right now, he needed some air. The art deco building behind him rose up unimpeded by any other structure or object into the steel grey sky. Green space on the rooftop stretched out beyond the doors and across the rooftop. This space wasn't open to tourists or the public. In a way, it was a secret.

Today it also proved to be secluded with respect to those who could otherwise access it.

The natural area up there still surprised him. It was so unusual. Amid New York City's concrete was a hidden and relatively inaccessible rooftop garden that was thriving.

There was a water feature, topiaries, trees, pathways, and a lush green lawn with a few small tables and chairs. Winter was approaching, and the trees within the roof garden's purview had already shed their leaves. The fragrant and colorful flowers that lined the garden pathways were no more. However, a winter garden had a magic all its own. This was especially true of a rooftop one in the heart of New York City at Christmastime. Marcos was able to fully take in the emergence of Christmas in the city below from the privacy of that rooftop winter garden.

He put his half-finished coffee and croissant down on the table and walked past the reflecting pool and out to the edge of the garden. The city at Christmastime lay below him, and it was a panorama only available from a secretive spot high above the city such as this.

This felt different from standing at the top of the Empire State Building. It was caged up there on the viewing level. That was how most tourists saw the city from above. This Rockefeller Center rooftop view was unique, freer, different, and much more open. *I want more freeness and openness in my life*, thought Marcos. He was trapped in a job that no longer held any joy for him and working each day in a city that was rattling his nerves and patience a little more with each passing day.

Who wanted to go through the process of applying for another job and all of the tedious bureaucratic motions that such an act would involve? he thought, looking out at everyone bustling on the streets down below him. He didn't want to be a part of that bustle or hurriedness any longer. Marcos sometimes thought about looking elsewhere, but always in the end decided against it. How could he sit at a desk again while some young, eager, and ambitious go-getter asked him leading questions that were purposefully designed to get him to slip and say something that would give them a reason to move on to the next candidate in their pile? He even hated the word candidate that they used in their "screening process." It all felt full of politics, insincerity, and deceit.

He wasn't going to apply for a job ever again if he could help it. He'd work here until he could retire, even if that meant hating his job now and for every day to come. It was the only option. Going for something different involved too much aggravation that he didn't want to deal with any longer. *It's a young person's game,* he thought to himself, looking out over the city again. It's not that he wasn't young. He still was, but there was a degree of naivete and trusting with youth, particularly those who were of college-age. They still felt ready to take on the world. At that age, one could sometimes still buy into what other people said to some degree. Often, one could still put up with what Marcos typically referred to as "the bullshit of it all."

With time and experience, it had become harder and harder to buy into the way that other people, often less qualified people in his opinion, told one to think or how it had to be. He had spent so much of his life in New York. Did he have the strength or patience at this point to build something new elsewhere? *At twenty-one, I was ready to go anywhere and do anything. Now, I still have dreams and hopes, but they're my dreams, not those of a company, government, or another person. I can't buy into those so-called "vision statements" that others come up with for me any longer.* He struggled with all of those emotions that morning as he stood there in the rooftop garden high above Rockefeller Center.

At that very moment, he felt the very real sensation of being caged in. It was related to that feeling which tourists experienced when looking out from the viewing platform at the top of the Empire State Building. However, they would ultimately be leaving their voluntary cage. High-speed elevators would soon whisk them down to the street level after their viewing and picture-taking moment at the summit of the building. Marcos would be stuck in his cage until the end of the day and then return there again tomorrow morning and for every working day going forward.

This feeling, though, was something much darker. It was the sensation of not being able to escape from a situation or that of not having the ability to freely leave at any given moment. It was the absence of having free will and that made him uncomfortable. He supposed that many people felt like that in their jobs, but that didn't make the sensation any better. The caged feeling was not even directly connected with where he was now in the rooftop garden. Instead, it was a haunting and overhanging premonition of what he would soon have to face inside the building behind him within the space of a mere few minutes.

Marcos shivered. *It's pretty cold up here too actually.* Of course, the cold was to be expected with the harsh near-winter winds coming in off the water and a temperature that was rapidly dropping. Manhattan was after all an island and very much surrounded by open water. He felt the cold of the city both physically and metaphorically. Marcos drew his coat a little tighter around him. Then he adjusted the scarf again that he had put on only fifteen minutes ago.

It felt special though, up there above Rockefeller Center. The rooftop garden was between Forty-Ninth and Fiftieth Street. Fifth Avenue was out in front. This made it the perfect place to look out over the city. St. Patrick's Cathedral itself and its two twin towers were now directly in front of him on Fifth Avenue. He continued looking out at the emerging spectacle below and savored his remaining minutes outdoors.

Wreaths, garlands, and lights were being strung everywhere. The city was beginning to embrace the Christmas season. Even the energy felt different now. Yes, it was still frantic. However, there was also a touch of hopeful optimism. That positivity wasn't always readily available on-demand at other times of the year. The traffic below moved in a continued steady stream.

Crowds of people drifted about hurriedly on the congested streets. Many carried shopping bags. Some had children. This vantage point made them all look like rapidly moving ants along a busy thoroughfare.

He remembered his first time in New York. It had been with his family at Christmastime. The experience had been magical. The city had been so different from all that he had known growing up in the rural bluegrass country of Kentucky. He had been to Louisville on numerous occasions while growing up. It was a city that certainly had its fair share of big buildings and urban sprawl. However, New York was a place incomparable in scope, personality, and environment. It wasn't the same as the feelings and sensations that he had experienced on those early trips to Louisville. At that time, it was the biggest city he had ever visited. Louisville indeed was the largest city in Kentucky. New York was vastly larger, more populated, and just being there filled one with a sense of the surreal and at the same time a feeling of possibility.

On that first trip to the city at Christmas, decorations, music, cold weather, and all of the Christmas shows created a New York that was a touch more hopeful. It wasn't much different from the New York that he presently inhabited. Of course, now it was years later since that first trip. Marcos worked there every day. A place that was once exotic had become his everyday experience. This kind of transition had a way of changing how one felt about a place and viewed it. New York had once been something distant, something glimpsed at when one was on vacation, and something that was unique and unattainable. He had now attained a life based in New York. It was a life he had once dreamed of having while living in Kentucky. It was also a life that now caused him to no longer be as optimistic, joyful, or to feel as warmly toward the city as he once had. However, Christmas brought those early positive feelings about the city back to him once more. Christmas made New York a different place and a better one.

Marcos looked out again in a different direction. He could now see the angels in the Channel Gardens below. The approach of Christmas had brought them back. Their gold trumpets appeared to jut out triumphantly and in a manner that had them seemingly strategically fixated toward the iconic Christmas tree. The famous tree had also now been turned on with the passing of Thanksgiving. A brightly illuminated star sparkled high above the gold statue of Prometheus and the famous ice rink below.

The tourists below still looked busy and endless as they moved through Rockefeller Center. Marcos remembered how excited they seemed when he passed them on his way into the office earlier. They were taking photos of everyone and everything. Selfies simply didn't exist on his first trip into the city years ago. Now, they were everywhere. Everyone had to document themselves beside every landmark. New York certainly had no shortage of landmarks. These provided the additional and, perhaps for most people, the more important benefit of making for good photo opportunities. That documentation requirement also demanded that those same photos be absolutely perfect for social media purposes. Perfect meant sometimes holding up others with one's own numerous retakes. Making those same photos look spontaneous on the third retake was an additional challenge. It also created a particularly tense situation when others were waiting to take their own photos behind you in an already overcrowded holiday environment. Marcos was glad that he was up there watching, rather than taking part in the chaos down below. Soon enough, he'd have to face his own unique form of chaos.

The doors on the other side of the rooftop lawn suddenly opened. A young woman with brown hair in a high-end (but ready to wear) blue pantsuit called out. "They're ready for you now." The silence was broken in an instant.

"I'm coming," responded Marcos walking back over to the table. He finished the remainder of the croissant and coffee quickly with a single bite and a large sip. It was time to face whatever was coming next.

CHAPTER 2

The hallway was long and lined with framed pictures on both sides. Each photograph was a metaphorical trophy. Each reflected a successful commercial building project by the firm. There were certainly a lot of them. However, that was not on his mind today. Marcos was looking forward to Christmas. He needed the time off and the feeling of being at home again. Home would still be in the city this year, not back in Kentucky where he had been raised. It still meant a break from work and being at home, even in the city, was a respite from the daily grind at the office. He couldn't believe though how many meetings were still being scheduled. There was one after another leading up to the holidays. Maybe the firm wanted to make their numbers before the coming new year. It was hard to say.

The interior of the commercial real estate developer's office where he worked was devoid of holiday charm. Well, that wasn't exactly true. There was a small and dilapidated plastic Christmas tree on the table where the clients waited. It sat next to an outdated pile of magazines. An administrative assistant had made a weak attempt to hang a garland across the doorway. The private offices were beyond that same doorway. Christmas didn't seem to be encouraged beyond that point.

Marcos continued down the hallway. He felt treated like an outsider and oftentimes a child in those offices. It was akin to a summoning to the principal's office. The disobedient student still had to report to a higher (and sometimes punishing) authority figure even after all of the years put in at this prestigious New York City firm. The numbers hadn't been reached this quarter. He knew that. It was probably the subject matter of the meeting, at least partially.

Sheila was the principal of the firm. She was already seated in the conference room with his coworker, Monique. Brad from accounting was there as well, and a few new and unrecognizable faces. They were probably clients or investors who had come to take part in the meeting. It would have something to do with whatever project they were a part of with the firm. Marcos was in no hurry to find out.

Sheila pushed a piece of paper down the table toward him and began immediately. "The Hamptons are a competitive market. We want to create value through a new commercial property purchase and development project. Ultimately, we are looking to build a modern, state-of-the-art, upscale retail site. The square footage should be enough for a few retail establishments and dining. You can see what our client is looking for in the document I gave you. We also want the project to be specifically located in Westhampton Beach."

She pointed toward the paper. Marcos looked thoughtfully at the figures and expectations. He began to say, "It's going to be a challenge to find that much available land near any village in the Hamptons. Then, there are all of the zoning regulations with the town. . ."

Sheila interrupted him. "This is a joint venture. We have a partner who we're going to be working with on the project." Her face contorted itself into a grimace. "The bottom line is that there needs to be a Purchase and Sale Agreement in my office before the new year." After a moment she continued. "If not, you probably shouldn't bother showing up here on January second."

Marcos glanced around the table anxiously. No one was coming to his aid. He didn't expect anyone to.

When you swam with the sharks, everyone was about their own self-interest and survival. In high school, teachers and counselors had told him to never be afraid to ask for help. They had said it was a sign of strength. In the nastiness of his day-to-day world, he knew that asking for help was one of the worst things that one could do. Sheila in particular viewed any sort of request for help or assistance as a sign of weakness. Weakness publicly displayed in that office lead to a frenzy of feeding and bloodlust among the other hungry sharks around him at each and every conference table or meeting. When there was blood in the water, no one was going to come back and ask why or what happened. They were just going to keep swimming and looking out for number one.

He had learned that lesson well and many times over throughout all of the years that he had spent working in this very competitive office.

Marcos gathered his breath. "But I've been one of this company's highest income producers."

Exasperated, Sheila pounded a fist onto the table. "It doesn't matter. It's what you've done today or better yet, now. That's all I care about. You're not getting any younger and maybe it's just that you can't keep up any longer."

"I'll deliver, don't you worry," said Marcos. He wasn't going to show weakness. He had to appear confident even if he didn't feel that way.

Sheila stood up. "I have nothing more to say and you don't, either. So if that's it, I have an appointment in Bensonhurst. I have to get going." With that, Sheila quickly got up from her executive office chair at the head of the table. She grabbed her bag and hurried out of the room with a secretary dashing behind her.

Marcos left the room also and went down the hall. He entered a door on the left leading into the employee lounge.

"Damn it," he said under his breath. "There goes the entire Christmas season. I was going to relax and enjoy the break. Now, I have to make that awful trip out to eastern Long Island. Then, I need to spend the next four weeks hunting around for commercial investment properties."

Monique came in a short while later and was the only other person besides Sheila and Brad who he recognized in the conference room. She walked over to him. "That's a bad break you got there, Marcos."

He sat at the table lost in his thoughts. "Oh, sorry, Monique. I wasn't paying attention. Yeah, that wasn't good news at all. Now the entire holiday season is finished for me."

Monique smiled. "But seriously, Marcos, spending Christmas in the Hamptons isn't the worst thing in the world that could happen."

"I had plans, Monique. I was going to stay here in the city. You know how dead everything is out there in the winter. That whole place revolves around the summer season. That's when all of the wealthy people and celebrities from the city go out to their mansions on the beach. The last thing I want to do right now is make that long trip. Spending weeks hunting around for properties in the freezing cold with everything closed down is not my idea of fun."

"I get it," said Monique. Marcos was still troubled by something that he wasn't talking about. She could tell. "What's bothering you? I know you too well, Marcos, and I know that you've got something else on your mind."

Marcos looked forward silently at the usually bare white wall in front of him. A tacky framed landscape print had been added recently to the center of it. It did little to actually improve the view or employee morale. "You know that comment about me not getting any younger . . ."

Monique nodded knowingly. "I heard that. That was harsh." She paused for a moment before continuing. "But you know that's how a lot of these companies operate, Marcos."

"I'm very much aware, Monique. Believe me, I am."

Monique frowned thinking about how everyone was getting older. She also knew what that statement in the conference room really meant for all of them. No one was safe from aging or the actions that a heartless company might take against them on a whim.

She continued. "They're always looking to make people who have been at the company a long time redundant. You know that, Marcos. They lay someone off who is older and then they replace them right away with someone young, eager, right out of college, and desperate for a job at half the price."

Marcos laughed. "You know, you're not helping Monique."

"I'm trying. I'm really trying," she replied.

Marcos paused and then after a moment said, "And what do you mean about someone older? I'm only in my late thirties."

Monique laughed out loud knowingly. "Neither one of us is twenty-one or twenty-five, Marcos. We might as well accept it."

She paused and looked back at him. "And neither one of us cares enough like someone who is twenty-one or twenty-five about whatever the hell this week's mission or vision statement is."

Marcos and Monique both laughed at her last statement.

"This is really turning into some awful Christmas already," answered Marcos in a frustrated tone as he continued to think about what had just taken place. He was looking at the already late hour on his Patek watch and noticed that the sun was beginning to set outside the single large window in the employee lounge.

"Well, I better get going too," said Monique picking up her papers off the table. She looked back at him one last time before walking out the door. "You know, Marcos, it might turn out better than you think."

"I hope so, Monique. I really do," he responded.

CHAPTER 3

The phone continued to ring persistently. Christmas music filled the spacious luxury apartment in Park Slope, Brooklyn. Monique stared intensely at the screen of her computer. *Gift cards for everyone this year,* she decided with finality after having spent the last hour drifting from one website to another. Last year a foul event had occurred. An ungrateful niece had been the recipient of a very well-thought-out gift that Monique had spent days agonizing over and then finally choosing. That same gift had then been "regifted" to another member of the family. Monique found out when she saw her original gift sitting conspicuously in the new recipient's home only a month after Christmas when she visited. No, that wasn't going to happen this time. She would get gift cards for everyone this year and be done with it.

The phone continued to ring. Whoever was calling didn't seem to be getting the message. She got up from the computer, crossed the room, and answered.

"Monique, it's me, Marcos," said a voice on the other end.

Monique answered gruffly. "Did you ever think that I might be busy and maybe you should try again later?"

"I know, Monique. I'm sorry. It's just kind of urgent."

"Well then, on with it. What is it, Marcos?" she replied, still looking at the gift card options on her computer screen.

"I need to find a place on short notice for four weeks out near Westhampton Beach."

Monique practically laughed out loud. "And you think I'm the one who can help you with this? Do you have any other outrageous requests or special wishes today, Marcos? Maybe a winning lottery ticket, your own personal unicorn, or a home with a helicopter pad that I can somehow accommodate you with?"

"That's not funny," answered Marcos jokingly, even though secretly he did kind of find her response a bit humorous. Of course, his request was pretty ridiculous in the first place and he was very much internally aware of that fact. "It's just that you know how hard it is to get anything in the Hamptons at a reasonable price. It's even more difficult on short notice."

"Marcos, you do know that there's no such thing as advertised Hamptons real estate that is 'reasonable' based on your standards, don't you? They don't even use that word out there," answered Monique.

Marcos knew she was right. The Hamptons, like other luxury real estate markets, liked to keep their prices sky-high, so it was kind of a ridiculous request to begin with. "Well, I just need somewhere that can be my base for four weeks. I need just enough time to hunt around for commercial investment properties and secure the deal for Sheila."

Monique seemed to be thinking. "Well, it didn't sound good in there. In fact, I don't think you're going to still have a job if we don't see to it that you succeed with bringing in a Purchase and Sale Agreement at some point during the holiday season. I think that would be the best Christmas or New Year's present you could give her right now."

Marcos was touched by the kindness in her words. "So, you do kind of like having me there in the office after all?"

"I definitely didn't say that," replied Monique in a jokingly indignant tone. She added, "I guess . . . maybe I just feel a little bad for you, Marcos. And . . ."

"Yes, Monique?"

"Well, I might be in a position to help you out."

"Now, that's what I'm talking about," exclaimed Marcos. He could barely contain his excitement. He knew that Monique would know someone out there who could help. She was the only shark in the water who would swim back to help him out in that office. Additionally, Monique was always attending various parties and real estate functions out east and seemed to be in the know about a lot of the people and events that took place in the Hamptons, particularly during the summer months. "Let me call a friend. I can't promise you anything, Marcos, but let me check into a few things."

"I'd be so grateful to you, Monique."

Monique was in a hurry now and wanted to wrap up her Christmas gift ordering by finally purchasing the gift cards that she had decided upon. "I know, I know. Listen, I have to finish ordering some gift cards. After I'm done, I'll make a few calls and get back to you."

"Thank you, Monique. I'd be forever in your debt if you could help me out with this."

"You'd be forever in debt, period, if you had to pay full price for a rental out there," replied Monique, laughing.

"That's very true, Monique. Very true." They ended the call and Monique went back to her computer and ordered the Christmas gift cards.

"Merry, merry something or other," she said grumpily under her breath as she pressed the checkout icon with her mouse.

4 hours later. . . .

A single warm light emanated from the thirty-fourth floor of a condo in the now cold and wintry gray landscape of lower Manhattan. Marcos was sitting at his desk working on paperwork that he had brought home when the phone rang.

"Marcos?" It was Monique. "I have some good news for you."

Marcos was surprised. He hadn't expected to even hear back from her in the same day. "That's great, what is it?" he asked questioningly.

Monique paused for a moment on the line. "Well, I don't know what you stepped in this week, but you have hit the jackpot this time."

"You're kidding me?"

"Nope, not at all. I have a dear friend who is actually going away shortly but happens to own a home right on the ocean in Westhampton Beach."

"Really? That must be an incredible home," responded Marcos, shocked at what he was hearing.

Monique paused. "It most definitely is. It's five bedrooms, four baths, and very contemporary. It's really beautiful. I've been to a few parties at the home."

"It does sound impressive," replied Marcos.

"Believe me, it is. There's an infinity-edge saltwater gunite pool, magnificent grounds that go right to the ocean, and so much else. It's all very modern and stunning. There's even private beach access."

Marcos was in complete disbelief. "That does sound incredible," he replied.

Monique continued. "Well, the owner was telling me how during the summer season, the house rents for somewhere in the neighborhood between seventy-five to one-hundred thousand dollars for one month."

Marcos went silent in utter shock. "You're kidding?"

"No, I am most definitely not. There are houses in the Hamptons and even a few I can think of offhand in Colorado that rent for even more. Anyway, they are willing to let you have it for four weeks for the rent that you would pay for a modest apartment here in the city. The owners are going abroad, and I told them you're a close friend and trusted associate from work." Monique then told Marcos in a hushed whisper the number for four weeks.

"That's unbelievable! Monique, I don't even know how to thank you for this," exclaimed Marcos excitedly.

Monique pushed the compliment aside. "Really, it's nothing, Marcos. You're a dear friend. I'm glad I could help. I do ask one thing of you, though."

"What's that?" replied Marcos.

"Well, you know how I love a good party. So, if you can get me invited to some of those fancy Christmas parties out there, I'd be a very happy individual this holiday season. I'm sure that there are bound to be at least a few taking place now and especially in the coming weeks."

Marcos laughed. "I most definitely will, Monique. However, I think you're the one who could much more effectively get me invited."

Monique gave an audible sigh. "Maybe so, Marcos. Regardless, you're bound to have a Christmas unlike any other. You'll be in the Hamptons and staying in an incredible home at what is always a magical time of year."

CHAPTER 4

A rural ambiance quickly sets in after a short drive to certain areas just outside of Westhampton Beach Village. It was here that Dani's family had established a small French bistro. It was no more than a mile away from the village and all of the summer activity that took place there. However, its unique location made it feel separated and a world away. The building itself was a picturesque red brick structure with a row of street-facing French front doors. A blue and white color scheme on the doors and columns that acted as partitions were complimented by a delicate lunette above each of them.

There was a small seating area in front of the doors that were separated from the road by a low blue retaining wall. Here there were tables and chairs and a standing outdoor heat lamp to keep the diners comfortable when the temperature began to drop with the approach of fall. A series of potted arborvitaes kept prying eyes off of both locals and celebrities who might stop in to dine alfresco. The wait staff wore white shirts and red vests and prided themselves on delivering impeccable service and artisanal meals to their guests.

Behind the bistro sat four acres of land carved out of the expanse of scrub pine forest. Here Dani grew mostly grapes along with fresh fruits and vegetables. These were all then harvested. Everything served at the bistro was very much in keeping with the farm-to-table ideal. Although the fields behind the bistro were now fallow with the approaching winter, they still held a beauty all their own. There was a wonderful sense of openness along with the occasional bird swooping down to gather whatever fruit and vegetable remainders might still be hidden within them. Picturesque rows of neatly lined (although now leafless) grapevines stood out against the contrast of the grey skies of winter and pine forest that met the field where the planting had concluded. Her grandparents had always wanted to establish a small winery on that land, but the funds had not been there. She hoped that she would be able to achieve their dream someday soon. As the bistro continued to prosper, it became more of a present daily thought in her mind.

Eastern Long Island was known for its winemaking and vineyards. Although the bulk of the wineries were on the opposing eastern north shore of the island, there were numerous thriving ones even on the south fork. Dani hoped to expand south shore winemaking and someday join in with a small and successful winery of her own. However, that dream would have to wait for now. At the moment, all of her effort and attention was being put into continuing to make the bistro a success.

Dani's family had bought the land, including the parcel where the bistro now sat, many years ago. At that time, property values were significantly less than what they were today. It had proved to be a good investment. The bistro had become a much loved local establishment in the years that had passed. Tourists loved visiting and having their coffee and meals outside while summering in the Hamptons. During the "off-season," locals loved stopping in, talking with Dani, and having a leisurely meal in a relaxed, elegant, and quiet setting. The area was still picturesque, calm, and just far enough away from the ever-encroaching suburban sprawl and development.

Down the road from the bistro there was even a thriving farm stand.

Dani would sometimes sell any extra fruits and vegetables that weren't being used in the restaurant there. It was a long red building that during the summer months had an abundance of fruits, vegetables, flowers, and hanging baskets. In the fall, there would be pumpkin and apple picking along with homemade apple cider. At this time of the year and with the approach of winter, there were stacks of chopped firewood neatly bundled for sale in the dirt parking field out front. This was paired with an abundance of wreaths, each sporting a bright red bow, and rows of live Christmas trees for purchase. Each tree seemed to be actively awaiting its new home for the holiday season.

Dani had thought about stopping by later today to buy a Christmas tree for her own home. At the present moment, her mind was instead focused upon the beehive of activity taking place in the kitchen. Mr. Perkins was a regular local customer and his salmon tartare was late. Although in many ways he was a lovable curmudgeon, he also inspired a sense of fear in everyone who worked at the restaurant.

At one of the stations, a new young chef was hurriedly placing the salmon into a container in which it could be seasoned. Dani rushed across the kitchen bearing some shallots and salt. Another young cook rushed over with the necessary olive oil. The team continued working on the last-minute order that was now late. At last, they added the crème fraiche along with the final sprig of green and pieces of a baguette needed to top the dish off. It was then plated beautifully and finally ready to be taken out to Mr. Perkins.

A young waiter in his white shirt and red vest approached the table cautiously. Mr. Perkins was already scowling at the delay. Dani poked her head out from the double doors of the kitchen discretely to check on the delivery of the order. Stone-faced, Mr. Perkins took a bite. The waiter stood by silently after asking him if he needed anything else. Suddenly, the hint of a smile came across the face of this hard-to-please guest.

He gave a quick glance over to the waiter. "Not bad, not bad. But where the heck are your Christmas decorations already?" Dani smiled at the scene before her. *Another disaster happily averted.*

She returned to the bustling kitchen. It had become a nice space within the past two years. Although the outside of the building maintained a traditional design, the kitchen had been fully modernized in a recent renovation. Each of the prep and cooking stations had a sleekness and sense of efficiency embedded in their design. On the other side of the room, the wine cellar had now been expanded to accommodate a much greater number and selection of varietals. Overall, she was very proud of everything that had taken place there and everyone working within it seemed to be as well.

There was indeed a lack of Christmas decorations. This was true both in the kitchen, which usually wasn't decorated very much anyway, and more importantly out in the main dining room. This was where the guests received their first impression of the bistro. This would have to be changed quickly with December already moving forward rapidly. She guessed that in a way, Mr. Perkins was correct.

It was for this reason that it truly felt like a destiny moment when Anton came bursting in through the front doors of the bistro laden with boxes.

"I come bearing decorations," he called out.

Dani's eyes expanded in sudden surprise. "That's incredible, Anton. You remembered!"

Anton put the boxes down. "Of course I remembered. Maybe we can get some of the chefs from the back to come out and help with all of these things."

"Well, they're kind of busy right now, Anton, but I'll definitely help," replied Dani. They proceeded together to move all of the boxes to a table in the back of the main dining room and began to unpack them.

Dani was ecstatic. "This was perfect timing, Anton. I was just thinking that we had better get on with the decorating soon. I didn't know how much longer the salmon tartare was going to be enough to keep Mr. Perkins and others like him happy and coming back for more during the holiday season."

Anton laughed. "Well, I did feel that with the sky getting progressively darker regularly and the threat of snow being featured more and more in the forecast, that it was finally time for us to brighten things up in here with some holiday decorations."

They began to unpack the boxes methodically. Anton had purchased a selection of beautiful table centerpieces with red candles flanked by fresh-cut evergreen branches. They would look beautiful with the red tablecloths and accompanying linen napkins that were also in the box.

The guests would be sure to feel the Christmas spirit while sitting at tables bedecked in this kind of holiday style. The restaurant itself required several wreaths and garlands for the windows in order for the entire space to be completely decorated.

Anton had already considered this while shopping. A selection of fresh pine garlands filled the top of the second box. As they were taken out, their wonderful pine scent quickly began to fill the main dining room of the bistro. Beneath them, there was an assortment of freshly cut pine wreaths. A few were designed with pine cones and poinsettias. Some of the other wreaths contained little sailboats and an anchor attached instead of a bow to their center. Finally, there were four wreaths made with seashells and artificial starfishes interspersed amidst the pine branches. This was paired with the colors of aquamarine blue, white, and yellow coral, all in a nod to Westhampton Beach's strong connection with the nearby sea and adjoining beachscape.

Dani beamed. "This is going to be the most festive Christmas that we've ever had here at the bistro."

Anton looked around at the room they were about to decorate. "I totally agree, Dani. I can't wait. Do you want me to get started with the decorating now?"

Dani cast her eye quickly over the dining room, which was still undecorated and the numerous tables filled with guests enjoying their lunch, set on the white linen tablecloths. "Yes, absolutely, Anton. Let's get started right away and make this atmosphere a lot more fun, Christmassy, and celebratory."

A few hours later, Dani decided that she had one more errand to run before heading back home. She would finally go and buy a Christmas tree for her house. It was a decision and action that she had been putting off for the past few weeks. She would go right now over to the nearby farm stand with its selection of freshly cut pine trees out front and purchase one immediately. In a way, she had to thank the not-so-gentle prodding of Mr. Perkins. It was his definitely-not-subtle encouragement to ramp up the festiveness that caused the sudden surge of holiday spirit now happily filling the second half of their workday at the bistro.

CHAPTER 5

This was not the time to think about Christmas. It also wasn't the time to worry about Sheila's demand for the perfect commercial property or the delivery of a Purchase and Sale Agreement before the new year. Finally, it wasn't the place or time to worry about anything else except the congested roads, rapidly changing lights, sharp turns, approaching tunnel, and endless traffic that lay out in front of him.

Entering or leaving New York City could quickly turn into a thrill ride. All of one's senses have to be fixated on the task at hand. Today for Marcos, that task was getting safely out of Manhattan and onto Long Island. The weather and traffic with its long list of continuous delays throughout the city and metropolitan area played at a low volume on the car stereo. He left it on as background sound to create an atmosphere of calm in the car. Sometimes he'd switch over to classical or smooth jazz. Marcos refused to listen to anything else while driving and navigating through the chaos.

He had picked up the passcodes and everything else needed for the rental house in Westhampton Beach from Monique last night at her place in Park Slope. A classic faux leather weekend bag sat on the backseat of the BMW. It contained all of those items along with just enough clothes that seemed reasonable enough to carry him through Christmas. *Hopefully, I'll be able to get everything settled in a week or two. I can then get back early enough to the city to enjoy some of the Christmas festivities in here.* He had grown tired of working in New York City. The parties and celebrations that took place at Christmas made it the most desirable time of the year to be living there. He didn't want to miss out on all of that by being stuck in the isolated Hamptons for the entirety of the holiday season. Marcos may have wanted to get out of the city, but if he had to live there, then there was no better and more inspiring time than Christmas to be in it and to take advantage of what it had to offer.

He brought his attention back to the task at hand. The area around Thirty-Fourth Street in Manhattan was busy, to say the least. It was a major transit hub and tourist starting-off point situated in the heart of Midtown, and it was the location of New York's Pennsylvania Station. The moving was slow as Marcos tried to maneuver the car through the lines of traffic congestion. Pedestrians hurried across the multiple crosswalks that intersected the major roadways. There was also the challenge of watching out for the speeding cars that were trying to beat the fast-changing traffic lights.

It would be a little less than seventy-seven miles to get out to Westhampton Beach. The duration of the trip would be just under two hours if the traffic was good. Marcos kept steering the car toward Seventh Avenue and was glad for the quiet of the interior cabin. Outside was the constant roar of trucks, vehicles, sirens screaming, construction taking place, and all of the less than pleasant sounds that can be expected in the heart of a busy city. He thought back to the rolling green hills, forests, white fences, and farmlands of his youth in Kentucky. He had wanted to leave it all behind for the excitement and possibilities of New York.

It was a young and perhaps idealistic dream. It was the same goal that he shared in common with so many people from all over the United States and the world. He had met many of those people during all of his years working in New York. Some had stayed. Many more had left long ago. The land of opportunity to them was now somewhere else, somewhere other than New York. Their new promised land was a place that was more affordable, greener, peaceful, and—above all—more sustainable.

The place that they had envisioned and come to in their youth was now for many no longer a place where they saw a viable chance at building a happy life. They, like Marcos, had gone through an evolution during their time in New York. He was still there and still fighting. He now wondered if he had stayed too long at the party.

Marcos continued driving toward the Queens Midtown Tunnel and shortly thereafter arrived on the Long Island Expressway. It was here that he would remain over the next sixty miles out to eastern Long Island. He flipped through the radio stations and settled on one of the twenty-four-hour Christmas channels. It would play non-stop Christmas music until Christmas day. Of course, he'd need a break from it at some point. There was only so much of it that one could bear to listen to over and over again. This only happened once a year though, so why not enjoy it.

The landscape alongside the Long Island Expressway changed with the miles covered. There were more buildings, congestion, and concrete closer to the city. Further east, were where the pine barrens and farms gradually became apparent. It truly did feel a lot more like the countryside when Marcos turned the car off at his exit for the route down to Westhampton Beach.

Things were changing fast now. There were farm stands, a lot more trees, open land, and more farms here and there. There were creeping signs of suburban sprawl both on and off of the expressway. It was still a far cry though from the city and Queens. It was nearing winter too, of course. Marcos envisioned how green the landscape must otherwise look out here at any other time of the year. The whole area had a significantly different feel from that of the city where he had just been a little under two hours before.

It really is rather remarkable how things can change within a seventy-something mile drive and a mere few hours. Marcos continued on and then reached the final stretch of road leading toward the shores of the Atlantic Ocean and the small community of Westhampton Beach, New York.

Marcos debated whether to turn off and make a short drive through the picturesque village but decided against it. It had been a long trip. Honestly, at this point, he felt tired and wanted to rest. He'd explore more of Westhampton Beach tomorrow. The best thing right now seemed to be to get to the house, unpack, and get some rest. Marcos decided to head directly for the rental property. Tomorrow, he could go exploring.

He reached Jessup Lane. It had a classic Hamptons feel with a seaside aura. That was the feel of neatly manicured and expansive green lawns; privacy hedges; and large, elegant homes set back at the end of a long gravel or paving stone driveway. Nature seemed to have been employed as an effective instrument in the landscape architect's toolbox within this region. The natural environment had been artistically merged with that of its less natural and human-created counterparts. Together, they both worked harmoniously in unison in a manner that achieved the dual outcome of privacy and pastoral ambiance between many of the properties that he had already passed since entering into the Hamptons. Nature or those spaces which were otherwise wild and open existed in a unique way here as well it seemed. Marcos could only describe it as a countryside, which in the Hamptons, felt very well looked after. It did not appear untamed or unending in its scope. There were always limits to where the countryside ended and genteel luxury began. It somehow felt different from how one may have typically thought of areas that were rural or otherwise considered countryside in other parts of the country. It was a countryside that was controlled, tamed, and groomed in comparison with that of its rural counterparts in other geographic regions. This area wasn't Kentucky by any means. Seeing nature again though and a bit of open land somehow made him feel a little better. It felt good and almost indefinably restorative to his spirit.

Jessup Lane finally reached the point where it made the very short trip over Moriches Bay. On the right, there were expansive views of the water. The landmass of Long Island and more specifically the community of Westhampton Beach lies in one direction situated on the bay. On the other side is the famous barrier strip of sand that stretches out in both directions into the sea and is traversed by Dune Road. That was where Marcos was heading.

He was over the bay and now at a traffic light which enabled Dune Road to be traveled either to the right or left. The vibe had changed quickly. There was a commercial feel that reminded him of certain areas on the Jersey shore. He had visited the New Jersey shore on numerous occasions with friends. There were parts of it that felt overly commercial and too developed. The shoreline in those areas seemed to take a backseat to endless strip malls, housing developments, and other commercial ventures that in a way almost blocked out the natural beauty of what he had come to see. That wasn't quite the case here on Dune Road, but at the traffic light, it did initially feel less than picturesque. Yet, there was still a very summer-at-the-shore kind of ambiance. It certainly wasn't summer right now though and the gray sky above and wind whipping outside continued to make that abundantly clear. This was especially true being right on the fringes of the Atlantic Ocean.

This was a prime strip of land separated from mainland Long Island, and the cost of the real estate very much reflected that sentiment. There were real estate agencies that specialized exclusively upon properties situated on Dune Road given its prestige, exclusivity, and the desirability of the properties located along both sides of it. There were both bay and oceanfront properties, which made it a highly desirable place to purchase real estate. The area had suffered significant destruction many years ago during the Hurricane of 1938 and was in many ways also a landmass that protected Long Island itself from the natural elements. It was a kind of first line of physical defense against the fierce nor'easters that occurred in this part of the world.

Dune Road was a little under fourteen miles and at times felt as though it could go on forever. It was tempting to pick up the speed a bit on the long straightaway. Marcos caught himself doing so, anxious to arrive at his destination. He slowed the car down to the speed limit of thirty miles per hour. Large waterfront homes were appearing on both sides of the road. The vibe had changed for the better. It wasn't just all commercial at this point. The sky was changing as well. It had gone from gray to a light blue, and white clouds seemed to drift lazily over this cold, winter beach environment. It didn't feel exactly like the "traditional" Hamptons out on Dune Road. It felt "beachier" in a word. It was very built up in this area on both sides of the road and at times impossible to fully see the ocean or Moriches Bay. Of course, one still knew that the water was there just beyond the buildings and homes that lined the strip of road.

He scoured the road in front of him. It was not always easy to drive and to look for house numbers, particularly when they're hidden at times from view by homeowners seeking to discourage visitors or prying eyes. Monique had said to look for a really big modern house that stood out from the rest. That advice didn't narrow the field given the plentitude of modern homes there. One was definitely coming into view up ahead and it looked significant. He felt almost certain that this had to be the place.

It could have been the home of an architect, a celebrity, or a supervillain who was doing a residency at the beach. The place was impressive. Glass, steel, and white exterior walls along with curved glass wings rose out of the sands of Dune Road. It towered over any neighboring properties. The number matched the one given to him by Monique. Marcos pulled the car up to the gate.

He could have entered the passcode, but for some reason, his finger slipped and hit the call button on the box. Surprisingly, a gruff voice came out over the speaker. "What the hell do you want?"

And a Merry Christmas to you too, asshole. "This is Marcos. I rented this house for four weeks."

There was silence. A few moments later there came a response. "Oh yes, yeah. Come in, Marcos. Monique let me know. I had forgotten all about it." The twin black automated iron gates slowly began to swing open. Marcos edged the car through them and down the tan gravel driveway which ran past some privet hedge blocking off the neighbor's view and then swung around to an expansive motor court in front of the huge modern home.

A short, stout, balding man in Bermuda shorts, a tank top, and a gold chain around his neck came running out. He looked like something out of a rap video gone bad. Additionally, he must have been freezing in that ensemble at this time of year.

"You can't park there," he started screaming. Marcos looked at the guy so as to suggest, well, where should I park then, in your living room?

"I'm having the gravel groomed by a service company later today," the man continued to shout. "Pull it up into the porte-cochere next to my Range Rover."

This guy is going to be tons of fun. He pulled the BMW up into the area on the right side of the home that the guy was frantically motioning toward.

Marcos got out of the car and walked up toward the front of the home. The stout man had been watching his every move and particularly how and where he parked the car.

"Name's Marvin," he said finally, extending a hand. Marcos shook his hand. "Let me show you around the place. I'm in construction and built this place on spec. There are a few offers on the table right now. I'm just waiting until when we get back after the holidays and then I'll see what I'm going to do."

Marcos looked at the man who was motioning for him to come inside. "Where are you heading for the holiday season?" asked Marcos cautiously, but in an attempt to be friendly.

"The boyfriend and I are heading off to spend the holidays with his family in Marbella," said Marvin as they walked into the entry foyer.

The main entrance foyer had terrazzo floors and high, sweeping ceilings. There were a few large modern art paintings with bright colors that popped on the wall. This all only added to a continued sense of occasion and feeling of arrival at this expansive property on a coveted Hamptons' road.

"José, if you want you can show Marcos the living room," called out Marvin suddenly. José came over from the other side of the room and took over briefly while Marvin fixed himself a drink. He was pouring out some top-shelf liquor into a glass at a built-in alcove bar adjacent to the foyer through which they had just entered. José was much younger and significantly better looking than Marvin. Marcos silently wondered how this relationship had come to pass, but then again, a lot of relationships were often otherwise unexplainable and shrouded in mystery. José proceeded to lead Marcos into the spacious great room.

There was natural light flowing in everywhere. The open floor plan caused one room to flow into the next and the minimization of actual walls created a sense of spaciousness. The room was double height and had low-lying oversized sofas and two perfectly placed ottomans.

On a large low table in the center of the great room sat a pile of books. They had Marvin's face very boldly plastered on the front cover. Marvin caught Marcos looking over at the table as he was making his drink at the small bar.

"I see you noticed my book," he called out.

"I just did," said Marcos. He looked at the title, *Winning at Life with Marvin*. "Sounds like a great book."

Marvin walked over to the table and pile of books with his drink and patted them proudly with his right hand. "It is. It's a hell of a read. Then again, I've had a hell of a life. You know what, kid, take one. I want you to have it. It might inspire you to greatness."

Marcos looked at Marvin incredulously. "Really?"

"Of course," responded Marvin without hesitation. He added, "You might pick up some pointers from me. You know what, go ahead and take two. That way you have one for yourself and another one for your inamorata."

Marcos went over and took two off the pile. "Well, that's very kind of you, Marvin."

"Don't think anything of it, kid," responded Marvin cheerily as he stirred his drink again.

Marvin walked over with his drink closer to where Marcos and José were now standing in the great room. "That's book-matched marble over there on the fireplace," he said pointing with his right hand that was also holding the drink simultaneously. Marcos walked over to where Marvin was pointing and ran his hand along the edge of the fireplace in the living room to feel the texture of the building materials employed.

"That certainly doesn't come cheap," commented Marcos.

Marvin was taking a sip of his drink. "No, it doesn't, kid. It definitely doesn't."

José walked ahead of Marcos and toward a floating staircase. He led the way up. Marcos looked around. "This will take us up to all three floors. Marvin had that oculus built into the top above it all," said José.

Marcos nodded. "This is impressive."

"Well, if you think that's impressive, look at these steps," added José. Marcos looked down. They were covered with faux leather.

"I've never seen that in a house."

José laughed. "Well, it's a rarity for sure. However, it feels great to walk on when you're barefoot and running around here during the summer."

They climbed the stairs. There was a modern artwork piece surrounding them on their ascent. It seemed to change in form and design as they advanced up the stairs.

José seemed to also realize that Marcos had noticed. "That's a custom art installation that I created. I'm an artist," said José.

Marcos gasped. "It's stunning, really stunning."

"Glad you like it," said José smiling. He continued up the stairs with Marcos and a few moments later Marvin rejoined them.

They all continued down a long hallway on the second floor. There were additional bedrooms up here besides the master, according to José.

"Are you ready for the showstopper?" asked Marvin. He swung open a door at the end of the hallway. "This is what they call the money-shot, kid," said Marvin triumphantly.

They walked into the master bedroom. Marcos observantly looked at the light-colored walls in the room. It was spacious with floor-to-ceiling windows and doors leading out to a second-floor terrace. Retractable skylights in the room let even more light into the space from above.

"Is that paldao wood?" he asked.

Marvin turned around and smiled. "It sure is. How do you know that, kid? You must be in a similar business. Not many people would realize a fine detail like that."

"I'm in commercial real estate," replied Marcos.

Marvin nodded. "Not a bad business to be in, not bad at all. Are you out here or in the city?"

Marcos' eyes wandered around the vast master bedroom. "I'm in midtown in the city. They just sent me out here for a short-term holiday project."

Marvin started heading toward the double doors on the opposite side of the room. "Well, there's plenty of money washing around out here as well. I'm sure you know that, but it's worth trying your hand at because there's a lot of cash to be made." Marcos laughed. "All you have to do is take a short drive around to realize that fact."

"Anyway, kid, everything in here is custom. A custom bed, custom sheets, custom furniture, you name it." There were endless views out toward the ocean and it seemed like a fantastic place to wake up each morning. Marvin continued the tour. The master had two connecting closets and a luxurious bathroom with a plunge tub. There was also an electric fireplace built into the wall. The room created a crescendo-like experience for anyone viewing it. The builder had been dedicated to exploiting the ocean vistas from the home at every opportunity and, at least to Marcos, it seemed well worth the effort.

They walked down a wing off of the great room when they came back down the stairs. Marvin opened a door on the left. It was a wellness center perfectly tucked away. There was a sauna, a state-of-the-art home gym, and a massage area.

"Not a bad place to spend Christmas, is it, Marcos?" said Marvin.

Marcos nodded. "It really isn't. It's not a bad place to spend any time of the year."

"Come with me." Marvin led José and Marcos out of the room and down a short flight of stairs.

Marvin turned on the light. "I didn't want to skimp in this department."

They were in a large wine cellar with warm-colored walls, dim lighting, and comfortable furniture. "We can hold up to two thousand bottles in here." Marvin pulled a bottle off the shelf and inspected it. "There's a lot of good wine even being made out here on the east end these days. You'd be surprised."

Marcos nodded. "I've heard good things about the wine production in this area and on the north fork."

"It's a pricey business to be in, but a good one in a lot of ways. We actually have the Hamptons, Long Island American Viticultural Area out here on the south fork," added Marvin.

"Let me show you the outside," said Marvin changing the topic at hand and anxious to show Marcos around the rest of the property. The indoor and outdoor spaces flowed together seamlessly via floor-to-ceiling glass doors that led to the outdoors from the living room. They pocketed neatly into the house almost immediately after Marvin touched a button on the wall.

Marcos, Marvin, and José stood together looking out over the infinity-edge pool, hot tub, tennis court, and green lawns leading down to the beach and the Atlantic Ocean.

"It really is beautiful out here," commented Marcos.

Marvin looked at him knowingly. "It is, but beauty does come at a certain price."

"Well, I have come to realize that for sure. I saw what you were asking to rent the place out in the summer for," said Marcos in an almost joking-yet-serious tone.

Marvin looked at first hurt and then just a touch angry. "Worth every penny," he responded curtly.

"Well, I don't know . . ."

Marvin interrupted his attempt at even suggesting that the wisdom of his asking price for the house should be challenged. "You get what you pay for and here, let's face it, you get a lot."

"I have to run inside quick and finish packing the last-minute things that I'm going to need," said José, interrupting the bit of tension that had suddenly developed.

Marvin continued. "During the summer months, José and I do like to get out on the water. I suppose that's just like anyone else out here. We're not really much different. We have the jet skis and the village marina nearby for taking a small boat out of. There's also paddle boarding and you've got both the bay and the Atlantic right here as well, so there are options."

It truly was the ultimate backyard.

"See that hot tub over there?" Marvin pointed toward a fixture at the end of the pool deck. "That can hold up to twelve people at a time. You should see some of the parties that we have out here in the summer. I've even got speakers placed in the pool. We have misters installed also so everyone on the terrace stays cool. When you're done, you can even go and relax in the Zen garden that a neighbor insisted I put in. I didn't want to, but at the end of the day, she was right. It helps keep me calm and centered. Look at me. If you had met me a year ago, you would have seen a totally different person. Now, I'm full of tranquility. I'm like a fucking rich beacon of peace of the beach."

Marcos didn't know about all of that. Marvin didn't really seem like any kind of beacon of peace and grace, but he nodded his head in agreement with him anyway. When he was young, his mother had always told him to be nice to rich people. She would say to him that you never knew what kind of doors they could possibly open for you. That had never happened yet for Marcos. He was still very much waiting on those rich people to open a few doors. It didn't seem to be forthcoming at any time in the foreseeable future. His experience in the world to date had instead revealed a world where most acted from a position of self-interest, rather than any sort of benevolent altruism.

However, she had also said to Marcos, "Don't bite the hand that feeds you." Marvin had indeed given him a very good break, with Monique's help, by letting him stay at this house over the holidays. So, Marcos thought it best to continue to stay on his good side.

Marvin continued. "Who knows, kid, play your cards right and maybe you'll even get invited out here someday to a few of our parties." He winked slyly at Marcos.

They moved on to the backyard side of another wing of the residence. There was a long beige-colored wall running along where the driveway swung partially into the backyard.

"What do you think that is?" asked Marvin.

Marcos looked at it, unsure. "A wall?"

"Wrong," responded Marvin in a very matter-of-fact tone. A moment later, it became evident that the "wall" was actually a bi-fold door that swung up to reveal an impressive car collection within a hidden space.

Marcos gasped. "Is that a Rolls Royce Dawn?"

Marvin smirked. "It sure is, kid. It's a beautiful convertible for traveling around out here in style, especially during the summer."

As they walked toward the doors leading back into the main part of the house, Marvin drew everyone's attention to a small building at the edge of the lawn.

"And that is the pool house, in case you want to put any of your friends up who come to visit you over the next four weeks," laughed Marvin. "Of course, it's pretty damn cold this time of year, so I don't think any of them would want to swim in the ocean right now."

José came back into the living room just as Marvin and Marcos walked in. He was flawlessly attired in an unstructured green blazer, white pants, and Oxford shoes. "Is my waistcoat done up alright?" he asked.

Marvin walked over and adjusted the lower button on it. "Now, it's perfect, dear."

José started moving the two bags toward the front door. "I think we better get going, Marvin, or we're never going to make it to the airport on time."

"Are you flying out of MacArthur or the city?" asked Marcos out of curiosity.

Marvin looked bothered at being asked this question when he was clearly in a hurry. "We're going out of Kennedy. There are no international flights to Spain out of MacArthur. I couldn't even countenance the idea of engaging with a connecting service at this point in my life, especially for a long-distance trip. Finally, they don't have any first-class lounges at the airport here on the island that are connected with our preferred airlines. José and I cannot and will not compromise on that."

Marcos smiled. "Well, I always did feel that good first-class airline lounges were underrepresented here on Long Island."

Marvin wasn't amused by the attempt at humor and looked at his watch. "Oh no, it's actually really late. I have to get going. If everything is good, which I don't see why it wouldn't be, I'm going to grab my things and head off."

Marcos put out his hand to shake Marvin's. "Everything is perfect. Thanks again for allowing me to stay in your home for the four weeks while I close the deal out here."

"You're welcome. Just don't trash the place, and maybe I'll see you sometime after we get back," responded Marvin.

Marcos smiled. "That sounds perfect."

Marvin hurried up the stairs to the second level to grab his things while José headed out to the front of the home.

Ten minutes later, Marcos stood outside the residence waving to Marvin and José as they sped down the gravel driveway in their Range Rover and out onto Dune Road. He went back inside and stood in the large, silent great room alone. He wished he was back in New York with friends and all of the holiday parties starting to take place there. This felt so empty and like such a depressing way to spend Christmas. He was in an empty mansion, spending the winter in what was generally considered a summer resort area, and very much alone. He walked up the floating staircase with its surrounding modernist art installation to the second floor. *So what happens now?*

CHAPTER 6

Dani had pretty much eliminated her commute to work these days. Home was now the historic red barn at the back of her vineyard, which bordered the scrub pine forest. The bistro itself sat only a short journey from the barn at the other side of the vineyard. It faced out toward the main road. She had worked for years lovingly engaged in the structure's restoration. At the same time, she wanted the inside to be made contemporary and comfortable for modern living. It was now a peaceful oasis. There were expansive views from nearly all of the rooms looking out over the surrounding natural landscape. Dani walked down the spiral staircase from the master bedroom in the loft. In the kitchen, she checked her Google Calendar. There was an appointment with a local resident who was considered an authority on building wineries.

It had been an unrealized dream of her family for some time. They had hoped to someday start producing wine from the grapes grown for years on their four-acre plot behind the bistro. Dani hoped today would be the beginning of making that long-held dream a reality. She had a legacy to uphold and a family dream that had now also become her dream. Her grandparents had been out here for years and the one thing that they wanted, which wasn't realized in their lifetimes, was that of establishing a winery. The early nineteen seventies had brought winemaking to Long Island. The growth of the wine industry on eastern Long Island had only sparked Dani's enthusiasm and continued passion for making that dream a reality while she was in charge. Her own wine label would be prestigious, put her business on the map, and with time generate a profit that would make the operation worthwhile. However, that wasn't at the forefront of her mind. She wanted to make her late grandparents proud of what she had accomplished. She also felt a connection to the land and the community of Westhampton Beach and wanted to leave both a little better as a result of her years of hard work.

The balsam fir Christmas tree in Dani's living room looked beautiful. Its white lights and red bows were set against the rich green pine needles of the tree. The abundance of natural light, the light wood floors, and the vaulted ceilings of the converted barn made the tree appear even more beautiful in its holiday setting. Dani was glad that she had started early with the decorating. She would still have to get around to hanging that wreath high above the barn's former entrance doors later today. *Oh well, there would be time for that.*

There was still a little time before her meeting with the winery expert. It would be just enough of a gap to take a leisurely stroll across the acreage en route to the bistro. He would be meeting her there shortly. Dani grabbed a straw sun hat with a black ribbon off of a hook by the door. She then headed outside into the beginning of the new day.

The morning was quiet and peaceful and the vines were not yet covered with snow. The first snowfall of the season would surely come soon enough. This was especially true now that December was in full swing. Dani started down a well-traveled dirt path leading out through the vines. Each curving grapevine twisted its way up from the Earth. They looked stark without their leaves and thick clusters of grapes waiting to be harvested.

There was a winter beauty even to those twisted stalks spaced equidistantly apart from one another. The symmetrical rows stretched out in all four directions from the path that Dani now walked along. It was the end of fall and near the beginning of winter. The sunlight was somehow different out here at this time of year. The vines, the endless scrub pine stretching off into the distance, and the peacefulness of the agricultural and natural landscape made this a very unique landscape on what can sometimes be a very crowded island.

She arrived at the back door to the bistro and went inside. The kitchen was already bustling with her staff preparing the morning breakfast orders. Benoit rushed over to Dani. "He's in the dining room."

"Already?" replied Dani. The appointment wasn't for another half-hour yet. Dani glanced at her watch. "I'll head right in."

She walked into the main dining room of the bistro. There were already a few guests scattered throughout at the various white linen-covered tables. There was optimistic energy to the morning. Bright sun streamed in, and there was the gentle clinking of china as tables were set and plates were cleared from tables with diners either getting ready or already enjoying their breakfast.

"Marcel!" She walked over to a table in the corner of the room where a middle-aged man with slicked-back black hair and a blue sweater and white pants sat. He had been a hedge funder in the city before buying and developing one of the major vineyards and wineries out here on the eastern end of Long Island. He was frequently called upon for advice by anyone thinking about getting into the wine business out east. Part of this notoriety was because of his much-publicized and touted successes locally in the industry.

Marcel stood up. "Dani, it's wonderful to see you again."

"It's always a pleasure, Marcel. Thank you for coming on such short notice."

"It's not a problem at all," responded Marcel.

Dani motioned toward the chair. "Please sit, Marcel."

They sat down at the small corner table. "Well," said Dani, "I wanted to talk to you about the possibility of getting into establishing a winery to go along with the vines on the property here. They've been growing for many years at this point. We've always sold the grapes to other wineries. I'd like to do something for ourselves at this point."

A waiter came over with glasses of water and orange juice. Dani took a sip.

"How many vines are we talking about?" asked Marcel inquisitively.

She looked reflective for a moment. "You know, Marcel, I don't know the vine count any longer. We're talking about four acres of vines roughly."

Marcel seemed to be holding back a muffled laugh.

Dani glared at him for a moment. "Yes?"

Marcel took a sip of the orange juice. "Well, you know as well as I do, Dani, that four acres is a small vineyard."

"Of course," replied Dani. She continued. "But I still think we could get a considerable number of bottles out of the acreage and that in itself might make it worthwhile."

"It probably wouldn't justify the investment, at least not immediately," added Marcel.

Dani thought for a moment. "How many bottles of wine would be potentially generated per acre of the vineyard if I went into this business?"

Marcel leaned back in his chair. "It depends upon how many tons of grapes come out of that acreage. Let's say you got two tons out of the harvest for an acre of property that you planted."

"Okay, so how many bottles does that give me?" asked Dani.

"Somewhere beyond one thousand," he paused and then continued slowly, "and four hundred and something odd bottles I'd say." He took a bite out of his muffin. "That's of course if you get a harvest of two tons out of one acre of that property."

"That's interesting," replied Dani. She continued. "Now what if I get ten tons out of that acre?"

Marcel took a pen out of his pocket and did some quick figuring on the paper napkin that had been placed under his glass of orange juice on the table. "Well, then you're probably looking at somewhere in the neighborhood of around seven thousand and maybe a couple hundred bottles in total, I'd say."

Dani looked out the window for a moment and then returned to the discussion. "So, what you're telling me is that even an acre could bring in somewhere between one thousand and some change to around seven thousand and something potential bottles of wine?"

"That sounds correct. But you know, Dani, there's so much else to consider before jumping into the business."

"I'm not stupid, Marcel. Of course, I know that," she replied impatiently.

"Just for a minute, though, let's consider some of the other factors," said Marcel knowingly. He ordered another glass of freshly squeezed orange juice.

He continued, "First, there are the zoning regulations and how the vines themselves are placed in the ground. That's all going to impact whether you can have the vineyard in the first place and then the amount that is going to come out of it."

Dani looked unimpressed. "Of course I realize that, Marcel. Those are the absolute basics."

Marcel continued. "I know, Dani, but then think about that period at the beginning where you'll be operating at a loss. There are all of those initial upfront costs of just getting into the business. You have to be able to weather that. In a way, I guess the bistro itself has to be doing phenomenally well financially to sustain the development of a winery."

"It's doing pretty well, Marcel, but you and I both know that there's always room for improvement," answered Dani.

Marcel paused reflectively for a moment. "Well, you can possibly make money in the future, but it is going to be hard initially, especially with so little land. Then think about the people that you have to hire along with the equipment. You've also got to keep those vines watered and free of pests along with incorporating your vineyard. These things all add up as far as costs go."

Dani took a sip of her water as Marcel continued talking. "Then we have to consider whether you've ever thought about starting your own wine label."

"I have," said Dani, "I think it would be fun to be able to come up with a unique brand and form of specific marketing for our wine."

"Well," said Marcel, "then you're going to have a whole other bag of issues. You also have to think about whether you're going to make the wine, Dani, or whether you're going to hire an outside winemaker."

"I haven't actually made wine yet at this point," added Dani.

"Well, then there's the cost of the winemaker. Of course, then you need a crush facility or somewhere to process the grapes and make the actual wine. You could work with other people who have vines and a small amount of acreage. At least in a cooperative type situation like that, the equipment costs would be less, because you'd all be using shared equipment to process your grapes together."

"I hadn't considered the idea yet of being part of a cooperative," said Dani.

"It's definitely a possibility," added Marcel, "but think about all of the other costs. That's the problem here."

Dani looked toward the window again pensively. "Maybe there's still a way."

"Maybe," said Marcel.

A woman in a flamboyant red hat sat at a table nearby and leaned over in Dani's direction suddenly. "Listen, hun, don't let him put the damper on your dreams. I've been an artist out here for thirty years. Everyone told me I was crazy for making art my vocation. You know what? I'm still out here, and I'm still painting. If I had listened to them, I would have given up years ago."

Dani smiled at the lady. "Thank you for the encouragement, that's very kind of you . . ."

"Vera, Vera Renaud," the lady added. "And listen, one more thing. You want to make bottles of wine. A lot of people are going to be in support of that. I think you'll have even more success with peddling alcohol to people than I ever experienced with painting."

They both started laughing. Even Marcel let out a little chuckle before continuing to prattle on about the obstacles to running a small vineyard and winery.

"Think about this, too. I know you're a big farm-to-table enthusiast," he continued.

"That's true. I definitely am," replied Dani.

"Well, if you want your wine to be considered 'organic' when it's marketed and sold, then you're dealing with the USDA. They have a challenging process for things such as wine to be certified as 'organic,' to say the least. This also has to be applied both to the grapes and to the actual making of the grapes into wine."

Suddenly, Marcel looked at his watch. "I didn't realize that it's almost noon already. I really should get going."

Dani stood up. She reached out her hand toward Marcel's. "Well, I do want to thank you for meeting with me this morning, Marcel. You've given me a lot to think about."

Marcel looked at Dani. "I don't want to discourage you. I just want to give you a realistic view of the whole process."

"I know, Marcel."

They said goodbye and Marcel walked out of the front doors of the bistro. It was already filling up with the lunch clientele.

Dani sat back down at the table and looked out over her bistro and all of the patrons that were coming in and leaving after they finished eating. A peaceful and otherwise inspired morning walk out in the vineyards had turned into this, a disappointment. She didn't know how she was ever going to come to realize the vision of her grandparents who had worked so hard just to establish the bistro itself where she was so successfully working and thriving today. They had so much more in them as well, before they passed on. They had so many dreams that they still wanted to achieve in Westhampton Beach. She wasn't going to let those dreams die. No, it wouldn't happen on her watch.

Dani's head was spinning with everything that Marcel had said, and not in a good way. She thought that this was probably the same reason why people joke about how creative people and lawyers don't mesh well together. The creative people see the big picture for their vision of something that they would like to see accomplished in the world. On the other hand, the lawyers are always the ones telling those same creative people all of the obstacles and reasons why that particular something can't actually be accomplished. Dani found the whole conversation kind of disheartening. She drank the rest of the orange juice in her glass and, letting out a heavy sigh, headed back into the kitchen. The dream of owning her own thriving vineyard and winery would have to wait, it seemed. She was somehow going to find a way, with or without Marcel's "advice" or help to make it happen.

CHAPTER 7

Meanwhile in Spain. . . .

The flight from New York City to Spain had gone well, and thankfully, been uneventful. Marvin and José were now enjoying the drastic change for the better in the weather that the south of Spain afforded them. This pleasing shift in climate was paired with the many sights of the affluent world around them in Puerto Banús as they walked together near the marina.

Puerto Banús had the warm and inviting feel of a well-to-do tropical paradise. There were of course the mandatory beaches. There was also Dalí's green rhinoceros sculpture, which lent a bit of eccentric character and artistic flair to the place. It was one of the first sights that José insisted that he and Marvin visit and take a picture in front of when they arrived. It was particularly exciting for José given his own respective artistic interests and endeavors. Marvin, on the other hand, was less than impressed but chose to humor José for the larger benefit of their relationship.

Puerto Banús was a purpose-built development in a location with stunning natural beauty paired with the wonderful weather of southern Spain. The focal point was its yacht-filled marina, which had an adjacent luxury shopping, restaurant, and nightclub district. Although the marina was the central scenic point around which Puerto Banús appeared to revolve, there were also beautiful, rugged mountains bathed in red and gold that rose in the distance, a bit further inland from the sea. Its location on the sea and many amenities, all within easy reach of nearby Marbella, made it appeal easily to an affluent clientele and enabled it to serve as a wonderful place to take a winter holiday.

José seemed to be lost in thought as they walked together in the bright sun that day. Suddenly, he turned to Marvin. "I never did get a chance to ask you about how you connected with this Marcos who you've rented our house to for the holidays."

For a moment, Marvin wondered if José was jealous. They had such a solid relationship at this point that it seemed highly unlikely. The inflection in his tone didn't suggest jealousy. It was rather a genuine curiosity as to how this somewhat odd and unexpected situation had entered into their lives back at home over the holidays.

Marvin watched as yet another Ferrari revved its engines and then started again after lingering at a red light on the adjacent roadway. "Well, you know Monique, of course," began Marvin. José grinned. This was a good sign. Now Marvin knew he wasn't jealous or angry with him.

"Without her, we wouldn't exactly be together right now having this conversation, would we?" responded José.

"Certainly not," replied Marvin in a matter-of-fact tone. He continued. "Monique and I have been friends for many years now and of course we work in related fields. She was actually the one who alerted me when the Dune Road property became unexpectedly available and where I would go on to build the house."

José was surprised. "I didn't know that. It must have been before we met."

Marvin nodded in agreement. "It was. You and I would meet about a year later when she introduced us at that party in Southampton."

José had a mischievous look on his face. "That's right. I'll never forget the Rosé and Refinance Mixer."

"Nor will I," said Marvin putting his arm around José as they continued walking. He continued. "Anyway, she called me about this guy Marcos who she works with. He needed a place to stay out in Westhampton Beach to close a deal for their company, which for whatever reason, had to be finished before the new year. I owe her a certain degree of gratitude. It's a matter once again of 'one hand washing the other' because you and I both know that's how business in the real world gets done."

José agreed. "Absolutely. Little ever gets done with these nonsensical committee meetings where no one can decide anything and even less gets done if you try to accomplish something through the so-called proper bureaucratic channels."

José, like Marvin, was no novice or fool in the actual business world, which differed so radically from the bogus pie-in-the-sky one that Marvin had been exposed to during business school. It was actually the reason he ended up dropping out, seeing little value in continuing and more value in actually making something of himself in the world. His gamble had proven successful and he had no regrets. José too had been through numerous business transactions in the hard-nosed world of art, and it had developed within him a necessary degree of self-protectiveness and shrewdness as the importance of his art continued to grow within the eyes of the community.

Marvin smiled. "I think we make such a good pair because we think so similarly."

"Well and because I'm sexy as hell," responded José laughing.

"And that," replied Marvin. He continued. "Personally, the whole thing sounds ridiculous to me. It just doesn't make sense, that this large building site their company wants to acquire is in a small place like Westhampton

Beach. There's nothing that I know of that would even meet what they claim to be looking for."

José looked quizzically at Marvin for a moment. "You think there's something else going on?" The palm fronds in a tree next to them crackled in the sudden cool, refreshing, and very welcome breeze.

"I don't know," said Marvin. He thought to himself for a moment. "Something doesn't feel right about the whole situation. There seems to be so much building and construction often taking place on the main drag off of Sunrise Highway into Southampton. There's plenty of commercial development there and it's a highly trafficked road with a lot of action. Now that would be a great place to catch the attention of tourists who are making their first sortie into the Hamptons after exiting off of the highway. Why the heck aren't they looking there? It all just seems idiotic to me. It's not how I would do business, at least."

"I agree with you Marvin, you know that," responded José. At that moment, a large white superyacht with tinted black windows released its lines and was starting across the harbor near where they were now walking. "Is this the right place?" asked Marvin pointing ahead to a spot near an approaching beach.

"I think it is," answered José.

Marvin looked out toward the harbor with its multitude of yachts all neatly docked in their respective slips. "I guess time has a way of getting the truth to come out. Sooner or later, I think we'll find out what's really going on."

José nodded. The topic had been summarily dismissed as Marvin and José picked up the pace walking toward the dock. The unanswered questions back in New York were not going to be allowed to interfere with the beautiful trip that José and Marvin had booked and planned to spend together in this warm, welcoming, and vibrant holiday location.

A short while later a catamaran carrying José and Marvin departed from the shores of Puerto Banús. It gracefully began its journey under the bright midday sun as it glided across the sparkling waters of the nearby sea on its short trip back to nearby Marbella where José's family lived. For now, everything that had, was, and might eventually take place in New York had to remain exactly there, in New York, and not here in paradise.

CHAPTER 8

He had never awakened in a setting such as this. The winter sunlight filled the master bedroom and he could hear the waves crashing out on the beach. New York City felt like a world away. Even Long Island didn't generally resemble this or hold the same feeling that starting the day here embodied.

This was different and somehow calmer. It was very much a place that was a unique world all its own. It was still early and only a little after sunrise. He got out of bed, put on some workout clothes, and headed downstairs. There was no need to break the morning routine just because he was in the Hamptons now for four weeks.

Marcos headed downstairs to the living room and then out onto the terrace. The air was crisp, salty, clean, and refreshing. He had heard of people "summering" in the Hamptons. It just seemed funny that he was in essence "wintering" out in the Hamptons now, for lack of a better term.

At the edge of the backyard, there was a boardwalk or catwalk, depending upon which term one preferred. It went across a section of the dunes with their undulations, salt hay, and reedy grass that blew gracefully in the morning wind. After traversing the dunes, the wooden walkway ended right on the beach with the Atlantic Ocean directly in front.

It felt incredible to be able to go from one's house and down to the beach so effortlessly in the morning and in a matter of minutes. It was so quiet out here too. This was paired with the sparkling of the waves under the recently risen sun at this very special and unique hour of the morning. Marcos took it all in.

It was so different starting the day out here compared to his morning routine back in the city. In there, the day started amidst a cacophony of sirens, the noise of cars, traffic, roaring sanitation trucks, and the feeling of unending restlessness everywhere. Here, it was just the quiet peace of the sunrise, the beach, and a sensation that there was no need to rush or be in a hurry about anything. Somehow life felt good again here. Marcos hadn't felt this at peace since he was a child growing up in rural Kentucky many years ago. Westhampton Beach was already helping him to connect with a part of himself that he hadn't made himself vulnerable to experiencing again for so many years now.

He realized that Westhampton Beach was special. Parts of Long Island could feel like an extension of New York City. Heavy traffic, a lack of open space, strip malls, and endless tract housing could all create a similar feeling of stress and restriction. This was paired with the high cost of living connected with living just outside of a major American city. People on Long Island that worked in New York were guaranteed heavy traffic and strenuous commutes by car or by train daily and that wasn't what he wanted. Marcos knew all of this from his many trips out to the island to visit friends and distant family members throughout the years.

He never really looked at Long Island as a place he would want to move to in order to escape from the city where his life was now. It felt too similar and too much of an extension of New York rather than a release from it. Yes, some areas were peaceful and beautiful, and it was inherently different from New York City. However, a good portion of western Long Island still felt like too much to him. It didn't light him up with any sort of passion that would suggest it as a serious place for getting away from a life that was ever wearing deeper upon his nerves and patience.

He didn't feel the inclination to go back to Kentucky either, after the life he had lived in New York City for all of these years. The dream though remained with him of someday attaining some sort of happy medium between the social events and activity of New York and the peace of a calmer landscape and location, wherever that might be. Long Island didn't strike him as the answer to that. This experience in Westhampton Beach was beginning to change his mind and already felt significantly different from the Long Island that he had seen and experienced in the past.

He walked down to where the beach met the water. The beach seemed to stretch on endlessly in both directions. He began the run. It didn't feel as though he was running toward any particular place or point. He just began to jog at a steady pace and before long was moving along at a consistent speed. Marcos made a mental note to remember which boardwalk entry point was "his." It would be very easy to take the wrong one upon returning from the run and end up in someone else's backyard.

Seagulls soared overhead and out over the water. The waves crashed as they roared in and then washed back out, one after another as Marcos ran and ran. It was as though running here was enabling so much of the stress from years of working in the city to gradually escape from his body. The stress, too, was going back out to sea along with the receding tide, little by little.

Yes, it was cold too out here and nearly winter. The cold was mitigated by how refreshing it otherwise felt and a feeling of renewal that was overtaking him. It was very different from what one would feel or experience on the very same beach in the heat or crowds of summer.

❦

Marcos reached the point of being about two miles down the beach from the house. He stopped to catch his breath. There was no one else around at this hour. It felt wonderful to know that if he wanted to, he could run on and on until he fully exhausted himself. It wasn't like a circular paved trail at a city park. Additionally, it wasn't a treadmill at the gym. This felt incredibly freeing and liberating. He had never started a morning like this. He could have never imagined running along the Atlantic shoreline after waking up in a large contemporary home on the beach. It was beyond anything he ever envisioned. It was remarkable to think about the difference in lives between people. There were people who were waking up to this kind of morning every day, which glaringly contrasted with what waking up in the city had been like for Marcos each morning up until now.

Marcos took some deep breaths, turned around, and began running back to the boardwalk that led to the rental house. A short while later, the entrance to that strip of wood across the dunes came into view once more. He slowed down to a walk and headed back to the house.

Once upstairs again, he went into the master bathroom to clean up. There was a walk-in shower separated from the rest of the master bath by only a single pane of glass. The walls were a luxurious white and veined marble. The warm water from the rainfall shower head paired with vetiver and sandalwood body wash felt utterly luxuriously. Marcos let it soak into his tired muscles after the long morning run.

After the shower, he toweled off, dressed, and went out to his car, still parked from yesterday in the porte-cochere. The gravel too of the driveway had now been groomed. Hopefully, Marvin would have no objection to him driving or parking on it now. He got in the car, headed out along Dune Road, and made the left at the traffic light. The car then made the short trip over Moriches Bay and back to the mainland.

He hadn't started a morning in such a peaceful and pleasant way since he couldn't remember when. There was no real rush this morning. He was taking it all in. A few minutes later the little and very picturesque village of Westhampton Beach came into view. He turned onto Main Street. The village itself was tree-lined (although at this time of the year the trees were now bare), appeared to be very pedestrian-friendly, and seemed to hold an inviting small-town ambiance. It had the feeling of how one would picture a quintessential and classical-looking New England village, yet with an almost contemporary flair. Considering the relatively close proximity of Connecticut, which was just a short trip across the water from the north fork, this made sense. The shops were all brightly decorated for the holidays, and even with the onset of the cold weather, it was a place that made one want to linger and spend some time. At this hour though, nothing yet seemed to be open.

Marcos continued driving on. *I really need coffee and something to eat,* he thought to himself as his stomach emitted a not-so-subtle growl as though to remind him. There did not appear to be a Starbucks or drive-thru chain restaurant in sight. These types of places existed even out here of course. However, they were not as prevalent. It was something unique about the Hamptons in comparison to the rest of the island. As a result, one was encouraged to eat locally.

It didn't help this morning, as he still really needed some coffee and breakfast. This was especially true before starting what promised to be a long day. Marcos had kept driving beyond the village and was now out near Gabreski Airport. There were some deserted sections of scrub pine forest in that area. Marcos wondered if he had gone too far and should turn around. He certainly didn't want to end up in the hinterlands, which was what Monique often jokingly referred to parts of eastern Long Island as constituting. A farm stand suddenly came into view. It had Christmas trees for sale out front, but that too was closed. There were no signs of life just yet. He continued a little further up the road.

Suddenly like a mirage on the horizon (although one that he hoped wouldn't disappear upon reaching it), Marcos spotted a pleasant-looking red brick building. Something was going on inside as well. The lights appeared to be on, and there were even three or four cars parked in the small dirt parking area out front alongside the road.

As Marcos pulled the car into the dirt lot, he noticed that the building was decorated for Christmas and it reminded him that the holidays were indeed fast approaching. He thought about it so little right now with everything else that was on his mind. Marcos didn't even know if he'd still have a job in the new year. Those kinds of concerns made it difficult to feel celebratory. They also resulted in him feeling a certain degree of indifference to any sort of holiday spirit, no matter how much he tried to feel otherwise. *I'll just take a chance and go in.*

He walked up to the red brick structure with its blue columns and white doors. Christmas had definitely arrived. Above each of the French doors outside was a wreath. Marcos noticed that one had pine cones and poinsettias while another featured small sailboats and a whimsical anchor instead of a bow. On the third set of doors, there was even one with seashells and artificial starfish set against the evergreen branches. He supposed it made sense given how close he was to the sea. The exterior of the bistro seemed to echo that thought perfectly with its well-thought-out and very welcoming decorations.

The place recaptured a sense of charm. It had character, which so many other mass-produced establishments lacked. It also reminded him of the little bistros that he had frequented when traveling through France many years ago. Now, finding one in Westhampton Beach rekindled that sense of nostalgia within him once more.

Marcos walked inside. The tables had centerpieces with red candles and evergreen branches in their center and were covered with red tablecloths. The silverware was polished and there were white linen napkins. Christmas music was playing even at this early hour and the wait staff in white shirts and red vests attentively fawned over each and every guest at a table. No one was left not feeling wonderfully looked after, it seemed.

Marcos was shown to a pleasant table adjacent to one of the bistro's front-facing windows. It was too cold to dine outside this morning. He had a nice view of the alfresco seating area and its privacy-creating potted arborvitaes. *I'll have to come back in the summer and sit outside there.*

Marcos scanned the extensive breakfast menu that had been presented to him by the *maître d'* when she seated him. At the top, there were the basics. These included cereals; bagels with cream cheese, butter, or salmon; fresh fruit; smoothies; and yogurt selections. There were also specialty items such as kippers, along with various egg dishes, customized omelets, and a wide selection of coffee and teas.

The eggs Florentine looked potentially appealing. It was served poached with fresh, locally-grown spinach over an English muffin. There was then a choice of hollandaise or a mornay sauce, with its richer cheese composition. Under hot breakfast items, the "Full English" looked even more appealing. It would be a hearty meal for sure. This was especially true given its inclusion of eggs, toast, bacon, and sausage. *It might be a good choice for the long day that I have ahead.*

There was a section on the menu though that he had never seen before. The category was labeled "viennoiserie." A waiter in a white shirt and red vest approached the table. "Can I get you coffee, tea, or anything to drink?"

"Just coffee please," replied Marcos. A few moments later the waiter came back with a hot pot of coffee and poured it into the cup beside Marcos on the table.

"I do have to ask you one thing," said Marcos looking at the menu again. He continued. "I'm unfamiliar with what viennoiserie is."

The young waiter looked confused for a moment. He looked at the open menu that Marcos was holding in his hands. "I just started working here yesterday. They lost a staff member due to a family emergency. As a result, I was hired right on the spot when I came in to apply after my classes at Stony Brook Southampton. I do know that there are things like croissants that are served under that category."

Marcos frowned looking down again at the menu.

"Actually, let me get someone," said the young waiter, anxious not to disappoint a guest and eager to preserve his gratuity. He hurried off and disappeared behind the swinging double doors that led into the kitchen. More people were now gradually starting to come into the bistro for breakfast as it became later.

A few minutes later, an elegantly dressed young woman with long, dark blonde hair came over to the table. "I'm Dani, the owner and chef de cuisine here. Is there anything that I can be of assistance with?"

Marcos looked up at Dani. She was smiling and seemed to carry positive energy with her that he was suddenly drawn to. "I was just looking at the breakfast menu and was unfamiliar with the term viennoiserie and some of the items listed under it."

Dani smiled. "That's perfectly understandable. A lot of people here ask us about that as well."

"Well, I'm glad I'm not the only one," replied Marcos.

Dani shook her head. "Certainly not. Actually, viennoiserie means 'things of Vienna.' Apparently, certain types of baked Vienna items gained a following and degree of notoriety in France at some point, from what I understand. These items under viennoiserie are uniquely French creations rather than Viennese."

"That's pretty confusing," replied Marcos.

Dani nodded. "It is in a way, I suppose. These items are all freshly made right here in our kitchen. They're sweeter as far as baked goods go and in a way straddle that delicate line that exists between where bread stops and the category of pastries begins."

Marcos interrupted. "So what does that generally include?"

"Oh, you've got croissants, brioche, Danish pastries, and a number of other items that all fall under that category."

"That's really interesting. I had no idea about any of that," replied Marcos.

Dani continued. "A lot of people don't, but we are trying the best we can to replicate a French bistro here in the Hamptons."

Marcos laughed. "Okay, so I've got a few more questions for you, Dani, while we're at it."

She nodded seriously now. "Go ahead."

Marcos pointed at the menu. "What is Cannelés Bordelais? I see that if I order them, I'll receive two."

"Those are actually small cakes that contain rum as well as vanilla. You will indeed get two with an order. Another bonus is that there's not even enough rum in them to give you a hangover."

Marcos laughed. "You think that's a bonus? Interesting. Well, it is the holidays so hopefully, I'd be forgiven if they did."

He looked again at the menu. "You certainly have a lot of different croissants here. What's the difference between le croissant au beurre and le croissant ordinaire?"

Dani nodded knowingly. Apparently, Marcos hadn't been the first person to come into her bistro and ask that question.

"Well, you see . . ." began Dani.

"Marcos."

"It's nice to meet you, Marcos," replied Dani, smiling. She continued.

"Le croissant au beurre has a composition that includes butter. If you're watching what you eat, maybe choose le croissant ordinaire. This is still a croissant but without the butter. In my honest and personal opinion, it's not as delicious, either."

Marcos nodded. "Well, I want to go with the chef's recommendation."

"Always a good decision," agreed Dani almost mischievously. She continued. "You know, though, you may even want to try le croissant aux amandes. It's delicious."

"Now, what's that?" asked Marcos.

"It's a delicious croissant, of course. That one has sugar and thinly sliced almonds embedded in it."

Marcos was debating which option to go with. Everything seemed so delicious. "This is a tough choice to make."

Something in the dining room had suddenly caught Dani's attention. "I'll come back in a bit," she said hurriedly and added, "I want to see how you enjoyed whatever you end up ordering. I just have to run and take care of something."

Before Marcos could say, "that's perfectly fine," Dani had rushed off. He was starving and more than ready now to order and finally eat something.

The young waiter came back to the table. "I'm going to go with the full English breakfast, a Danish pastry, and a le croissant au beurre from the viennoiserie portion of the menu."

The waiter scribbled everything down hurriedly onto his notepad. "That sounds perfect, sir. I'll have it out to you shortly. Do you need a top-up on your coffee?"

Marcos looked at his now half-empty cup. "Yes, that would actually be wonderful."

"Very good. I'll be right back to fill that up for you," responded the waiter.

The food arrived shortly thereafter. The waiter placed the full English in front of him and then two croissants and the Danish pastry on a smaller side plate.

"I think I only ordered one croissant," said Marcos.

The waiter nodded. "Yes, you did. Dani wanted you to try le croissant aux amandes as well. It comes with her compliments."

Marcos was unexpectedly surprised and pleased at Dani's kindness and generous hospitality toward him as a complete stranger in her bistro. "Please tell Dani that I said thank you for this."

The waiter refreshed his water glass. "I will, sir. I believe she'll be out to visit from the kitchen before you leave."

"That sounds wonderful," responded Marcos. He happily embarked on his delicious breakfast as the waiter headed off to another table in the now nearly filled dining room.

Christmas music was playing and all of the centerpieces, evergreen garlands, wreaths, and festive table cloths created an ambiance that was starting to make Marcos feel a little bit of the holiday spirit. Dani came out from the kitchen and walked over to the table just as he was finishing his meal.

"How was everything, Marcos?" she asked.

"It was all just perfect, including the music, the food, and the whole environment in here. I also want to thank you for that almond croissant. It tasted absolutely amazing."

Dani grinned. "Well, I'm glad you enjoyed it. Hopefully, you'll come back and I can introduce you to some much more complex French cooking and meals in the future."

"I'd like that. This is actually my first time in Westhampton Beach."

"Really?" said Dani in disbelief.

Marcos nodded. "Yes, I'm just in town for about four weeks over the holiday season."

Dani rubbed her chin. "There's a lot to see out here. A lot of people think it's just a summer destination, but it's a beautiful place to be year-round."

Marcos was quickly finding out just how correct she was. "I can believe that. I haven't seen too much yet. It has been great so far just being in a place near the ocean and with so much nature and a laidback lifestyle. It's completely different from how I've been living back in New York City."

Dani was in complete agreement. "It's a different way of life." She paused for a moment. "If you'd like, I'm free on Saturday and would be glad to show you around the village a bit."

Marcos couldn't believe how nice she had been to him with first the croissant and now this. "I'd really like that a lot, Dani." It felt odd saying her name and addressing her so personally. Yet at the same time, he felt an unexpected spark of joy within himself just by using her name.

She picked up a stray plate left on a neighboring table. "Well, then it's settled. Meet me here at say ten o'clock on Saturday morning?"

Marcos stood up from the table and realized that he may have just gone up a belt size. "Ten on Saturday will be perfect."

Dani smiled. "Great, Marcos. I will see you then."

They said goodbye and Marcos headed out to his car parked in the dirt lot in front of the bistro.

As he walked out to the car, he felt as though Dani had already known him for a lifetime. There was something so unique and different about her. He couldn't place it, but it was there, nonetheless. The older he got, the more he trusted his instincts over the reasoning of his mind. There was definitely something special about Dani, that he knew already instinctually. When she said his name too, it felt as if they had already been friends for years and knew each other deeply.

He hadn't remembered feeling this sensation regarding anyone in such a long time. It was so different, new, and unexpected. Stopping at a bistro in search of breakfast on a near winter morning had resulted in a chance encounter that for some reason felt incredibly deep and significant. It was strange because little had been exchanged between them other than an explanation of items on a breakfast menu, a complimentary croissant, and the offer of a weekend tour of Westhampton Beach. Yet, it did feel significant and that was something that Marcos knew deep down, even though his reasoning and logical mind would have had him otherwise write it off as meaningless and just a nice business owner being friendly to a stranger.

The small field was now filled with cars and it would have been impossible to find a parking space at this point. He was glad that he had arrived early and had the opportunity to meet Dani. She was special. He knew that deep down even though they had just met. A car was already behind him with its blinker on and waiting to seize his coveted parking spot. Marcos backed out slowly and started down the road back toward town.

He had planned to stop in at two particular real estate offices. At the first office, they had a variety of land available for mixed-use, retail, and industrial purposes. Overall, it was a very limited selection along with the acreage available. Some of the land was located too far off of any road that would generate the kind of traffic that Sheila was hoping to bring in.

At the second real estate office, a lot of the property that was zoned commercial was under an acre and already had some sort of small building or office on it. Additionally, this particular office was mostly offering leasing options on the properties listed and that was out of the question. Sheila wanted to build. The selection that was being offered was nothing like what she was in the market for with her client. This was turning out to be more difficult than he initially thought. He knew it would be hard, but this was looking impossible.

It had been a day of mixed feelings. The morning had been great and the afternoon less than spectacular. He had an idea. Marcos drove back to the farm stand out near Dani's bistro. People were milling about outside purchasing fresh evergreen wreaths and trees to bring back home. Marcos parked and got out of the car. There were so many evergreen trees out front that it was hard to choose. He kept thinking about how much he was looking forward to Saturday and to getting to know Dani better. He had been given a touch of the Christmas spirit this morning thanks to Dani and the wonderful breakfast at her bistro. He wanted to keep that feeling alive even if he hadn't been successful this afternoon in finding an appropriate commercial property for Sheila and her client.

A half-hour later, there was a blue BMW slowly moving through Westhampton Beach with a stately balsam fir tree tied securely to its roof and bound for a house on Dune Road.

CHAPTER 9

There was a starkness to the winter landscape and vineyards along the north fork this morning. Dani drove and drove. Christmastime at the bistro was always a busier than usual time of year. She had planned out all of the specialty menus for the holidays last night working late. Now, she needed a release. The south fork of Long Island, where Westhampton Beach was located, had wineries. She needed the drive today and instead headed over to the north fork for a change of pace. Being on the north fork always acted as a consistent visual reminder for her of her own dream and that of her grandparents before her. It was there that the vineyards physically appeared in her reality, one after another along the narrow two-lane road that snaked its way east. Every time she was over there, it reminded her of what a dream fulfilled, namely that of a successful winery and tasting room, could look like when finally actualized. It made her vision for her life a little bit more real by seeing it all in person.

Dani continued driving. The greens of summer had been replaced with the subtle beauty of the browns and grays of winter. The landscape had changed and so had she. She had started youthful and starry-eyed out here.

The world of running a bistro had changed her. It made her see the world a bit differently now than she did in the past.

She saw a faded political campaign sign from the fall that had been forgotten and fallen to decay on the side of the highway. It reminded her of how she had never very much liked politicians. She didn't care for the ones locally or nationally. Dani drove on past the sign and yesterday's con job. There would be a new one next November. She had toughened with the years out here and with running a business. She remained a dreamer and visionary at heart despite everything. The holidays reminded her of how far she had come and how far she still had to go. They also reminded her to keep that visionary and dreamer spirit alive within herself no matter what she had to face as the years passed.

There was a quiet that seemed to have descended over the north fork. Everyone appeared to be keeping themselves inside for the winter now. The tasting rooms with their outdoor pavilions, seating, and live music seemed to have entered into a quieter and more reserved season. There were still tastings of course, but indoors, and with fewer and generally more local people. The steel-blue gray skies still stretched on above the rows and rows of symmetrical vines that made their way down toward Long Island Sound.

The small towns interspersing the vineyards were now more often places to be passed through by travelers. In the summer, they would be locations to stop, linger, and explore. Many would shop and perhaps have a refreshing gelato at an outdoor table or go on to take a swim in the sea that exists ever presently around an island such as this. There was even one particular street along that route called "Love Lane" and by its very name invited the transient passerby to stop, explore, and consider the possibilities.

Dani thought about her own life as she passed that particular street. She hadn't thought seriously about love in her life for some time now. Occasionally, someone would appear attractive to her, but that was it. It stopped there. Everything was about the bistro these days and she didn't feel that there was time for a great romance or even a minor one right now. A relationship required a lot of energy and commitment. Many often ended in disappointment, in her experience. She didn't want to put that much effort out again only to be hurt. Dani had been burned in the past and wasn't going to lose out again by making a large investment in someone else that ended up not having any sort of positive return. At least with the bistro, she could put effort and energy into it and expect to see some sort of return or beneficial outcome. She couldn't be sure that this would be the case with any particular relationship. One knows so little about another person upon even entering into a solid and committed relationship with them. Dani liked facts and she liked knowing about anything that she was entering into. A relationship meant taking a chance with no guarantees. The only chances that she wanted to take right now were those related to following her dream of establishing a south shore winery. Nothing else—with the exception of the bistro—mattered any longer.

It is beautiful over here, thought Dani before rolling down the window and letting the cool air blow into the car. The winter now offered a quieter and more subtle beauty than what tourists would experience passing through in other seasons.

She thought about how it seemed that there was one last burst that occurred each fall. It was the time of the harvest, festivals, farm stands with pumpkins, apples, cider, and corn mazes here. Then, with the disappearance of the tourists, came the gradual and subtle move toward winter. Everything became progressively quieter and calmer as the cold set in over the agricultural landscape. Many would retreat indoors and were not to be seen until the spring came again to the two eastern Long Island forks that jutted out into the water.

Dani stopped in to purchase some locally produced wine for the

Christmas and New Year's celebrations at the bistro at a friend's vineyard. They sat in the large, vacant tasting room with its shelves and shelves of bottles and empty tables and talked for a while on this cold December morning. Christmas and the new year were ever closing in on them rapidly. This was in addition to the advancing cold of the winter. It was a realization that was very evident to both of them on this particularly frigid December morning in the tasting room. Dani and her friend had gone out to the barn prior to the tasting where the wine was stored. There were a variety of tanks and barrels. Dani's friend had diligently let her watch as she topped them up, which was part of a routine that took place every four to six weeks over the winter months due to evaporation. The barrels themselves were after all porous, and she had a barrel in reserve to top off any wine that had evaporated from the others. Anything that was left at the end of the winter would then be broken down into smaller containers. These included carboys and kegs and that too would then be sold. Dani appreciated the economic efficiency, diligence, and close connection with the wine that she witnessed at her friend's winery. The warmth of the tasting room inside had been a welcome relief when they finally went back to talk and to catch up on life.

"These vineyards are clocking in at twenty, ninety, two hundred, and over five hundred acres. What are you going to do with four acres? You have to have more acreage and investment capital for a successful winery and for the project to be worthwhile. Stick with your bistro, which you are succeeding wildly at. Why do you always insist on pushing the envelope?" said Dani's old "friend" expertly. She had clucked away knowingly and dispensed more words on why things weren't possible for Dani, but just happened to have worked out for her.

It always struck Dani as interesting that people who were succeeding in a particular business had a propensity to tell others why they couldn't succeed or make money if they tried to enter and work within exactly the same field. Of course, deep down Dani did realize that she needed more land and money. Just once though, she wanted to talk to someone who was also optimistic about her dreams rather than just another voice saying why it couldn't be done

They had stood out in the field in front of the tasting barn with the bare grapevines behind them saying goodbye. A frigid wind swept across the field and Dani hurriedly loaded the boxes of wine bottles into the car while her friend hurried back inside the tasting barn. She drove off again, making the little over twenty-mile drive back to the south fork of Long Island and Westhampton Beach.

Dani did feel better after the drive. Seeing the vineyards during the winter and even being inside her friend's tasting room reminded her of her dream. The sky and the open winter landscape that she traversed always held a certain restorative effect for her as well. There was no traffic or significant tourism now, so the drive back ticked along relatively smoothly.

A few hours later, she was back in the kitchen of the bistro. Dani had put most of the wine away into the wine cellar and was chopping cilantro, peppers, and bunch carrots. These particular carrots had a certain degree of sweetness to them and were favored by guests in her bistro over certain other varieties. Everything was quiet. During the winter months, she closed the bistro early. At this hour, everyone had gone home, including all of her employees who would have usually filled the big, and now empty, kitchen.

Dani kept working at the counter. She always wanted to keep her French active. "Haché, haché, haché," or "chopped" could be heard audibly as she worked away steadily into the evening prepping food for tomorrow's guests. There was a sudden knock at the side door of the kitchen.

Who could that be at this hour? Dani was tired from the drive earlier and the long day. She just wanted to finish up some of this prep work for tomorrow and go home. *I have to see who it is.*

She went to the door and opened it. "Mark!"

"Dani!" replied a jubilant voice.

Dani hugged the young man standing at the door. "I thought you were still in Spain."

"I was. I just got back in town last night. I had to come see the best boss that I've ever had while I was here. I also brought you a gift from Spain."

It was a bottle of wine from the famous Rioja wine-making region in Spain. It was the perfect gift as Dani had always had a certain fondness for wines from that region. There had also always been a certain something between Mark and her. Of course, he was significantly younger. Yet that spark was always there. She hugged him. He had been working out and had a much leaner physique from when she had last seen him two years ago. At that time, he had worked as her poissonnier, or fish chef, in this very kitchen. Spain had been good to him.

Mark looked like he was withholding something standing there in her kitchen. "I have big news."

Dani's eyes opened wide expectantly. "What is it? I need to know."

Mark sat down on one of the stools. "Well, myself and a few other investors are opening up our first restaurant this summer right on the water in Montauk." Montauk was at the very end of Long Island's south fork and was located in the town of East Hampton.

Dani drew back jokingly, as though she were hurt by what he had said. "So, this is supposed to make me happy? Now, I'm going to have yet another competitor to contend with out here during the busy and already competitive summer season."

Mark shook his head. "You know I couldn't and wouldn't compete with you, Dani. This bistro and its owner are the best. Anyway, there's nearly a two-hour drive between the bistro here in Westhampton Beach and where we'll be opening out in Montauk."

Dani began to smile. "Well, you just stay in your lane and, of course, no one can contest what you said about this bistro being the best."

Mark laughed. It felt like something more, though, when he had said that she and her restaurant were the best. Maybe there was nothing to it. *I'm probably just imagining it.* Something in his intonation seemed to carry greater weight and felt like a reference that went beyond merely referring to her bistro.

The subtle and playful chemistry that had always existed between them was clearly still there. Spain hadn't changed that. Dani would always shake her head and dismiss it when they worked together and say that he was too young. It was her default position when she did feel that perhaps there could indeed be something between them someday. He certainly looked tan and fit after spending time over in Spain. It was a refreshing change to see someone looking like this out here and at this particularly cold and frigid time of year in the near-winter Hamptons.

"I really am happy for you, Mark. You'll do great out there in Montauk. It's a nice place with a good dining scene."

"Thank you, Dani," said Mark.

"I have something for you too," replied Dani.

Mark grinned. "You didn't even know I was coming, though. How could you have had time to get me a gift?" He of course realized that she couldn't have possibly gotten him a gift beforehand. Dani would have had no idea that he would be dropping in, or even that he was back in town from Spain.

She hurried outside quickly leaving Mark standing in the kitchen. It was cold out there today. Dani came back in with one of the nicer bottles that she hadn't yet unpacked from the trunk of the car and had purchased at the north fork winery earlier.

She presented the bottle to Mark after shutting the side door tight to keep out the increasingly cold wind outside. "Merry Christmas, Mark."

Mark knew instantly upon seeing the bottle that this was indeed a very good wine that Dani had given to him. "I'd very much like to share this bottle with you, Dani. It's a special wine and should be shared with a significant person." He still had the same charm from when he was just twenty-one and had started working in her bistro.

"I was actually going to say the same thing about this bottle that you brought me from Spain," replied Dani.

Mark looked as though he was coming up with a plan. "You know what? It's the holidays. If there's ever a time to celebrate another year and toast new beginnings, then this is it. Let's just open them both."

Dani laughed. "See, it's that kind of innovative and progressive thinking that led me to hire you in the first place."

"Well, I wouldn't be where I am now without all you did for me, Dani. You taught me everything that I know about working in the restaurant business."

Dani looked directly at Mark. "Well, you were always intelligent, hardworking, and . . ." She paused for a moment and then continued, ". . . eager."

They suddenly locked eyes with each other in the silent kitchen of the bistro. Her use of the word "eager" seemed to linger and hang in the air between them.

"You were a great boss," replied Mark, changing the subject a bit.

Suddenly, Dani returned to the moment. "I'd say we could drink them out in the dining room, but I still have a cleaning service coming in tonight."

"I'm renting a place in Bridgehampton right now while I launch the restaurant. It seems foolish, though, to drive out there just so we can hang out and drink wine."

Dani looked thoughtful for a moment. "If you want, we could go and have them at my place."

"Are you still living in Sagaponack?" inquired Mark.

"Actually no, not these days. I'm right behind the bistro, in fact."

"Where? You're kidding!" Mark couldn't believe what he was hearing.

Dani continued. "Remember that barn in the back of the field?"

"Of course," replied Mark. "We used to use it as a warehouse for the bistro."

Dani laughed. "Well, that's home now."

Mark looked incredulous. "How? I thought you would have had that old thing taken down by now. It was in pretty bad shape."

Dani shook her head. "Nope. I had a local architect come in and completely restore and convert it. It really came out nice."

Mark was obviously impressed. "I'd love to see how it looks now."

Dani grinned. "Well, I would be happy to show you. Just grab that bottle, and I'll switch off the lights when we walk out."

Mark grabbed one bottle and Dani the other one. They walked out into the now leafless rows of grapes stretching out into the fields behind the bistro. They continued into the winter sunset and headed toward the far back field and the converted barn.

"How was Spain?" asked Dani casually as they walked along the path through the vines.

Mark was looking straight ahead at the evening sky in front of them. "Spain was nice. It's like the Hamptons in a way."

"Come on now," said Dani in disbelief.

"No, really, it is. The Hamptons has its own unique rhythm and way of life. It's not just what the summer visitors come to see and experience. It's the same in Spain, really. It's a way of life that is all its own. I miss it. If I am working in New York, then I can't think of a better place to be than out here."

Dani nodded her head. "I do agree with you on that. It's special out here, especially at Christmas."

Mark added, "There really is something unique about this place." They approached the doors and headed into the converted barn, which was now Dani's house.

As they walked into the entrance foyer, Dani went to turn the lights on. Suddenly, the sound of Sinatra singing a Christmas song came out of a hidden speaker or speakers embedded somewhere in the room.

Dani was slightly embarrassed. "I'll turn that off." She realized that she had accidentally turned on the music system and the song that she had been listening to earlier before leaving for work.

"No, please leave it," responded Mark. He clearly enjoyed her taste in music. Mark grinned. "I always liked some of his recordings from when he was performing at The Sands in Vegas myself."

"Well, you're quite a hip cat then, Mark," answered Dani. She almost couldn't believe that she had let that expression escape from her lips and felt just a touch ridiculous for having said it out loud. She thought about his comment about liking Sinatra. That was a bonus for Mark. She knew there was a reason why she had always liked him. There were the looks too, of course, but liking Sinatra recordings from The Sands Hotel in Las Vegas many years before his time was very next level and only added to his appeal.

They walked into the living room with its high vaulted ceilings and light wood flooring. Mark's eyes went about the room taking it all in. There was a stone fireplace on one end with a flat-screen television above it. On either side were two large floor-to-ceiling windows with views out toward the fields and grapevines. Two large beige sofas were separated in the middle of the room by an elongated and low coffee table. There was a black iron spiral staircase closer to the entry foyer which led up to the master bedroom in what had originally been the loft area of the barn.

Mark was amazed. "I think this looks better now than it ever did as a warehouse space. I bet the original farmer who built this never could have imagined it looking like this."

She turned the dimmer on the switch to a warm setting as the recessed lighting came on. The wind was now picking up outside. Darkness had arrived, but they could still hear it whistling through the symmetrical rows of grapevines in the fields. Winter was indeed coming.

"I'll light a few candles," said Dani, moving over toward the coffee table in the center room. She lit a vanilla and pine-scented candle, and the warm, comforting scent slowly began to drift up and into the air of the living room.

Mark looked at the candle burning on the table. "I've always thought that candles add something nice and kind of comforting to a space."

Dani nodded in agreement as she put her coat and Mark's into a nearly hidden closet close to the spiral staircase leading upstairs.

In the corner of the room near the fireplace, the Christmas tree looked wonderful. It had tasteful warm white lights, a red tree skirt, and added so much to the large space, especially when it was on at night.

Dani started heading into the other room. "I'll just get a bottle opener from the kitchen, Mark. Make yourself comfortable."

Mark placed the bottle of wine from the north fork next to the bottle he had purchased for Dani from the Rioja region of Spain on the coffee table. He then took a seat on the sofa on the opposite side of the Christmas tree.

Dani came back from the kitchen with the bottle opener. She looked at the two bottles on the table and hesitated for a moment. "What should we start with?"

"Hmmm," said Mark. He continued. "Maybe we should drink the north fork one first since we are on the east end."

"I would have to agree," responded Dani. She opened both but poured two glasses from the bottle that she had purchased earlier in the day. They sat there in the great room with the dim recessed lighting, the high vaulted ceilings, the warm lights from the Christmas tree, and the wind whistling outside through the vineyard and raised their glasses.

Dani put her glass against Mark's. "Let's toast new beginnings."

Mark smiled. "I cannot think of a better toast right now than that."

They clinked their glasses and sat down.

They talked of adventures in Spain and interesting happenings where wealth, celebrities, fame, summer experiences, and memories collided together in the Hamptons. Mark certainly had a lot to catch up on from Dani, having been gone for two years now. There always seemed to be something interesting to talk about when two interesting people who were connected to two fascinating destinations came together. Both had lived and were continuing to live in places that many people wondered about. Both were interesting people themselves. It made each of them a constant subject of fascination to others who could never possibly fully understand them. People at the bistro, both locals and employees, had wondered if there was something between Dani and Mark. It had been a subject of local speculation and gossip. No one was really sure. With time and with Mark having left for two years, all of that idle talk seemed to have now vanished.

However, here at Christmas were two friends who could now catch up together on life in their own unique way.

"You've done well for yourself, Mark. I'm proud of you," said Dani.

Mark smiled. "I'm grateful for that. It means a lot coming from you."

Alcohol loosens one's inhibitions. Perhaps the passing of another year and the unknown of a new one does too. Christmas is a fixed point on the calendar that acts as a powerful reminder of that fact. Dani and Mark had finished the first bottle of north fork wine together and were now getting ready to move onto the Rioja region bottle. They told one story after another. There were stories about Spain and stories about life on Long Island's east end. There were stories about their own lives and what had transpired in the time that had passed while both had been following their own storylines.

"It's really cold by this window," said Mark suddenly. "Maybe I've just gotten too used to the warmer weather abroad. Is it okay if I move over to that chair?"

Dani laughed while holding her wine glass.

"Or you can just sit here if you'd like," said Dani with a faint hint of mischief as she pointed at the vacant space on the sofa next to her.

"I guess I'll take option number two then," laughed Mark.

He moved over next to Dani after pouring a glass for each of them out of the Rioja bottle.

Dani took a sip. "We've always had a good working relationship, Mark."

Mark nodded. "We certainly have. I wouldn't have left if things hadn't come up in Spain."

Dani put her glass down on the table for a moment. "I know that. You have to go where the best opportunity is. We all missed having you here, but you did the right thing. It's good to have you back, though."

Mark took a large sip from his glass. "It feels good to be back, really good."

The wine was impacting them both. She looked into his brown eyes and put a hand on his shoulder-length black hair, which touched the very edge of a fitted blue polo shirt. He had more life experience now. They both had. Right now, he was the same attractive twenty-one-year-old who she had hired all those years ago. They had worked side by side together up until two years previously. Neither had ever acted on any feelings that might or might not have been. In a moment, their lips met almost instantaneously. The moment itself felt brief and yet like an eternity all at the same time. Everything that had been left unsaid had now, at long last, finally been said.

As soon as the moment had passed, Dani and Mark sat there in the silence of the great room. So much had changed in both their lives. For a moment, they had both acted as though nothing had. The reality was that things had changed for them both and all of a sudden, that truth became abundantly clear.

Mark looked into Dani's eyes. "I have to tell you something, Dani. I met someone while I was over in Spain."

Dani didn't say anything. There was nothing to say at that moment.

Mark continued. "Mariela and I met for the first time during a festival while I was working in País Vasco, or the Basque country. We were both a part of the same comparsa."

Dani looked confused. "What's a comparsa?"

Mark leaned back. "A comparsa is basically a group of costumed individuals who are traveling together from place to place, aiding and taking part in creating the celebratory atmosphere of the festival that is occurring in the area."

Mark took a deep breath and continued. "Anyway, we were both carrying los gigantes, which are a popular tradition in a number of places, actually. They are these giant costumed artificial figures that are carried through the streets during certain festivals in Spain and elsewhere. That's how we met. One thing led to another then and we ended up in a relationship together. She's coming over here next month."

Dani didn't know how to respond to that statement. Was there even a response needed? Mark's comment had once again confirmed her existing feelings toward relationships and any thoughts of a great romance potentially coming into her life. Once again, she was glad that she hadn't become too invested. Here was the proof once more of what would have happened if she had entered into this with him too deeply at an earlier time.

"Stay here tonight, Mark. There's no point in paying a car service to drive you back to Bridgehampton at this hour."

Mark nodded his head. "Thank you, Dani."

She got up from the sofa and halfway up the spiral staircase turned around. She looked at Mark still sitting there in the great room, but alone now.

"And Mark, I do appreciate you telling me the truth rather than letting things go on any further."

"Of course, Dani."

Dani paused for a moment, looking at him sitting there in her great room one more time.

"Goodnight, Mark." Dani continued up the stairs to the bedroom.

"Goodnight, Dani," called out Mark.

He put a blanket over himself and soon after fell asleep on the sofa. It was just him now in the great room beside the warm glow of Dani's Christmas tree as it stayed on through the night. The wind continued to blow outside. The official start of winter and the arrival of Christmas, and all that it did or did not have to offer, moved ever closer.

CHAPTER 10

Saturday had arrived faster than he could have believed. Yet, at the same time, Marcos had been anticipating seeing Dani again all week and was glad for its arrival. The brief encounter between them at the restaurant had felt special and unique. She drew him in. Her outgoing personality, intelligence, and obvious business acumen made him want to know more about who the person behind the bistro really was.

He had completed his morning run on the beach, came back to the house, cleaned up, and was now ready for something strong to get the day started before meeting her at the bistro at ten. He made a strong cup of espresso in the large chef's kitchen. Only Arabica beans would be used this morning in his coffee. He believed in using the best and strongest of anything whenever it was available. It was a very personal choice and one that he felt brought him success. He thought back to Dani for a moment. She seemed like a person who followed a similar ethos, namely never settling for less than the best in anything that she put her mind to.

After the brewing was completed, he found some high-quality porcelain espresso cups and saucers that Marvin had tucked away in a cabinet under the center island and took his morning cup of coffee into the double-height adjacent great room. The great room was a little cold, and it reminded him of how it had been colder than usual outside during his morning run. He was now into his second week out here in Westhampton Beach and noticed that there was a significant drop in the temperature from when he had first arrived.

Marcos put down his espresso on the large, low table in the center of the room. It was placed directly next to Marvin's pile of books about winning at life, which were all still sitting there. Seeing those books reminded him that he was now into the second week and still had not found an appropriate commercial property that would meet Sheila's expectations. He turned on the electric fire in the book-matched marble fireplace to warm the large open space up a bit. Marcos looked outside through the floor-to-ceiling windows and noticed that it was snowing now. It must have started while he was showering upstairs. This was the first snowfall of the season, and it had happened so unexpectedly. Westhampton Beach seemed to be the place where unexpected experiences were happening in his life one after another. The unexpected meeting with Dani, finding a bistro that was open at that hour of the morning, and now being able to experience the first snowfall of the season were all positive and unexpected events. Not being able to find an appropriate property for Sheila was also somewhat unexpected, he supposed, but definitely not something that he was happy about.

Marcos looked at the snow falling outside. *That explains the cold.* He sat down on one of the low-lying plush oversized blue sofas and reached for his espresso. The snow was coming down steadily on the lawn and beach further off in the distance outside, and he enjoyed his cup of espresso along with the now blazing electric fireplace. It was quickly making the large room significantly more comfortable. After the espresso was finished, he went back into the kitchen. Marcos washed the dishes and then headed up the floating staircase alongside José's custom art installation to the master bedroom to get dressed for his morning meeting with Dani.

As Marcos approached the bistro, he noticed all of the grapevines and fields stretching into the distance behind the building until they eventually reached the scrub pine forest. They were all now covered with snow, and this was especially noticeable between the rows of vines as they stretched their way toward the pink and cobalt blue hues of the horizon beyond.

The morning crowd was already having breakfast and starting their weekend when Marcos walked in. At the front entrance, he was warmly greeted by the *maître d'*. She recognized him nearly immediately. Upon asking to see Dani, Marcos was ushered down a hallway with pictures on the wall of various celebrities who had at one time or another eaten at the bistro. He was then led to a back door entrance, which went into the kitchen. Dani was busy giving instructions to the sous chef when Marcos walked in.

She waved happily and called out to him. "I'll be right over."

A few minutes later, Dani came over, gave Marcos a quick hug, and said, "Just let me grab my things and we'll get going. It's good to see you, Marcos."

"It's good to see you too, Dani," he replied. Marcos kept thinking to himself about how alive and full of energy Dani seemed. She carried with her a positive energy that seemed to radiate from her very being and impact everyone around her. Even the staff working in the kitchen seemed to be more optimistic, solely because of her influence and presence in the room. Dani and Marcos walked out into the cold and got into Dani's car with her driving.

It was a relatively scenic and short drive from outside the village. The grand homes of the Hamptons with their hedges and rolling lawns looked particularly attractive with a dusting of snow upon them. The patches of forest and fields that would sometimes come into view also looked very pretty as they sported this first snowfall of the winter.

Dani stopped at a traffic light. "So, how are you enjoying being out here in Westhampton Beach, Marcos?" It was the first real question that she had asked of him since she had asked him his name during their first encounter at the bistro.

Marcos looked out the window at a shingled elegant home set back far from the road in the distance as they paused at the light. "It has been a nice change, actually. It's different from being in the city, but in a very good way."

Dani nodded her head. "I agree. It is nice out here." She seemed for some reason to be preoccupied and thinking about something else in the moment. Marcos didn't know for sure, but just for a brief few seconds, she even appeared a bit melancholy. It was startlingly different from how she had just appeared in the kitchen when all of her staff had been gathered around her and Dani herself had been completely engrossed in her work. She seemed to be thinking about something now, and whatever it was, it didn't appear to be something pleasant.

They continued driving. "So how long have you been out here, Dani?"

Dani smiled now and seemed to return from whatever had been on her mind. "I've lived here for most of my life at this point. My family started the bistro years ago and bought the land even further back before the current building was a place that served food."

Marcos leaned back in the seat as they continued driving. "That's wonderful. It is an incredible bistro that you have here."

Dani turned on the right turn signal. "I'm very proud of it. Hopefully, in the future, we can expand into winemaking as well and get a tasting room going and all of that. It's a big business out here. It would be really nice to have a winery next to the bistro, especially during the summer months."

Marcos thought about what she had just said for a minute. Here was someone who had already achieved so much and ran a very successful bistro in the Hamptons. However, she was still striving to achieve more. There were still dreams and hopes in her future. She still wanted something bigger. It felt so inspiring to hear this from her and to be talking with someone who always wanted more out of their life. He then thought about her relatively small plot of land where the bistro sat, and a shadow of doubt came unexpectedly across his mind concerning the real dream of Dani's that she had just expressed to him.

"Doesn't that take quite a bit of land?" asked Marcos a bit confused.

Dani nodded. "It does, but I own the four acres behind the bistro. I know it's not enough for the winery that I'm envisioning, but we'll see what the future brings."

Marcos looked ahead at the snowy roads leading ever closer toward the village. "Well, I'm sure anything you attempt will be a success, Dani." Seeing the determination in her eyes as she told him about the land behind the bistro that she owned made him believe that she could accomplish anything that she wanted to achieve in her life.

"Thank you, Marcos," she replied. Marcos suddenly had a thought. It was a different kind of thought and one that was completely separated from Dani's dream. It related to the real reason why he was out in the Hamptons, which was something that he purposefully let himself forget from time to time. This was especially due to all of the positive experiences that he was otherwise having since arriving in Westhampton Beach.

He hadn't realized that all of the land with vines on it behind the bistro was still a part of Dani's property. She had said it came in around four acres. That was really about the size of the property that Sheila was looking for. Additionally, in all likelihood, it had some kind of farm or commercial zoning designation. If it was zoned as commercial property and he acquired it, this all might help it to go faster through the approval process with the community. The idea was starting to grow into a realistic potential possibility in his mind. All of this was definitely something to think about and consider seriously. It had nothing to do with Dani's dream, but it had a lot to do with his survival at the company and whether or not Sheila would keep him on in the approaching new year.

They were soon nearing the edge of the village of Westhampton Beach, New York. Dani wore a black felt fedora, which covered her long, dark blonde hair, tan driving gloves, a red coat, and patterned scarf. She pushed her sunglasses up above her eyes to get a better view of the wintry road ahead and proceeded to ease up a bit on the gas.

"So, I know I asked you about how you like it here. However, the really important question is what brings you out here to Westhampton Beach, Marcos?" asked Dani suddenly as her eyes scanned the buildings of the village just ahead. She sounded much more business-like in that moment. Her question was put forth with a tone of authority. It was a voice that she might have used in the boardroom when facts had to be presented about something or the truth needed to be laid out bare without any unnecessary trappings.

"Business is the main reason that I'm out here right now. My company sent me out here for four weeks as part of a project that they're looking to bring to completion," answered Marcos.

"That has to be challenging," added Dani. She continued. "I mean, wrapping up any project during this time of the year when so many people are taking off for the holidays can't be an easy task."

Marcos nodded in agreement and thought that this was a nice-looking little village that was coming into view. "It certainly is. Without a doubt, it most definitely makes everything a lot more challenging both for me and for the company."

The picturesque little villages in the Hamptons are each different in their own way. As a whole, they all possess a seasonal beauty, which is distinct to each one of them respectively, at this time of the year. There is an essence which they hold that cannot be experienced at any other time except at Christmas. Driving into the village, Marcos first noticed the cars parked at angles along an attractively landscaped Main Street, in front of classical-looking, but contemporary New England-type village shops. It was different from pulling into the acres of a large asphalt parking lot in front of a big-box retailer.

These shops and restaurants had a certain specialness and interest surrounding them. One wasn't certain exactly what kind of atmosphere, items, or experiences would be found inside. They were in a sense like people, with each one being unique, different, and special in their own respective way. The standardization of national chains was not there of course and that became a part of the pleasure of the experience and its corresponding uniqueness. The buildings themselves had character and the experiences inside seemed to be awaiting discovery by the pedestrians who found themselves anxiously peering into their windows with anticipation as they strolled along the sidewalk out front.

The next apparent visual was the profusion of wreaths, red bows, and Christmas lights. The trees along both sides of the street were bare now. Regardless, there was still life to be seen. People continued to mill about outside the quaint shops and restaurants even in this cold weather. They seemed to enjoy being out in the winter sun, which appeared to give off a piercing and even brighter light that was somehow different now as compared to other times of the year.

Summer was different there as well. It was a time when most were outdoors. There were live concerts occurring at places along Main Street and there was a focus on an outdoor lifestyle, as well as that of coming from or going to the beaches nearby. Both Christmas and summer emerged as two unique times in the Hamptons when one could take a visual, postcard-like snapshot of a unique lifestyle. It was the character of the place itself which made this visual possible, and it was certainly unique and not available everywhere that one may travel. The Hamptons were just that: different. Each community possessed a certain degree of charm and feel about it that was all its own. These small villages in particular had not succumbed to standardization and as a result still possessed a strong degree of character. They had the added benefit of existing within the context of a beautiful natural environment, which formed so much of the framework around which life in the Hamptons existed.

"Do you mind if I stop at the post office first, Marcos, before we go on our tour? I have some Christmas gifts that I really need to get mailed out." There were four brightly wrapped packages sitting on the backseat of the car.

"No problem at all, Dani," replied Marcos as she continued driving the car along Main Street. They got out of the car and walked inside. It was an older building and very well maintained and architecturally attractive. All of a sudden as Dani approached the counter with Marcos, she felt a tap on her shoulder.

"Dani!" said an excited voice.

"Fran! How are you?"

Dani had known Fran for a few years now. She worked for a magazine out here in the Hamptons, along with various other pursuits that were far more lucrative and kept the estate of the moment paid up. However, the magazine and covering what was going on in the Hamptons was her real passion.

Fran was exuberant. "I'm doing very well, actually. House number six has just been purchased, so you know how that is."

Dani laughed, "Well, I don't actually, but I can certainly imagine, Fran. I'm so glad to hear that everything is going well, though. I feel like it's only at this time of year that you run into your neighbors so frequently here at the post office."

"I know, and that's so true, Dani. It's kind of the place to come to catch up on the gossip and what's going on out here right now. Summer will be here soon enough and that's always the busy time of year for all of us," added Fran.

Fran suddenly noticed that Marcos was looking at a painting on the wall of people from another time. The people in the image appeared to be sailing, hunting, golfing, spending time on the sand, and playing tennis, all at the beach.

"That painting came out of the New Deal Era," said Fran knowingly as she pointed at it with a gloved hand. "Artists who didn't have work had the opportunity to create art. The government was actually behind it, if you can believe that. It was nice because it acted as a tool for beautifying buildings that belonged to the general public, such as this post office."

"Thank you, and that's really interesting," said Marcos continuing to look at the pleasant seaside image.

Fran smiled a bit smugly. "You are most welcome."

Dani looked over at the mural as well. *The way that the people were dressed and everything about the scene clearly reflected a different and much earlier time in Westhampton Beach.*

Fran turned toward Dani. "If you have time, Dani, and would be interested, I'd like to do a piece on you for the magazine. You could talk about running the bistro and life out here in the Hamptons, something like that."

Dani thought for a moment. "That might be nice. Let's do it. You let me know and we'll set up a date for the interview."

Fran continued. "I don't want everything that we cover to be just about the celebrities and what they're doing out here. I want to expand our reach into what more of the local people are working on and what their lives look like."

"Well, that's very generous of you, Fran. Let me know when the time comes and we'll most definitely make it happen," replied Dani.

Fran was holding a shopping bag in her hand along with the receipt from the mailing that she had just completed. "The new house is over on Meeting House Road here in Westhampton Beach as well. I've had my Feng Shui expert in already, so it's all good now. When the weather gets nicer in the spring, you'll have to come over and see it. Maybe we can even do the interview there."

Dani held the door open for Fran as they walked out of the post office. "I'd like that a lot, Fran."

Fran pulled the haute couture stylish scarf tighter around her neck. "We'll play bocce ball while we drink wine and catch up. I like a low-impact sport where I can have some wine and get in a bit of exercise all at the same time."

Dani laughed. "Now, that's my kind of workout as well."

"Happy Holidays," called out Fran as she began heading off in the opposite direction down Main Street.

Marcos and Dani got into the car and moved it down the street and closer to the performing arts center. Dani was looking out the window at the snow-covered village as they pulled into a parking slot on Main Street. "It's kind of a beautiful morning. Maybe we should just take a walk through the village."

Marcos agreed. "That sounds perfect."

They got out of the car and began their walk through the village of Westhampton Beach. The village certainly had a scenic quality to it. The buildings were tasteful and pleasant to look at. Everything was very neat, clean, and well maintained. Many of the businesses had spaces or porches out in front indicating that in the summer people were encouraged to linger or to spend time outside interacting with their neighbors and the local community. Marcos felt that it all kind of suggested taking a more relaxed and leisurely approach to life and enjoying one's experiences, rather than merely going somewhere to purchase something or to eat a meal and then getting into your car and driving off to go back home.

Dani's long blonde hair was blowing a bit in the wind under her black fedora. The red coat showed up strikingly against the white of the snow all around them. She seemed elegant, attractive, and endlessly interesting to Marcos. His reverie was suddenly broken by a voice.

"So, have you already done all of your Christmas shopping?" asked Dani unexpectedly and in an almost doubtful questioning tone. He winced at the thought of what she had just reminded him of. It also reinforced how little time there actually still was before Christmas to complete it.

"Actually no, I haven't. I was hoping to get back to the city in enough time to do it there."

Dani looked surprised. "It's never good to put off things or wait too long. You never know how things are actually going to go."

"Those words sounded a bit prophetic, like someone with personal knowledge," said Marcos jokingly.

Dani laughed. "I had a friend who I caught up with last night. Unfortunately, we both put things off a little too long. When we did get around to finally acting on something that we had both been thinking about, well, it was too late, and let's just say the opportunity was lost." Dani seemed lost in a moment of reflection.

Marcos looked at the prints from their shoes side by side in the freshly fallen snow on the sidewalk. "That's good and very true advice," agreed Marcos. He continued. "You know, in that same spirit, I probably should just buy something out here in the village for a good friend of mine back in the city."

"That's the spirit," said Dani proudly. She looked in the window at a shop they were about to pass by along the sidewalk. "Let's take a look in there.

I've bought some good gifts for people in this store throughout the years. They have a good selection."

Marcos opened the door to the shop, the inside bell above it rang noisily, and they walked in.

The shop itself was pleasant inside with a wide selection of gifts and locally-themed items. Dani and Marcos walked throughout the various displays looking at each item on offer. Marcos came across some nautical-themed salt and pepper shakers, as well as a few additional and whimsical sets of kitchen-related items. *These would make great gifts for Monique.* She loved entertaining at her home in Park Slope and this would bring a nautical summer vibe to her place in the city. Dani was looking at some decorative summer-themed pillows nearby.

"I bought a Christmas tree for my rental house at the farm stand near your bistro, but I haven't actually bought or placed any decorations on it as of yet," said Marcos almost absentmindedly.

Dani looked at him in disbelief. "Well, don't you think you should get around to decorating it sometime soon? You don't have all the time in the world before Christmas at this point."

"I know, I know," replied Marcos.

He explored another corner of the shop and saw some beach-themed Christmas decorations. *These look kind of nice.* Dani had already gone up to the counter and was paying for her items. Marcos came up there shortly afterward and purchased a platter, pitcher, salt and pepper shakers, and a variety of beach and nautical theme decorations for his tree back at the house. It certainly wouldn't cover much of the tree as a whole, but it would be adequate for the short time that he would be out here. It would also be nice to take them back to his home in the city after Christmas and those decorations would always serve as a reminder of his winter in the Hamptons.

Dani and Marcos walked out of the shop laden with packages and continued along the snow-dusted sidewalk.

"This is a nice little village," said Marcos aloud.

Dani nodded. "Well, the thing is that everything is close. If you live in the area, you can come into this nice, quaint little area easily. You then have this great ambiance and can have breakfast, lunch, or dinner in a nice setting, or even see a show and take care of any shopping all in the same trip."

Marcos agreed and replied, "And it's all very compact and in a very pretty setting. This is so different compared to driving to a supermarket, multi-screen mega movie theater, or a big-box national chain store. The vibe here is completely unique."

They stopped at the car to drop off their packages and then continued walking.

"I'm getting a little hungry," said Dani suddenly. She added, "Usually, I'm at the pass in my kitchen at this time of the day. I'm standing there checking all of the food and making sure that it is beautifully presented before giving it over to the wait staff to be brought out to the guests. This is a very welcome change being here in the village with my new friend Marcos."

He grinned a little hearing this from Dani. "Well, I feel very fortunate that Westhampton Beach's premier chef de cuisine could take a little time off to show a stranger around her town."

Dani smiled. "I know a pretty nice place where we can have lunch."

A snowplow rumbled by along Main Street as they walked a bit further and then eventually went into the restaurant that Dani had in mind.

They were quickly seated in a lovely back room that almost looked like an upscale screen porch in a home. There were French doors along one wall leading into other parts of the restaurant and then large windows that looked out over the snowy village. The space had ceiling fans above that had been turned off for the winter and square back chairs. The tables themselves had white linen tablecloths and napkins on them. Marcos couldn't help but think that these didn't look quite as festive or seasonally appropriate as the way that Dani had chosen to decorate her dining room for Christmas. The red tablecloths, evergreen centerpieces, and candles throughout her dining room at the bistro put one in much more of a Christmas mood.

The menus were brought over and Dani and Marcos studied their contents. All of the choices looked excellent and making a final decision was not going to be easy for either one of them. Dani ended up going with the steak and Marcos with a cod entrée. A short while later the appetizers were served followed by the entrees that they had each ordered.

The cod was tastefully seasoned and herbs and noodles completed the dish perfectly. Dani's steak had a pat of butter seasoned with herbs that rested upon what appeared to be a perfectly cooked dish. This was complemented by sweet potatoes in a mash composition and a bit of broccoli and stewed rhubarb. They began to eat.

"This has been a really nice day so far, Dani. I'd also like to raise a toast to you for your graciousness in taking me around your town." Marcos raised his glass.

Dani put her knife and fork down and raised her glass as well. "Thank you, Marcos, for giving me this opportunity to get away from work and to have a day out again. It has been a while and this was some much-needed fun. However, it's not over." Their glasses clinked.

"Well, I'm glad to hear that," said Marcos. He liked how alive Dani was. She was intelligent, dynamic, and ambitious. These were all attributes that he had always valued in himself as well as in others.

They both continued eating their entrees. All of a sudden, Marcos noticed that Dani was frowning as she worked at her steak.

"Is something the matter?" he asked.

"This is a lean cut," responded Dani, preoccupied as she worked at her food.

Marcos was confused. "Is that a problem?"

"Yes, it is a problem," responded Dani.

"How do you know?" asked Marcos.

"Do you see how difficult this is to cut? That's because it's dry, and that's a result of the cut being too lean." Marcos looked at her steak on the plate. He didn't notice anything wrong. In fact, it actually looked wonderful. However, Dani was not pleased.

"How can you differentiate between a lean cut and one that isn't?"

Dani wasn't feeling like playing question-and-answer games with Marcos. "I don't really like trivia," she said in a bit of a snarky tone.

"Sorry, I apologize for asking," responded Marcos.

Dani looked up from her plate. "I shouldn't have said that to you, Marcos. Actually, you asked a very good question. It's just that if the chef had chosen a cut with more marbling in it, the taste would have been so much better, the cut wouldn't have been so lean, and everything could have been perfect. I always look for cuts with enough marbling before I present anything to a guest."

"Oh, I see," answered Marcos, not completely understanding, but thinking it best to move on to another topic. It had to be difficult dining in someone else's restaurant when you had one of your own. Marcos imagined that it would make anyone much more demanding of someone else's restaurant as a result. This had to be particularly true when one ran an eating establishment at such a high level and demanded perfection like Dani did with her bistro. It would be hard for most other places to measure up to the standards that she had set.

After the check had been presented and paid, Marcos and Dani went back outside and continued their walk. The day had slipped by faster than either one of them had realized. Initially, Dani had thought she'd spend an hour, maybe two at the most, taking this stranger around her town. Now, it was already late afternoon. Neither person was tired of the conversation with the other or of just walking together through a picturesque village that had just experienced its first snowfall of the year. They, therefore, continued to walk and visit the various shops and places scattered throughout the village.

As the evening approached, the temperature was beginning to drop. Both Dani and Marcos could feel this change. They walked just a bit closer together trying to stay warm while laughing and talking about their experiences to date. The street lamps were coming on and it paired wonderfully with the warm glow of lighting from the shops and businesses along Main Street.

"Would you care for a hot chocolate, Dani? If there was ever a night for it, this would be it," asked Marcos suddenly as they were nearly back to where the car was parked.

Dani's eyes opened wide in a sense of happy surprise. "I would love some hot chocolate tonight. It's the first snowfall of the season, and what better way to celebrate it. I know just the place."

Dani led Marcos to a place with a selection of cakes, pastries, and of course hot chocolate on the menu. However, this was not just everyday hot chocolate. Instead, it was an upscale version made from fine European Belgian hot chocolate and created at a consistency that gave it a much smoother and sweeter finish than anything out of a can or packet. This was then paired with a selection of choices for customizing the hot chocolate. There was the usual whip available, but also a variety of chocolate, star anise, peppermint, and cinnamon garnishes.

"This is delicious," said Marcos, taking a sip.

"See, I told you this place was good!" laughed Dani. She continued. "I have one other thing to show you before we head back." They left the shop and walked down to the village green.

The Christmas tree was lit and it was now dark. They took a seat together on a nearby bench near the gazebo with their hot chocolate.

Dani looked at the tree reflectively. "I sincerely do like this time of year. There's something hopeful and optimistic about it."

Marcos took a sip of his drink. "I agree. If I were in New York City right now, I would have missed all of this. There's the Rockefeller Center tree and all of that, but this is more peaceful." He paused for a moment. "It's more special too. If I had been in there, I would have been one of thousands looking at a lighted Christmas tree, but not actually sharing that moment with anyone. In New York City, especially during this time of year in midtown, you can feel anonymous. It's the kind of place where you realize just how many people there are in the world because you yourself become lost in the endless crowds. Here, you feel like an individual. You feel as though you count and that you matter in some way."

Dani tightened the lid on her cup with a gloved hand. "I think there's a lot of truth in that. I couldn't live in there. I don't like feeling completely anonymous or another number. People know me here. I'm recognized for what I do and you know, for me that's important. I have a lot of ties here."

Marcos nodded. "I think that's important for everyone and something that is lacking today. People don't value each other."

Dani nodded her head in agreement. "I like that we're around the same age and can acknowledge something like that. It takes some time in this world to come to that kind of conclusion."

They both sat together in the silence and peaceful quiet of the lights from the large lit-up Christmas tree on the snowy village green drinking their hot chocolate. Each was lost in what seemed to be their own personal reflections on a year that would soon be in the past. It was quiet and the sky was dark here at night. Yes, there was the rumble of the snowplow, the occasional car, and the sound of people talking, including others who had come to see the tree and menorah on the village green. However, it was significantly different from how Marcos remembered and knew the Christmas season to be back in the city.

Dani finished her coffee and then pulled an object out of her coat pocket. It was wrapped in silver paper. "I purchased something for you to help get your Hamptons Christmas season started."

Marcos was surprised. He took the small package in his hands and began to unwrap the bright silver paper. The object inside was a ship's wheel. It had a compass lodged in the center of the decoration and a gold string for hanging it on the tree. Marcos didn't know how to respond to this incredibly thoughtful gesture. "Dani, this is absolutely perfect. I don't even know what to say."

Dani looked at the wheel in Marcos' hands. "This will encourage you to continue to steer your own course and to follow your own direction going forward. You know what is best for your ship and for your voyage."

Marcos' eyes were fixed on the beautiful object in his hands and the very special meaning that Dani had now assigned to it. "We barely know each other, and yet I already feel as though you know more about me than most other people," replied Marcos.

Dani smiled. "I feel the same."

She continued. "You'll remember your time out here for years to come whenever you look at your Christmas tree and see that ship's wheel. It won't matter what your coordinates are or where you are at that time in your life. It will always bring you back to being this age and having hot chocolate with a stranger who became a friend. You can always come back to this Christmas tree, this moment, and this bench again just by looking at this decoration on your tree."

Marcos was speechless. It was all so meaningful and unexpected.

"Dani," he said. "I've learned so much from you already. You taught me about viennoiserie, different types of croissants, and that more marbled cuts will be tastier at restaurants. Now, I feel like you've even helped provide me with guidance for the path ahead in my own life with this beautiful Christmas ornament. It just feels like when I'm spending time with you that I'm learning more than any college class could ever offer."

Dani grinned. "And it'll be far more useful in real life."

They hugged, but not like it had been when they had greeted each other at the bistro earlier that morning. No, this held something else. This time there was a distinct indication that both Dani and Marcos felt something special developing toward each other. It remained to be seen where their journey would take them from that bench at night on the snowy Westhampton Beach village green in front of the Christmas tree.

CHAPTER 11

It had been one of those very special and rare days that doesn't come around very often. When it does, it quickly embeds itself as a memory that one looks back upon for a lifetime. The day and evening spent with Dani had been nothing short of magical. After the first snowfall of the season, he had been taken on a tour of a Hamptons village with a beautiful stranger. Earlier that day, he had woken up in a modern Dune Road mansion listening to the waves crash on the shoreline, gone for his daily run on the beach, started the morning at a French bistro, and ended the evening on a bench with hot chocolate within the warm glow of a Christmas tree on the village green.

Marcos felt that his life was taking on an otherworldly and almost dreamscape quality. It didn't even feel real. It was only for a four-week period that he would be out here in the Hamptons. Eventually, he'd have to wake up at the end of that time and return to the city. The holidays would be over then, another year would have passed, and the realities of a rushed time-strapped existence and work life would be upon him once more. Marcos wanted this moment right now to last. He wanted to live just in the present for now and not think about the future, New York City, or anything else for that matter. He only wanted to focus on these wonderful experiences that he was suddenly having out here in the Hamptons and this captivating stranger who had come into his life so unexpectedly and had been so gracious and kind to him.

He was lying in bed in the master bedroom and heard the morning sound of the waves crashing on the beach. It was a wonderful way to wake up each day. *I won't think about any of the stressors right now. I'm waking up to another beautiful morning in the Hamptons, and last night was a winter's night unlike any other that I've had previously. I need to think about all of that.* He closed his eyes, laid back, and continued to listen to the sound of the waves breaking outside.

Suddenly, the mobile phone on the bedside table began to wildly vibrate. The name "Sheila" appeared. *Shit.*

He reached for the phone and answered, "Hello?"

The voice on the other end was unmistakable and seemed in a hurry. "It's Sheila, Marcos. Have you found anything for me yet?"

Marcos paused on the line for a moment.

"So, I guess the answer is no?" said Sheila hurriedly and with a touch of annoyance.

Marcos thought for a moment. "There is one potential property I'm looking at, Sheila, that meets your criteria and the client's."

"Tell me about it," she snapped back.

"Well, it's not for sale yet."

"Then why are we considering it?" she interrupted.

Marcos almost lost his train of thought with the interruption, but then continued. "I think there might be a possibility of the owner considering selling."

"That sounds pretty uncertain and unreliable to me. Have you looked into zoning? You know what these local politicians and town boards are like."

"Not yet," said Marcos. He continued. "It's a bistro, and at least that parcel should be zoned commercial. There are then four acres attached to it that are being used as a vineyard right now."

"So the zoning might have to be changed and approved on those four acres?" asked Sheila.

"It's possible," replied Marcos.

Sheila was growing more impatient. "Why does the owner want to sell?"

"I don't know yet if she wants to. You'd have enough property for the development and the frontage is on a major and busy road out here. You could even potentially do a pad site if it was approved because there's enough space."

The line went quiet. Obviously, Sheila was meaningfully considering what Marcos had just presented to her. "Just make it happen, Marcos. I don't have to tell you what your employment situation will look like in the year ahead if you don't."

With that final veiled threat, Sheila hung up the phone abruptly.

It seemed as though there was no other choice now. Sheila was interested in the property and was probably passing the news on to the client already. *I have no choice. I have to find a way to get Dani to sell the bistro and attached property.* She didn't seem to be someone who had any intention of selling or of moving anywhere anytime soon. How could he possibly convince her that it would be in her best interest to give up the bistro and the vineyard and sell?

Then again, money did have a way of speaking brashly and loudly. Maybe she would see the logic in walking away from the property with a healthy all-cash offer. There were certainly much more affordable locations than the Hamptons. Additionally, there was no shortage of places where she would be able to get a lot more for the money with the proceeds from the sale. Finally, Long Island was well recognized for its high taxes. There were a lot of compelling reasons that he could present to Dani for selling the property and severing her ties with New York State. He remembered the words of one real estate broker in New York City when he had first started his career. He was trying to sell his first commercial property and she was already a well-seasoned broker in the field at the time. In a quiet moment, before the transaction process had begun, she had said to him sagely, "When you try to sell a property in New York State, everyone has their hand out and wants a piece of the action." She had been right. Armed with all of these reasons, maybe he could eventually make a convincing argument to Dani for selling and moving somewhere that would be more supportive of both her bistro and longtime dream of someday opening and operating a winery. *I'll have to see what I can do.*

He got up and went downstairs to the chef's kitchen to make a cup of espresso. After it was prepared, he went into the great room and saw Marvin's books sitting on the table. They always seemed to be there looking at him. Marcos laughed a bit to himself. *Maybe I should flip through one of them one of these days and see if there are any suggestions for a situation like this.*

All of a sudden, the phone rang again. It was certainly turning out to be a busy morning as far as people wanting to talk. It was Monique.

"So, Marcos, how's luxe living out in the Hamptons at Christmas treating you?"

She always has to start with a biting comment, thought Marcos, laughing to himself. "How many times do I have to tell you, Monique? They're regular people in the Hamptons and want to be treated like everyone else."

He could hear Monique laughing on the other end of the line. "Yeah, sure, Marcos. Anyway, how are things going out there, seriously?"

Marcos didn't know where to begin. "Well, first off I want to thank you for getting me this amazing house for the four weeks. It's more than anything I could have imagined."

"You are welcome, Marcos. That's the power of connections and influence at work right there with securing that place for that price. I can't tell you how many people used to tell me that they worked their way up the ladder, paid their dues, and that connections had nothing to do with their success. That's horseshit and most of them are liars. Connections have everything to do with nearly everything. I learned that when I finally stopped listening to the people who told me that I should focus on climbing the ladder instead of building my own connections. That's what they had been doing all along and was their secret to money and success. That's how it's really done," replied Monique.

Marcos felt Monique had drifted a little off track. He liked that she was a shark and a fighter. He needed people like that on his side. However, when she started talking about something that she believed in passionately, it could quickly turn into a lecture, which could go on for an indefinable amount of time. He redirected the topic back to the magic of her securing such an incredible house for him to stay in for four weeks over the holidays.

"Seriously, how'd you do it?" asked Marcos.

Monique didn't seem to want to reveal that kind of information to him but then changed her mind. "Let's just say that you have a guy in construction who is lacking in any kind of fashion sense. However, he has incredibly deep pockets. Then you have a handsome, lonely artist who just moved here from Spain. I may or may not have had a hand in bringing those two dichotomies together." She laughed.

"Well, I do like your style, Monique. That certainly sounds like some kind of Christmas miracle to me that you were able to make a relationship like that happen," replied Marcos.

"Well, it was really more of Marvin's early Hanukkah miracle, but moving on. I like to bring good people together," said Monique.

Marcos took a sip of his espresso. "Since we're talking about people meeting other people and coming together, I do have to tell you that I met someone pretty special out here."

Now Monique was interested. "Are you serious? You, Marcos?"

"I am quite serious, actually," he replied. Marcos continued, "There's this chef de cuisine who owns a bistro out here. We spent the day together yesterday touring the village in Westhampton Beach."

"Is she married, single, or otherwise attached?" asked Monique inquisitively.

"I don't know. I don't think so," replied Marcos. He added, "but there is one problem."

"So there's one problem besides not knowing whether she's in a relationship?"

"Exactly," responded Marcos.

Monique paused for a moment, "And that problem is . . . ?"

"Well, you know who we work for?"

"Sheila?"

"Exactly. Well, you know why I'm out here. I have to deliver that commercial property before the new year."

"That's true," responded Monique.

"Anyway, the one property that meets Sheila's criteria is the bistro owned by this chef de cuisine."

"Okay, I'm listening," said Monique, very interested in what was coming next.

Marcos continued. "Well, it would involve the purchase of her bistro, the four acres attached to it, and having it all bulldozed and redeveloped for Sheila and her client's project."

Monique gasped. "You have a way of getting yourself into bizarre and interesting situations, Marcos. I don't even know what to tell you with this one."

"I know," he responded.

There was a brief moment of silence on the line and then Monique continued. "Why don't you just tell her about all of this and what's at stake?"

"You mean that I'm going to lose my job if this doesn't happen? Why would she care about that? She barely knows me."

"No, no, no. I mean just tell her about what the offer is, how much she would get in return, and see what happens," replied Monique.

"I guess there's really no other way," said Marcos.

"There isn't. Since you two spent so much time walking outside yesterday in the village, why don't you take her to Rogers Beach where you can both walk and talk out the whole situation?" said Monique.

Marcos paused for a minute. "Where's Rogers Beach, Monique?"

Monique laughed. "It's right there near you on Dune Road."

"Oh, well that's certainly convenient."

"You bet it is," replied Monique. She continued, "I have to get going, Marcos. Invite her to the beach for a walk, tell her the situation, present her with the offer, and see how it all plays out. What's the worst that happens, she says no?"

"That is true, Monique. I'll give her a call after we hang up."

Marcos and Monique hung up a few minutes later, and Marcos sat in the great room thinking about their conversation while looking out at the snow on the pool deck area, lawn, and beach beyond, and all the while considering what to do next.

He thought about calling Dani. They had agreed to speak with each other again soon after their evening together on the village green beside the Christmas tree. This call didn't feel in keeping with the spirit of that night or in sync with whatever they had or could potentially go on to build together in the future. This had a business motive behind it and that didn't feel right. Marcos wanted to see Dani, of course. It wasn't that at all. He wanted to be able to see her as much as possible during the short period he still had remaining there in the Hamptons.

Suddenly, he thought about the ship's wheel decoration with the compass that she had given him. He had left it upstairs in the anteroom off of the master with all of the other decorations that he had purchased when he had come home late that night. Marcos looked at the tree that he had procured at the farm stand near Dani's bistro. It stood bare in the great room next to the book-matched marble fireplace.

I have to go upstairs and get the decorations and hang them on the tree now while I'm thinking about it. He hurried up the spiral staircase and found the decorations, including the one from Dani still sitting on the counter. He brought them back down to the great room. Marcos walked over to the Christmas tree. There was a branch protruding at the highest and most central point of the tree. Taking great care, he gently wrapped the gold cord that was attached to the ornament from Dani around the branch and secured it in place. The otherwise bare Christmas tree now had its first ornament. That ornament was a single ship's wheel with a compass, and it now sat in a prominent and highly noticeable position on the tree. It was striking and even more meaningful because of what Dani had said about it when she had given it to him. Marcos then proceeded to put the rest of the decorations on the tree below it.

He did want to see Dani. Seeing the ornament again reminded him of how much he had enjoyed their day and evening together. He would also have to tell her about the business proposal. There was no other way. This felt necessary even if he wasn't adhering to what his true internal compass was telling him. Marcos clicked on "contacts" and selected Dani's number.

After four rings, there was an answer. "Hi, Marcos! How are you?" She seemed to always be filled with a refreshing sense of positive enthusiasm.

"Hi, Dani. I'm good. How are things at the bistro?"

"Busy as usual," she replied. "It's the holidays and we're always even busier in here at this time of the year."

"Well, I'm certainly glad that everything is going well there. I really enjoyed our village tour the other night."

"I did too, Marcos."

Marcos continued. "I was wondering if you'd like to go walking at Rogers Beach this coming Saturday morning. I know it'll be cold out there, but I'd like to see you again while I'm still out here and have the opportunity to do so."

Dani interrupted. "Actually, Marcos, I was going to call you this evening and ask if you wanted to go out on my boat with me tomorrow. It's nothing special, just a small pleasure craft, but I have it tied up right here at the Westhampton Beach Marina. There's the possibility of the weather turning, but often the forecasts aren't correct. Do you maybe want to see how it is on Saturday and if it looks alright still go out on the water? You can get a nice view and see how beautiful this area really is. It's a different vantage point and worth seeing."

Marcos didn't expect this sudden proposal from Dani. He certainly wasn't going to turn down any opportunity to spend time with her. "I'd love to, Dani. When were you thinking we'd go out on the boat?"

There was a pause on the line as Dani contemplated when she would be free enough from her responsibilities at the bistro on Saturday to spend a day out on the water. "Is ten again good, Marcos?"

"That works great for me," he replied.

"Wonderful," said Dani. She continued. "We can still do Rogers Beach as well, but let's get out on the water, weather permitting, before we get any further into the winter. The beach will still be there when we get back."

Marcos laughed. "Perfect, Dani. I'm looking forward to it, and I'll see you at the marina at ten on Saturday."

After the call was finished, Marcos walked out to the snow-dusted terrace to get some fresh air. The clean, cold beachside air out there felt refreshing and restorative. Marcos took in a deep breath. He went back inside and looked at the single decoration from Dani high up on his Christmas tree. It stood out from all of the other ornaments that he had purchased.

The wheel itself seemed to be a suggestion that perhaps this was now a new journey that he was on here in the Hamptons at Christmas. He hoped for smooth seas and a minimal number of squalls on the winter ocean of life in the Hamptons that lay in front of him.

CHAPTER 12

Marcos drove out to East Hampton the following morning to experience a different part of the Hamptons as a whole. The trip might even have the added benefit of clearing his mind and perhaps spark some new ideas about the commercial property acquisition problem back in Westhampton Beach. He thought it might be a good place to purchase a gift for Dani as well. Marcos wanted something with a sense of occasion and gravitas about it. He wanted a gift that would reflect the unique time of year when they had first met and the special and unrepeatable moment of their first unexpected meeting in Westhampton Beach.

He thought about the symbolic and significant gift she had given him. The ship's wheel with a compass in the middle carried so much weight and meaning. This was not only because of what it represented, but even more importantly because of the person who had chosen it and given it to him at Christmas, no less. Marcos continued to drive and was now within close range of East Hampton.

Each of the communities that make up the collective entirety of what is known as the Hamptons possesses their own very unique and specific sense of charm and character. Westhampton Beach doesn't feel like Southampton, and so forth. There are even places that refer to themselves as "The Hamptons" of this or that place in an attempt to boost business and the prestige of that particular locale. Marcos had often seen this in various publications and media outlets and secretly wondered what exactly that meant.

Did it mean that the area had a beach or other specific Hamptons-type lifestyle? Was it a place requiring significant capital to live in and out of the price reach of most? Did it mean luxury, estate, and compound-like living? The questions seemed to go on and on in his mind.

Regardless, Monique had encouraged him to go out and explore other parts of the Hamptons while he was out there anyway if time allowed. She had told him not to be "that guy" who just identified with one particular town or area of the Hamptons exclusively and dismissed all the rest as not up to par. He decided that today he would indeed follow her usually sage advice and do just that by heading out to East Hampton for a change of scenery.

The village was now approaching. East Hampton had an elder statesman-type sensibility or aura about it in relation to its other Hamptons village counterparts. Maybe it is because of its traditional association with "old money" in the Hamptons. However, the exclusivity of the strong old money association feels, at this point, a bit dated and inaccurate in reality. Having significant money seems to instead be a more realistic portrayal of the criteria required to be able to buy into any highly sought-after locale within the Hamptons region of Long Island.

The village green, town pond, and Old Hook Mill were the first places that came into view as Marcos entered East Hampton. The village was very picturesque, particularly now at Christmastime, in a Norman Rockwell painting or early colonial American kind of way. Its layout was reminiscent of a traditional New England village. Yet, it wasn't all colonial or old in its bearing. Yes, the colonial architectural elements were very much there in various buildings still standing throughout the area and those fashioned to look that way. However, there was also a glossiness and modernity to others that made both the old and new blend perfectly together in a harmonious and charming architectural whole.

Old Hook Mill had its sails festooned with lights and a green wreath festively adorned its single front door. The wreath stood out against the field of white, upon which this windmill from 1806 sat with its gray shingles now dusted with snow and its accompanying picket fence. Marcos imagined it must look particularly striking at night with the white lights on the sails against the pitch-black night sky and the blanket of snowy field along with the village green stretching out in front of it.

There were small, decorated pine trees placed in between the larger trees and benches that lined the streets of the village. Marcos parked the car, got out, and started walking and taking it all in. The village did have a certain elegance and sense of refinement to it. A few moments later, he came upon a large white-columned church building situated amidst a field of snow. There was a clock and steeple at its summit. He decided to go in to get out of the cold for a bit.

There was absolute quiet in the sanctuary as he sat down in an empty back pew. The building itself didn't have the grandeur of vast space or sculptures aplenty like one would see at St. Patrick's Cathedral in the city. Neither did it have the auditorium or rock-concert type ambiance of the megachurch, where he had last attended services many years ago as a youth growing up in Kentucky. Finally, there was no steady stream of tourists coming in with their cameras and necks craned looking skyward at the ornate interior designs of a vast structure. No, this simple, relatively sparse space was typical in design of a traditional New England church. The structure's interior seemed to quietly suggest to Marcos that, at least, one should perhaps focus in upon the moment at hand,

and then maybe extend that focus to look a bit backward and then forward over one's life to date.

It being near Christmas and the end of the year, there was certainly no better time to engage in both of these long-range considerations. The career and life in the city in the world of commercial real estate had been an all-consuming whirlwind for Marcos. He was always busy and didn't have time to reflect on his life, or at least that's what he told himself until now. Yet, even in there, he felt an inner sense of emptiness that he could no longer run away from. It was particularly poignant when he returned home to an empty and cold home amidst the city's stark concrete canyons late at night. In a city with so many people, he still felt largely alone and unnoticed. Marcos' early years in Kentucky hadn't felt or been like that. There he always had friends and family nearby. He questioned why he had decided to move to New York City each year more and more. It had been a decision made hastily in youth and one's perspective tends to change with greater experience and the passing of the years, it seemed.

He looked around the interior of the quiet sanctuary. Marcos silently wondered if Dani felt similarly. He really didn't know. Dani's life, too, was extremely busy out here in the Hamptons, and she also was working all the time. However, the experiences that they had already shared together reminded him of that sense of companionship and feeling of being valued and appreciated that was now so pointedly absent from his life.

Marcos knew one thing at that moment, though. He did want a simpler life and one that was calmer and closer to the land. He had fallen out of love with the city that had been his home for so long now. He couldn't describe the sensation that was coming over him exactly. He thought about the life that his grandparents had lived on the farm and making bourbon at their distillery. There was something very special about that, which his life in New York City didn't possess.

Here, in this church, he suddenly realized that he missed all of it, as well as having people around him who had been so important to him growing up. He stood up from the pew, put his jacket back on, and walked out to the snowy street once more. Marcos hadn't thought about his life so philosophically since he couldn't remember when. Life in New York had consumed him and he no longer questioned things, even whether he was still happy, until this moment in East Hampton.

He purchased a cup of strong coffee and continued down the snowy sidewalk in search of a place to buy a gift for Dani.

Marcos walked into a small jewelry store that was well-decorated on the outside with various forms of evergreen boughs, red bows, and warm white lights. In a front display window facing the sidewalk, there was a selection of tasteful jewelry, appropriate for holiday wear, on display. He walked inside. The warmth of the small shop was a welcome break from the cold December weather outside.

"May I help you with anything?" inquired a well-dressed salesperson who had been, up to that moment, arranging pieces on a three-tiered island in the center of the store.

"I'm looking for a special piece of jewelry for a friend," said Marcos, casting a discerning eye over the many items on display.

"Is it more of a gift for a friend or a romantic partner?" asked the salesperson curiously.

"It's for a friend. So, I'm thinking something more in the nature of a pin, necklace, or something like that."

A smile came across the face of the salesperson. "Perhaps, if we select the right gift now, you'll come back to us for a ring or additional piece of jewelry later."

Marcos smiled. "Well, I don't know about all of that. I guess, though, that anything is possible."

The salesperson laughed. "Believe me, I've seen it happen more times than you would believe in here."

Marcos nodded in agreement. "I'm sure, especially at this time of the year."

The salesperson carefully adjusted the last small, blue-boxed item that she was putting into place on the tiered display. "It really is true, you know. The holidays have a way of encouraging people to take that next step in their lives."

Marcos looked down at a necklace on display. "Well, nothing says 'next step' like a piece of fine jewelry, I suppose."

The salesperson looked at Marcos, now giving him her full attention. "Well, it's more about what the piece of jewelry represents to someone than anything else. Of course, I'm biased." She laughed and then continued. "However, that just makes picking out the right piece even more important. It also makes my role in the customer's decision more difficult." She smiled sagely, as though this process was something that she had gone through many times in this very shop with many different people, all of whom had a variety of differing expectations connected with their jewelry selection.

"We have some holiday-themed necklaces over here if you care to take a look," said the salesperson motioning toward the other side of the shop. Marcos followed her and saw a variety of sparkling pieces on display behind the glass. The prices varied as widely as the types of pieces on display. Out of all of the items, there was one with a snowflake that caught his eye.

"Would it be possible to see that one?" asked Marcos, pointing at the necklace. The salesperson took it out of the case and placed it gently on the counter to show Marcos. He looked at it intently. It was a tasteful snowflake on a necklace and was absolutely perfect. Marcos didn't even hesitate as he normally did when purchasing something over a certain price point.

"This is the one," he said definitively.

"That's an outstanding choice," replied the salesperson approvingly. "I would have selected the same one myself if I were buying a gift for a friend at this time of the year. It's actually the last one of that kind that we still have available."

"Really?" asked Marcos in disbelief.

"Absolutely. They're very popular this year. You do know what they say about snowflakes?" questioned the salesperson.

Marcos looked confused. "I'm afraid I don't."

The salesperson selected a small blue box to package the necklace in. "Well, there's an old Zen proverb that states 'A snowflake never falls in the wrong place.'"

"That's fascinating," replied Marcos.

He thanked her for all of her help, they commented on the weather briefly, and a short while later he left.

As Marcos walked out of the jewelry shop and headed toward the car, a group of carolers dressed in Victorian costume had gathered on the village green near the frozen town pond. They launched into a chorus of "God Rest Ye Merry Gentlemen." Marcos couldn't help but feel a little bit better about everything that had recently taken place in his life despite the difficulties with work. He thought about his new friendship with Dani and how special that was becoming to him as he continued to walk toward the car to the singing of the carolers wafting through the now brisk night air. It was all accompanied by the warm yellow glow of the street lamps along the sidewalks of East Hampton, the snowy blanket coating the village green, and the snowflake necklace, now tucked carefully away in the pocket of his blue dress coat. He looked forward to a night of peaceful winter dreams upon returning to his new home for the holidays on Dune Road back in Westhampton Beach.

CHAPTER 13

It was now already 10 a.m. on Saturday and the day when Dani had suggested that they meet and go out on the boat. Marcos drove down to the Westhampton Beach Village Marina. One of the nice things that he had discovered about this community was that everything was relatively close. There never seemed to be a long commute or the hassle of being stuck in traffic to get anywhere. *How different things are seventy-something miles away.* He was also sure that the traffic situation would have been significantly different if he had been out here during the summer months, which was the busy season. Right now though during the winter, there was no problem getting around at all, and he arrived at the marina quickly.

The weather reports had all indicated that a fierce nor'easter winter storm was heading directly up the coast toward them. The current weather conditions suggested exactly the opposite. It seemed like a perfect near winter day in the Hamptons. The air was crisp and cool. The sun was shining overhead and the water in the marina and beyond looked completely placid. Dani and Marcos had both agreed to take their chances over the phone earlier and had jointly decided to take the boat out anyway despite the forecast.

Dani showed up a short while after Marcos had arrived and parked. She got out of the car exuberantly.

"This is such a beautiful day!" she called out to Marcos enthusiastically as she hurried over to his car.

"It really is, Dani. It's so good to see you again."

They hugged. It felt wonderful to be able to see Dani and to feel her positive energy this morning. With her there, it felt like even the darkest day would somehow be a good one. Dani motioned toward the slips where the various vessels were docked.

"Let me show you my boat," she said. They walked toward the water and found it quickly. The marina itself was a comfortable size, meaning everything was accessible and if you had a boat, there was no difficulty in getting to it easily.

They climbed aboard and Dani put down all of the bags that she had brought out of her car that were filled with provisions for the day ahead.

"Let me help you," said Marcos. They started unpacking everything and putting the perishables into the refrigerator on board. A short while later, Dani suggested that they had better set off. Marcos untied the boat while Dani took the helm and started the engines. A few minutes later, Marcos was back on board and they were ready to set off.

The boat moved slowly out of the slip and toward the open water side of the marina. The calm water of the departure route was bordered by beautiful homes and properties. Many had rolling green lawns that stretched down to the water, and some even had their own private docks that discretely jutted out into the water they were passing through.

The boat continued to move slowly along from the marina and toward the bay. Marcos hadn't been on a boat in a long time. It seemed he was always busy in the city and never had the time any longer for something like this. However, being out here today reminded him once again of the romance that he had always felt toward sailing and being out on the water. It felt good to finally return to something that he had always loved during his youth.

Even though it was nearly winter, the view of the surrounding Long Island coastline was beautiful. Winter brought with it a different kind of beauty. Marcos couldn't stop thinking to himself about how this didn't even feel like the Long Island or New York that he had been familiar with for so long now. Being sent out to Westhampton Beach for the holidays had completely changed his viewpoint and mindset about so many things, it seemed. It had also brought him back to the things that he had loved about his youth. These were things that seemed to have otherwise faded out of his life.

Dani pointed toward the barrier island and Dune Road from their current position on Moneybogue Bay. "My grandparents used to drive all the way out here from where they lived near the city during the '40s. They would spend the day going to the beaches off of Dune Road, having fresh seafood at one of the restaurants, and even eventually had their engagement here. We have an old black and white photo of them sitting on a rock somewhere along that stretch of sand that parallels the road. Our family has a lot of history connected with this place. I mean, just look around, Marcos. It's really magical, isn't it? I couldn't imagine living anywhere else."

Marcos nodded in complete agreement. "It is, and that's pretty special, Dani. I can see why this place means so much to you."

They continued looking out at the beautiful natural landscape around them while Dani piloted the boat. She then continued. "It's more than the place. I mean, it's beautiful and all, but it's my family's connection to it. It's the generations that have been here before me and who have felt something special toward it. That really makes it so much more meaningful for me."

Marcos nodded as he took in everything around him.

Dani had just told him how important this area was to her. Her family had so much history here. *No, I can't bring selling the bistro and property up to her now.* He watched her expertly increasing the speed of the engines and maneuvering the boat across the bay. She had so many interests and talents and constantly kept him amazed. He felt as though he was starting to develop real feelings for her. He had never before met someone quite so captivating.

He returned to the conversation. "I feel the same way about where I grew up in Kentucky."

Dani looked at him in surprise. "I didn't know you were from Kentucky, Marcos. I figured you were just another New Yorker trying to extend their business reach into the Hamptons."

Marcos smirked. "No, there's a lot more to me than just being another employee working at a big New York City company."

Dani smiled mischievously. "You see, this is the kind of stuff that I would have been interested in knowing about you from the time that we first met when you wandered into my bistro."

They passed under the bascule bridge, which went over Moriches Bay. It was the same route that Marcos had become so familiar with every day when he traveled back and forth between Westhampton Beach Village and Dune Road. It was different looking up at it while being down below now on the water. He was surprised at how quickly he had become accustomed to all of this. This was his world now, it seemed. Well, it was his world for the next few weeks at least. *How can I go back to New York City again after all of this?* He felt an unexpected bout of melancholy taking in all of the inspiring landscape that surrounded him, knowing that before long he would have to leave it.

Dani moved away from the controls for a moment and reached into the refrigerator. She handed Marcos a specialty type of bottled water and lemonade. Marcos took a sip of the bottled water first.

He was pleasantly surprised. "This is so good, Dani. Wow."

She nearly laughed at his unexpected reaction to what was her everyday choice of bottled water. "I'm glad you like it."

Marcos took another sip. "It reminds me of the amazing limestone water in Kentucky that my grandparents used to use to make their bourbon."

"Your grandparents made bourbon?" Dani was surprised. "I feel like I'm learning more and more about you by the moment. It's too bad I don't get a few drinks in you instead of lemonade and find out more about you a whole lot faster than the rate that we're moving at with spring water."

Marcos laughed and nodded as he took another sip. "That would be interesting. Seriously though, my grandparents had a farm in the bluegrass country outside of Louisville. I was practically raised there. It's where I spent most of my childhood."

Dani was becoming interested in the fascinating and surprising background of this handsome stranger and pseudo–New Yorker who had so unexpectedly wandered into her life.

"I have to ask you then, Marcos, about what life was like growing up on a farm with a distillery in Kentucky as a child. To me, that sounds like a pretty interesting childhood. I mean, it's not just that. To be honest, I've always been interested myself in owning land that produces wine and in someday opening a winery, so I'd love to know more."

Marcos was excited. "Really? Wow, we do have a lot in common. I'd love to hear from you then first, Dani. I can't believe this."

Dani took a bite of one of the snacks that she had unpacked. "No, no. I insist. I want to hear about you, Marcos."

"Well, I was fortunate to grow up in a place with a lot of natural beauty and freedom. There's a freeness in the countryside that you don't get in the city."

"I can agree with that," said Dani.

Marcos continued. "Anyway, the bluegrass country outside of Louisville is beautiful. I was also lucky to be raised predominantly by my grandparents on their farm."

Dani interrupted. "It's just so odd hearing that from you, Marcos. You strike me as so 'big city,' and now I'm learning that you grew up on a farm. Anyway, sorry, please keep going."

"It was definitely a contrast with where I'm living now, that's for sure. They instilled a solid work ethic in me. Fifty acres of their farm was planted with blue corn that we would use for the corn component of the bourbon. I'd help out a lot. As I became older, I even got into helping them more with the distillery side of their business."

"Now that must have been interesting," noted Dani.

"It sure was. I learned a lot about the bourbon-making process. I even helped them with deciding upon the mash bill some years."

"What's that?" asked Dani.

"Well, the bourbon gets distilled later on from the mash that is created. However, fifty-one percent of it has to be corn. The other grains that make up what's called the 'mash bill' in addition to the corn are up to the producer."

Dani smirked. "So, what were your favorite additional grains of choice, Marcos?"

He laughed. "That's easy. Wheat. I'm a classy guy, after all. A high wheat bourbon has a smoothness and softness to it."

Dani came right back at him playfully. "So, what you're telling me is that you're smooth, sweet, and elegant?"

"Damn right," answered Marcos right on cue as he laughed out loud.

Dani began to laugh as well and was impressed hearing Marcos talk so passionately about something so unexpected and seemingly out of character for him. She liked people who were passionate about whatever they chose to do. If they had a sense of humor about it, that was even better. In her book, Marcos was winning on both counts.

Dani grinned. "Well, if I ever open my winery, you might be a guy worth having around."

Marcos waved his hand as though dismissing the very suggestion of it out of hand. "That's very kind of you, Dani, but I don't see myself leaving where I'm working in the commercial real estate field anytime soon."

Dani adjusted the collar on her jacket. The bright sun over them out on the water was getting to be a little too much. "Well, honestly, I don't know when or if I'll have the opportunity to own and then get my own winery and tasting room up and running."

Marcos stretched out his legs. "I guess there are still possible unexplored paths ahead for both of us. Hopefully, we'll both get the opportunity to travel down a few of them at some point in the future."

"I hope so," responded Dani.

Marcos continued with his story. "Anyway, being young at the time, I believed that you had to go to a place like New York for the real opportunities. The problem is sometimes everyone is going to the same place and those opportunities never really existed there in the first place, or if they did, they begin to dwindle when a crowd starts to gather."

"So, did you find them when you finally got to New York?" asked Dani with a tone of meaningful curiosity.

Marcos assumed the facial expression of a serious poker player on the professional tour circuit. "Yes, I did, but they weren't what I thought they'd look like."

"But aren't you happy that you've achieved your dream, moved to New York, and been successful?" asked Dani, puzzled.

Marcos paused in thought. "I'm not happy with my life in the city. I've tried to believe that I am, but I've experienced enough to know that I'm not. I still want to chase the dream of being successful, but on my own terms. I also want to do it in a place where I matter and where I'd have some kind of authentic meaning in the lives of others. I'm a number in New York and replaceable to them. When I grew up in Kentucky, there were at least people who knew you and expressed some degree of interest in your life, hopes, and dreams. I don't feel that now. In fact, I feel very little working in there day after day and year after year."

Marcos hadn't expected to say any of that to Dani. It came out of his mouth unexpectedly. He barely even knew her, yet he was pouring out emotions and feelings, which he had kept inside for so long now. It felt suddenly cathartic to release all of them. He had never before expressed all of those pent-up feelings about New York or his life there to someone else.

He continued after a brief pause. "I've become used to working with and serving a very specific type of clientele. I am accustomed to the very unique, specific, and often demanding needs of New York's wealthy investors and developers in the commercial real estate field. The thing is, it all just leaves me feeling empty now. I don't have the passion that I did when I started in the field. I'm the person who gets the transaction done, but I'm anonymous and there's a hollowness to it all. I used to feel like I accomplished something meaningful and useful by the end of the day when I helped my family out on the farm and at their distillery growing up. The work that I'm doing now doesn't hold that same sense of satisfaction, at least not any longer for me."

Dani nodded. "Well, I can relate to what you're saying. I think that's why I've always been drawn to running a bistro and to the idea of planting grapevines and making wine. My family wanted me to go into law when I finished college. I'm really glad that I didn't now. I meet a lot of unhappy lawyers who come into my bistro regularly. There's something healing and very positive, though, about working with your hands and actually making or building something. It gives me a feeling of satisfaction that I don't think I could get doing something else in an office. I don't know how to describe it. It's just different from what I would imagine the work of someone working in commercial real estate in the city to consist of on a daily basis."

"You're right, Dani. You're absolutely right. You must have moments though where you doubt certain things?" questioned Marcos.

Dani nodded her head in agreement and looked deeply into Marcos' eyes. "Of course. There are things I don't enjoy, but I think that's with everything. The difference is there is a greater feeling of being a part of a small community with the work that I do and the community that I'm a part of out here. I'm invested in the place. My family has roots here. My grandparents always wanted to see so much come to pass for us as a family. A lot of it has happened, of course. However, that's where my biggest doubt or moment of questioning things comes in. I just feel that there's so much more waiting for me out there, Marcos. You must feel that way too sometimes. It's that sensation that you need to make something happen before time runs out." Dani looked off toward the wintry marshland of the nearby shoreline.

Marcos looked at Dani. He thought about what she had been saying about building upon something that her family had started. "I think it's amazing that you want to continue to build upon your family's legacy, Dani. I do. Don't you want to follow some of your own dreams, though, things that your family may not have even considered pursuing, because it wasn't something that they were interested in?"

Dani was still looking off into the distance. She slowly returned to their conversation and made eye contact with Marcos. "Of course I do. I have my own dreams. It's just that the family's dream has become one of mine as well. I'm a part of that legacy and have a responsibility to see certain things through to completion."

Marcos respected how dedicated and close Dani was to her family. He had always been close to his family as well, so it felt special that she had a similar relationship with hers.

Dani cut the engines and they found a place to pause her boat in the water. Marcos and Dani walked out to the sofa on the flybridge and took a seat next to each other with their drinks and snacks. The conversation quickly picked up right where they had left off. Both individuals were becoming increasingly interested in learning about each other during this moment of calm out on the water.

"How did your family end up out here in Westhampton Beach?" asked Marcos as Dani took a sip of her lemonade. A tea room out east, an escape from the ever-encroaching expansion of the city and its suburban counterparts, a quest for peace, a need for open land and clean air, and a desire to grow a few grapevines and a garden had all led Dani's family to discover Westhampton Beach, New York. Dani explained it all to Marcos as they sat there in the middle of the calm bay. *It feels so good to finally be able to share the stories behind my life with someone else.* She couldn't remember how long it had been since she had opened up to someone like this so freely and uninhibited.

"Relatives of my grandparents lived out here at the time. My grandparents wanted clean air, beautiful scenery, open land, and a peaceful life. My grandmother always had the dream of opening a little tea room on eastern Long Island. Maybe that's why I ended up going into the restaurant business," said Dani. It did seem like a plausible explanation, to her at least, for why she had chosen the path that she had in life.

Marcos agreed. "I think we are drawn to certain people, places, and even career paths in our lives for sure."

Dani adjusted the bracelet on her arm. "Anyway, as early as the Nineteen Fifties, there was a lot of tract housing being built on what were farms across western Long Island. My grandparents were starting to feel boxed in. Long Island, even back then, was starting to feel like it was getting too built up. They felt that in no time the island would parallel—in its own unique way, of course—the density of population, level of development, and amount of congestion that took place nearby in New York City. Of course, land values in the Hamptons weren't what they are now."

"That's for sure," interrupted Marcos.

She added, "Well, four acres, an old commercial building, and a barn became available on the property behind where our relatives lived. My grandparents had been coming out here on weekend trips since the 1940s, as I already mentioned. Anyway, they took a big chance and bought the property. My grandfather now had more than enough room to plant grapevines and vegetables. My grandmother opened the little tea room that she had always dreamed of and became very successful."

Marcos interjected a thought that came to him. "I think you have that same entrepreneurial spirit as your grandmother. The love of nature and open land feels like something your grandfather would have had as well."

Dani grinned. "I think I'd have to agree with you on that. Well, I would end up spending hours during my youth exploring the open woods and fields out here. There was a lot more of it back then. There were so many pheasants, deer, rabbits, and other types of wildlife. It was beautiful. It was also so different from living close to the city on the western end of the island. Unfortunately, a lot of that open land from my youth no longer exists. Land has become so prized, expensive, and limited here in a lot of ways. I think that's why I'm so passionate about the preservation of open spaces."

"I am too, Dani," agreed Marcos.

Dani thought for a moment and then continued. "You know, Marcos, I once read a piece by a columnist in the city who had recently visited the Hamptons to cover one of the myriad of events that take place out here during the summer high season. The reporter went on to describe the Hamptons as rural and a place where development was scarce. I actually winced when I read it, Marcos, I swear. I have personally seen how much development has taken place here, even during my lifetime. The Hamptons are pretty far from being the wide-open spaces of the Midwest or the vast forests of western Pennsylvania. The reporter didn't realize that it is a place that has tried to maintain a countryside ambiance. However, it is also a place always in danger of losing that carefully cultivated image and feeling altogether, if far-sighted precautions to preserve it aren't taken."

Marcos nodded, reflecting on everything Dani just mentioned. He then thought about what he had said previously when he had agreed with her. He really did care deeply about open and wild spaces. That was what had made his youth in Kentucky so wonderful. He couldn't have imagined growing up without it being all around him. It was experiencing and living within the opposite environment, namely that of New York City, which had caused him so much internal emotional pain. Yet, he was going to try to eventually sell Dani on something that he didn't believe in himself. The whole notion of what he needed to propose to her was so inherently contradictory with his personal beliefs and feelings. *Who is this person that I've become?*

Dani continued speaking. "Anyway, I would eventually start a French bistro in the same building where my grandmother's tea room was located. I like to believe that I'm carrying on her legacy. We've been a part of this community for all of these years. I just think coming out here to live was the best move that our family ever could have made." Dani looked content and happy as she looked out over the sparkling blue cold water around them.

"The only thing is I still don't feel fulfilled professionally or accomplished in the way that I always envisioned," added Dani.

"How can you ever feel that way about yourself?" interjected Marcos. He continued. "Look at how incredibly successful you are. You're talented, beautiful, and not many people have achieved the level of success that you have and at such a young age."

Dani smiled cautiously. "That's very nice of you to say, Marcos. It's just that I think about how my grandparents saw and always talked about the growth and development of the wine industry here on the east end of Long Island and particularly over on the north fork. They always felt that having a winery and tasting room would be the next step on the journey for our family. It's something that the whole family can do together and build upon."

"I believe in you, Dani, and I have no doubt that you will achieve it," said Marcos.

"Thank you, Marcos. I appreciate that a lot." She got up and walked back to the helm and the electronic controls for the boat. Dani took a deep breath. "So, do you think we should keep moving forward?"

He smiled at the obvious double meaning of what she had just said. "I can't think of any better direction to head in," he replied, smiling broadly.

Dani started the engines again and pushed the throttle forward. They were soon off again across the water.

Dani continued speaking as she piloted the boat. "Do you remember those scrub pine forests that you saw behind the bistro and fields that I own when you came by the other day?"

"Of course," replied Marcos.

"Well, that land was part of the property that our relatives owned and it was them who initially convinced my grandparents to move here all those years ago. Thankfully, an open land and agricultural property preservation group purchased it all after they moved away. It should stay that way indefinitely now."

Marcos thought back to how beautiful, natural, and untouched the landscape had looked behind Dani's bistro. "That sounds like a really good thing," he agreed.

Dani nodded. "I think so. I'm sure some developer would have loved to put a huge development on it many years ago if it hadn't been secured for protection."

Marcos was well aware that any acreage, and especially one that was sizeable, was a very hot real estate commodity in the Hamptons and could easily obtain a good asking price.

Dani stretched her arms. "There's a lot of those kind of efforts going on out here right now, thankfully. Hopefully, it will slow down some of the tide of ravenous land development. It's really the only way, I think. This area would look like so much else of Long Island if it wasn't for that kind of work taking place."

Marcos told Dani that he agreed with her. Deep down, he kept thinking about what he knew he would have to propose to her at some point or another. How could he do it knowing her feelings about land preservation and keeping open spaces just that, open? He knew her feelings now for sure. She'd never go along with what he would have to ask her. He couldn't even imagine her saying, "Oh, sure, Marcos, tear down my bistro, pave over the four acres of vineyards, and go ahead and put in a nice commercial shopping and dining district. It's okay because at least the scrub pine forests that my relatives were able to get preserved years ago will still be there." Just the thought of it sounded ridiculous, even to Marcos.

He decided to change the subject. "So, tell me then, what is the dream that you're personally waiting on to happen in your life right now?"

Marcos took a sip of his lemonade and there was a feeling of anticipation in the expression on his face.

Dani paused. "I'd like to continue to expand the bistro, of course. I would like for it to become an even bigger success here in Westhampton Beach and hopefully throughout the Hamptons, ultimately. I also want to be the first one in my family to establish a successful south fork winery and tasting room. I may not be able to compete with the big Wall Street money that finances some wineries, but I can still have a level and degree of success that is uniquely and all my own."

Marcos nodded, appreciative of what she had just said. He admired the dream that she was so wholeheartedly pursuing. "Is there anything else though, Dani? Is there anything that is just yours that you've also wanted to see happen in your life?"

She laughed and was almost taken back by his question. *Was there still something else that I wanted to tell him?*

At first, she tried to deflect the question and responded with a laugh by saying, "This is getting really deep out of nowhere, Marcos."

Of course, she knew that their whole conversation thus far had been one of substance. It had been one of those conversations that a person only has with someone they genuinely trust. She also knew that the conversation had somehow been leading the entire time to what was the most important question that Marcos had for her and that she had for herself as well. It was a secret that she didn't know whether she was ready to reveal. She also didn't know if it should be disclosed to someone who was merely a stranger to her a few days ago but was now fast becoming a new friend in her life.

Dani paused and almost appeared unsure for a moment as to whether she was going to respond truthfully. Deep down she knew that there was indeed something more that she wanted. She decided to go ahead and tell Marcos.

Dani took a deep breath. "I'd like to find someone to share those successes and happy moments of life with me, ultimately. But it's just . . ." Dani stopped.

"You can tell me," urged Marcos.

"Well, I just haven't been that lucky in past relationships. I would put a lot more into them than what I got back. I'm not sure that I want to try again at this point."

Marcos leaned over and hugged her. "You deserve to have that in your life, Dani. You have so much to offer anyone and deserve to receive so much in return from any relationship that you're in."

Dani looked at Marcos. "I know. I just feel like the door is closed right now."

Marcos stared deeply into her eyes. "I think you're going to find the right relationship and with someone who values the amazing person that you are. Please don't close the door on something that could come in and be incredible someday."

Suddenly, Marcos had the sensation that he wasn't referring any longer to some unknown or nameless third party that hadn't come into Dani's life yet. No, he had the distinct realization that he was referring to himself in that moment. He was the one who wanted to be in a meaningful and equally-giving relationship with Dani. Of course, he had no idea whether she wanted the same with him at this point. More and more during his time in Westhampton Beach, Marcos was coming to realize what really mattered and was most authentically important to him in his life right now.

Dani smiled for the first time since they had begun talking about their dreams out there on the deck. "Thank you for that, Marcos. I promise I'll keep the door open." She paused, chuckled, and then added, "just a crack, maybe."

Marcos began to laugh as well and they embraced each other again with a strong hug.

"Un abrazo fuerte amigo mío," said Dani smiling.

"What?" replied Marcos unsure of what Dani had just said in a barely audible tone. "It just means 'a big hug, my friend.' I learned it from a friend of mine who recently visited me after living in Spain for a while."

Marcos smiled. "You see, you're already letting new experiences and interesting people into your life. First your friend from Spain and now me." Dani laughed.

Marcos continued, "But seriously, leaving the door open is going to lead somewhere exciting and worthwhile, Dani. I promise. I really feel that way."

"I think you're right, Marcos. Thank you for the advice. It really helped," responded Dani, smiling broadly.

The weather had held up so far. Dani suggested they go a little further and take the boat out into the open waters of the Atlantic beyond the barrier island. This would give Marcos a different view of the area as a whole, but now from the Atlantic side. It would also be an opportunity to see more of the Long Island coast by increasing the speed of the engines and covering a greater area, which she couldn't do to the extent that she wanted while they were on the bayside.

They both agreed that it might be fun and the trip across Moriches Bay had been perfect. It didn't look as though the weather forecast had been correct. Dani started the engines again and they moved out into the open water. Neither knew what was waiting ahead of them.

CHAPTER 14

A short while later, as they neared the Atlantic, the sky began to grow darker.

"We can always turn around if the weather gets bad," said Dani as they continued. Marcos agreed. He wanted to see as much as possible of the beautiful beach-filled coastline of Long Island while he had this opportunity to be out on the open water with Dani.

Suddenly, out of nowhere, the weather began to rapidly change for the worse. It felt similar to the approach of a tornado in the Midwest, where the sky turned dark with a rapidity and speed that was different from the more gradual and progressive occurrence of a regular storm's arrival. The sky continued to grow darker faster. Snow began falling from the iron-grey atmosphere above them. Even the water no longer felt as calm beneath and alongside them. The wind picked up and began to howl. The fierce nor'easter that had been predicted had now arrived and ahead of schedule.

At the helm, Dani had the radar laid over the GPS so both could function simultaneously and be within her view while she piloted the small boat. All reports were now indicating that the weather was only going to grow worse. It had become so bad that neither Dani nor Marcos were able to stand on the outside decks any longer. The wind and blinding snow that was now taking place could have easily blown them both overboard with the level of sheer ferocity that it was taking on. Dani decided to keep the autopilot functionality on but first ensured that the boat was sharply and rapidly turned back toward what they thought would be the more protected waters of Moriches Bay as opposed to the open Atlantic.

Even the bay offered very little respite for them now. It too was churning in violent turmoil. As they gradually entered back into it, wild waves began to slam against the boat. Dani asked Marcos to watch the helm while she ran outside to grab objects off of the exposed decking that could now easily be blown off into the turbulent winter waters of the storm. With a snow jacket fastened securely around her, she ran outside. Marcos couldn't even see Dani out there, even though she was probably only a mere few feet in front of him. All visibility was now completely obscured by the blinding snow.

Suddenly, there was a scream. Marcos ran out onto the deck. A tremendous blow of high water had risen over the bow and unexpectedly slammed into Dani while her back was turned away from the starboard side and had knocked her down flat onto the hard teak decking.

"Dani!" shouted Marcos. "Are you okay?" He ran over to her. She barely moved. Marcos went to lift her up. He struggled as the water continued to slam against the boat. This was combined with the piercing cold and endless, rapidly falling snow. Marcos carried her into the salon and laid her on the sofa. She opened her eyes gradually after a few minutes.

"What happened?" asked Dani groggily as she looked up at Marcos.

"There was a wave of water, Dani. It hit you out on the bow."

"I'm okay," she insisted and tried to get up. She couldn't and fell back down onto the sofa.

"Just rest, Dani. It's alright. The boat is on autopilot."

"I've got it," she said again as she fought to get up. She fell once again onto the sofa.

Marcos grabbed a warm winter blanket and placed it over her. The boat was now rocking back and forth and shaking violently. Marcos felt incredibly queasy. He thought he was going to throw up right then and there. He cursed himself for agreeing to the idea that they should push on and go further out into the Atlantic on a day when they both knew that there was an approaching nor'easter.

Dani had a hand pressed firmly against her head. She was obviously in great pain. Marcos ran back to the helm to check on the engines and the GPS. *How much longer is it going to take to get out of this nightmare and return to the marina?* He looked at their navigational position on the electronic map. Suddenly, he heard Dani shout out in a voice that was exhausted and yet still powerful.

"Turn on the stabilizers, Marcos!"

Marcos had no idea how to do it. He looked around frantically at the control panel. He couldn't see a thing outside any longer and the shaking of the boat was becoming unbearable. The GPS indicated that they were approaching Moneybogue Bay again. That didn't mean much if this shaking kept up. He'd be violently ill and passed out on the floor before too much longer himself if the turbulence continued. Marcos continued looking around next to the wheel and joystick. Finally, he found the switch for the boat's stabilizing mechanism.

The water continued to slam hard against the little boat, although with a little less intensity than before. The boat was gradually becoming stable and the equipment was thankfully doing its job and not a minute too soon. Marcos looked intensely at the GPS and radar overlay next to the boat's wheel. They weren't too far from the marina now, thankfully.

Unexpectedly, Dani came up from behind him as she limped through the sliding doors and into the helm area. Marcos stood there alternating between looking out into the blinding snow trying desperately to see something and looking down at the electronic control panel where his hands were positioned and ready to make any adjustments that suddenly became necessary.

"I can take it from here," said Dani, putting a hand on Marcos' shoulder as though to urge him to move away from the controls.

"Dani, are you sure? You're in no condition right now to operate a boat."

"I have it," she replied determinedly. Dani sat down at the controls again and Marcos looked on. He deeply admired her determination and tenaciousness. It couldn't have been more evident than in that moment on the helm and after all they had just been through.

The boat was in the straight path of water now that headed back into the basin of the Westhampton Beach Village Marina. Dani took the boat off autopilot and eased up on the engines. She didn't want to create too much of a wake as the boat eased its way back into the marina. She continued expertly navigating the vessel into its slip. The intense pain that she was in was still evident on her face. However, she pushed on even after cutting the engines. Marcos climbed off via the boat's boarding platform and worked quickly to tie it up to the anchorage. He could still barely see with the snow and fierce wind. It slammed against him now, rather than the boat, as he struggled to tie it up. Finally, the boat was properly secured.

The marina was close to the village, very well-maintained, and there were a number of nice boats in their slips along the three sides for docking of the square boat basin. Marcos looked around at the now quiet marina, which sat poised in the middle of the fierce winter storm taking place around it. No boats were going out in this weather any longer. He smiled to himself after he had finished tying the boat up as he thought back to how Dani had corrected him earlier that morning. He had mistakenly referred to her boat as being "in port" at the marina. She had quickly told him, "This is a marina, Marcos, not a port. It doesn't have any large freighters bellowing out steam or cruise ships with passengers in Bermuda shorts and Hawaiian shirts coming and going and asking where their tour bus is. The port of Miami isn't the same thing as the Westhampton Beach Village Marina."

They had both laughed out loud when Dani had made that ridiculous comparison. Marcos felt a little more nautical after everything that Dani had already taught him about the boating world. Of course, he felt like an old salt now after the terrible winter storm that they had both just endured and survived together.

Dani came out from the helm and stepped onto the dock carrying the remainder of the bags of provisions that they had brought with them when they had started out earlier that morning. They had anticipated a relaxing day out on the water today. Now, as they returned early in the evening, things couldn't have gone and been more different. She set the bags onto the asphalt. Both Dani and Marcos took a collective deep breath. They were both incredibly grateful and relieved to be back safe and on solid ground in Westhampton Beach once more.

Marcos' jacket was soaked through with snow and seawater. However, the blue velvet box inside his zipped jacket pocket had successfully made it through everything. He had nearly forgotten about it with all that had transpired. Marcos reached inside and pulled out the box. Dani saw Marcos doing something and walked over closer to him.

"The Christmas anchor decoration with the compass that you gave me has become so special to me, Dani. I came out here as a stranger and you made me feel welcome. I want you to know how much I value that and everything it represents to me. I feel like it means even more now that we know each other better," said Marcos, looking at her.

Dani smiled. She looked tired, but even now, there was optimism in that smile. Her hair was soaked and tossed about from the storm, and like Marcos, she was soaked completely through from the snow and seawater.

"Thank you for what you just said, Marcos. Seriously."

Marcos handed her the blue velvet box. "I feel like this has even more significance after everything that we went through today."

Dani carefully opened the box in her damp hands. Inside was a necklace with a silver snowflake pendant. A strong smile broke out once more across her face.

"This snowflake is for you, Dani. Every time you look at it, hopefully, it will remind you of your strength, the storm that we made it through together, and the beautiful memories that we shared out on the water earlier today before the storm."

Dani lifted it out of the velvet box and handed it to Marcos without saying a word.

He placed it gently around her wet neck. It now hung shining brightly over her soaked jacket.

"Thank you, Marcos. It's beautiful. I don't have any words for what this means to me right now."

"Sometimes no words are necessary," replied Marcos, wiping some of the saltwater from his eyes. At that very moment, they both leaned in and kissed each other passionately.

Dani looked exhausted after the ordeal they had been through out on the water that afternoon. The snow continued to fall even as evening approached. They were both glad to have arrived safely back in the marina before darkness set in. It could be especially tricky driving home in the Hamptons at night with the dark sky laws that served as an attempt to control light pollution. The pavement around the marina where they had been standing was no longer visible, and the boats in their slips were also covered with a solid layer of snow.

"Please let me drive you home, Dani." Marcos was genuinely worried about her and especially about her driving home at night after all she had already been through.

"I'm okay, Marcos. I really am."

Marcos didn't believe her. "Are you sure? It's no trouble at all."

Dani smiled. "I live in the opposite direction from you. I'm fine, believe me." Even though she looked exhausted, Dani was coming back to being her old self once more. She was a determined and driven person and always believed in staying in the game and continuing to move forward, even after she had been through something difficult. Her experience with the nor'easter was no exception to that rule that she lived by. "You need to get home too, Marcos. This weather is only getting worse," she added. They hugged each other for one last time that evening. Dani then got into her car and drove off in the direction of Westhampton Beach Village.

Marcos took one more look around the surrounding marina and at Dani's boat, now quiet and sitting motionless covered with snow in its slip. He couldn't believe what an unexpected day it had been. His admiration for Dani had only increased with everything they had been through together. They had shared their secret hopes, dreams, and goals with each other for the first time. Marcos couldn't help but feel that the sharing of those "secrets" had been something very special, unique, and rare. His world felt as though it was changing fast and for the better, it seemed.

Of course, Marcos still didn't know about the situation with work and Sheila. With regard to everything else, he was beginning to feel a degree of happiness that he hadn't experienced since he couldn't remember when. A large part of that change taking place within him was due to one remarkable person.

CHAPTER 15

Dani was on her way to meet with Fran at her new home on Meeting House Road. Fran had called the other day. She had a little free time this morning and wondered if Dani would care to drop by. There wouldn't be any bocce ball or wine just yet. Maybe though Dani could answer a few questions for the interview, they could have some coffee together, catch up, and schedule something more formal if additional time was needed for the interview later on.

Dani was still hurting from being slammed onto the deck by the powerful wave that had come over the bow during the storm. When Fran invited her over she went regardless of how she felt. If she had declined the invitation, Fran was one of those individuals who might not ever schedule another one. Marcos had also called earlier that morning to check in on her. It had meant a lot. She had told him that she was recovering and feeling significantly better now. The pain was still very much with her in all honesty. She decided to try to focus her mind on the day ahead as best she could.

As Dani drove through Westhampton Beach on her way to Fran's, she noticed how different the privet hedges looked in the winter. They now enabled one to see more of the outline of the grand homes that lay behind them. These particular homes, with their double-topped chimneys and shingle-style architecture, were very much how people pictured homes in the Hamptons to be. Of course, there were a variety of architectural styles even out here. However, it was the shingle-style that seemed to come to mind for most people when they thought of what a home in the Hamptons during the summer should look like in its most idealistic form.

All of a sudden there was a beep coming from Dani's hands-free phone. It was a text message from Fran. She notified Dani that her personal assistant Morgan would take care of the gates being opened and let her inside when she arrived at the residence. This had all become such a common and expected part of her world. She almost expected privet hedges, personal assistants, gates, and luxurious surroundings when she found herself invited to someone's home out here. Of course, that wasn't true every time. It was accurate enough most of those times to leave a lasting impression upon her and to create a kind of general expectation of how things would be. Dani began to think back to her first experiences in the Hamptons. Heading to Fran's always made her reflect upon her earliest discoveries of what it meant when one was in the Hamptons.

One of the first events that she had ever attended out here came to mind. It was the first time that she had seen that there was a distinct Hamptons summer fashion style. Dani had always thought that it was something the media created in order to sell certain types of clothes from a particular designer. However, there really was a Hamptons summer look, and she had seen it in person back then. There was a wonderful event she had been invited to as a guest because of her position as a premier chef in the area.

Dani had been directed to park in a dirt field alongside a farm. The farms here too looked a little bit more dandified, kept up, photo-friendly, and meticulously attended to appearance-wise than, say, what one would experience in a more rural location such as upstate New York. This was not one's usual trip or experience in the countryside. When she got out of the car there was a small group of people already waiting for golf carts to shuttle them in to the main event.

This was to be held on the water underneath tremendous white tents. Everyone waiting was immaculately attired in what can only be described as Hamptons summer style. It was a purposefully relaxed-looking type of attire, but one to which everyone realized great effort had been expended in its creation. A few of the men she saw on that day had on bright pastel shirts that were opened at the collar with white, pink, blue, or red pants. Some sported sunglasses and watches to complement the look. She even noticed that one of them was wearing monogrammed velvet day slippers that appeared to have a pink satin lining. Some of the women were wearing white, beige, and floral patterned sundresses, off-the-shoulder blouses, and a few even sported designer sun hats. They too had chosen outfit appropriate accessories including nautical necklaces, earrings, bracelets, and, of course, designer handbags. It was glamorous, yes. However, it was done in a casual, "I'm-not-really-trying, but-I-really-am" sort of way.

There was a tone established as the next group climbed into a golf cart driven by a young man in a white dress shirt with a black bow tie. As the golf cart took them from the farm parking field and moved them closer to the event location, Dani noticed the rows of privet hedges, the chimneys rising from the shingle-style homes, and the perfectly manicured green lawns. She knew then and there that the Hamptons was not just a place, but a kind of unique style and way of life.

Looking out at the road in front of her now, she unexpectedly thought about Marcos. Besides being attractive, he had a wonderful outgoing personality. His well-defined body, blond hair, and hint of stubble hadn't been missed. She appreciated someone who took care of themselves in addition to being intelligent and attractive. *He's only out here briefly, though. There probably isn't even anything there as far as relationship potential, and even if there was, where would it lead?* She had been very attracted to Mark, but he was younger and hadn't had all of the life experience that she had. Yes, he had worked as a chef in Spain, but even that was still limited compared to the wealth of experiences that Dani had already been through in her life up until this point. That was the thing, though, that was so appealing about Marcos. He had lived more of life just like her, and as a result, they could talk about more topics, shared experiences, and commonalities together.

Additionally, their day together out on the water had been nothing short of magical. They had more in common with each other than she ever would have initially expected. He seemed to enjoy spending time with her as well. She was certainly enjoying spending time with him. Did he think there could be anything between them? Did she think there could ever be anything between them? The questions ran through her mind rapidly. Dani thought about their subtle flirtation over the subject of bourbon. *Yes, there did seem to be something there in that moment. Then again, maybe he was just being friendly. No, it really did feel like something.* Her instincts were telling her that now and she trusted them implicitly. Well, if there was something developing, she was glad for it. Dani hadn't been that open with anyone in a long time. Marcos brought it out in her. He had been extremely open with her as well. It didn't feel like just friends the way they had been interacting with each other. Of course, they weren't just friends. Dani suddenly remembered the passionate kiss that they had shared when he gave her the necklace. She had nearly forgotten all about that moment. Maybe it was due to the pain she was still feeling and everything that had happened. All of these thoughts continued to cross her mind as she continued driving.

Fran's house was coming into view. It was a shingled Queen Anne style home set far back from the road. The front gates swung open with her approach and she drove to the front motor court. At the door, Morgan greeted her.

"Fran is expecting you," said Morgan pleasantly as she guided Dani down a long arched hallway. In another room, Dani could suddenly hear the sound of someone saying, "Armando, Armando, that feels so good, keep going."

It's none of my business, thought Dani as she continued following Morgan into a large light-filled living area at the back of the house.

About ten minutes later, Fran came out, looking a little tired and flushed, but nonetheless refreshed.

"Welcome. Welcome, Dani. As you can see, this is my new little Hamptons *pied-à-terre*."

Dani looked around at the vastness of this new home that Fran had just acquired. It was hardly a small *pied-à-terre* or secondary home, but when in the Hamptons, go with the flow.

"It is beautiful, Fran," said Dani.

"Thank you. Would you like a drink or anything?"

"Maybe just a club soda with some lime," replied Dani.

"Wonderful," replied Fran. She sent Morgan scurrying to bring them both drinks, and they sat by a pleasant bank of floor-to-ceiling windows looking out over the backyard pool area.

"I do apologize for my lateness, Dani. I was working out with my personal trainer and he certainly puts me through the paces."

"I didn't know you had a trainer."

"Yes, we've made great progress together," replied Fran. She seemed anxious to change the subject.

Before they began the interview, Fran said, "I want to expand the people who we cover in the Hamptons and move beyond just celebrities, just like I told you when we spoke at the post office."

"I'm glad I can help in some way," replied Dani.

"So, shall we begin?" asked Fran.

Dani smiled. "Yes, of course, Fran."

The first question was relatively simple.

Fran asked, "Why did you choose Westhampton Beach as the place where you'd like to be a chef and run a French bistro?"

"I grew up here. I mean, a good portion of my childhood was spent in the city. It always felt more like home out here, and it was in the Hamptons that we were always all together as a family. It's the quality of life, the sense of community, and the natural beauty that made me want to ultimately stay here. When I became a chef and developed my interest in French cooking, I knew that there was nowhere else that I wanted to start my career. My family had started the bistro years ago. Well, it was actually a tea room at first. As a result, it was the natural progression for me to bring my passion for cooking to both the bistro and the community, which held a significant place in my childhood," replied Dani.

"I like that answer," said Fran. "It will endear you to the people as one of the community."

"But I am one of the community," responded Dani.

"Yes, yes. I know, dear. Moving on." Fran continued with her next question. "What is a technique used at the bistro that you feel is not given enough importance and consideration by those considering or already in the cooking field?"

Dani thought for a moment about this technical question that Fran had just flung at her. "I'd say braising. It's incredible how a cut can be transformed into something very tasty and wonderful through this process. You'd be surprised. Yes, it takes time and patience. However, doesn't everything significant and worthwhile require those two components?"

Fran nodded approvingly.

The next question came quickly. "The dishes at the bistro are so elegantly presented, Dani. You're known for creating elevated dining experiences. I noticed even the vegetables are served with a certain 'look.' What is the strategy that you have underlying this approach?"

Dani thought for a moment before responding. "Presentation makes the meal in many ways before we even begin to eat it. So, we are always striving for excellence at the bistro. This extends from the presentation of the meal on your plate, to how it is served, and finally—and most crucially—to how it tastes. We even decide what cuts to use for our vegetables in the presentation or for cooking purposes. I might use a large mirepoix cut back in the kitchen—"

Fran interrupted. "Can you clarify this type of cut for us, Dani?"

Dani continued. "Yes, of course. The vegetables will not be chopped as finely using this type of cut if I'm, say, preparing a sauce for one of our dishes. However, we may use a brunoise cut instead with vegetables that we want finely chopped and presented tastefully on your plate in the dining room."

"That's very interesting," said Fran, already looking at the next question on her sheet of paper.

"If you could live and be in the restaurant business anywhere other than Westhampton Beach, where would that be?" asked Fran before taking a sip of her drink that had been sitting on the table.

Dani paused for a moment. This was certainly not an easy question for her to answer. "I used to go out to Park City, Utah quite a bit as a teenager with my family. The scenery is beautiful and they have a thriving dining scene. I think other than Westhampton Beach, it is one of the few other places where I'd consider living and opening a bistro."

Fran asked Dani a number of other questions before arriving at the one that she had clearly been looking forward to asking from the very beginning of their chat.

A mischievous look now suddenly came across Fran's face. "Now, I'm going to ask you a question that a lot of us have all been wondering about. Is there anyone special in your life at the moment?"

Dani almost shouted. "Fran! I don't really want to answer that kind of question about myself for a magazine."

Fran was not to be deterred. "People love that kind of material, Dani. They like something gossipy or a personal tidbit here and there about the person being interviewed. Why do you think we write so much about celebrities and what they're doing out here? That's what a lot of people like and that's why a lot of them pick up the magazine in the first place."

Dani looked exasperated but decided to give in on this, at least a little. "Fine, I'll answer it. However, I'm not giving any details to be printed about my love life or lack thereof."

"As you wish, Dani," said Fran, pen in hand, ready to capture whatever came next.

Dani paused and reflected within herself for a brief moment. She thought about Marcos and about the kiss they had shared, as well as the silver snowflake necklace that he had given her. She thought back to their walk through Westhampton Beach Village and the evening spent in front of the Christmas tree on the village green. Then there was the experience on the boat in the storm and that first magical moment when they had met at her bistro. There definitely was someone in her life and someone who was becoming more and more significant to her with each passing day during the present holiday season. She couldn't let Fran know about all of this. It was still too personal, too private, and too much of an unknown. Dani's face took on a resolute expression. She would have to keep quiet about all of this for now. It was too soon. "There is no one romantically significant in my life at the moment," she replied to Fran determinedly.

Fran decided to continue pushing the envelope. "Would you like there to be?"

Dani decided to continue with the farce that she had decided to create and jokingly snapped back. "That's no one else's business but mine, Fran." Dani then decided to let a little more slip out. "If the right, successful, intelligent, and kind sort of person came along, I'd stay open to the possibilities."

"Now was that so hard, Dani?" said Fran grinning.

"Well, it wasn't exactly a day at the beach. I suppose it's okay, though." Dani felt proud of herself for not having let anything escape to Fran about her developing feelings and connection with Marcos, this stranger from New York City who had so unexpectedly come into her life.

With that, Fran now seemed ready to conclude the interview for the day. "I think we have enough to run it right now, Dani, without any additional follow-up needed or extra questions."

Dani felt relieved. "That's good news, Fran. I hope that we're still on for bocce ball and wine in the spring."

Fran smiled. "We certainly are, Dani. Of course. Right now, I need to get back to Armando. He does depend on me." She motioned toward herself. "All of this doesn't just happen magically, you know."

Dani laughed. "I suppose not. Anyway, Fran, it was a great pleasure as always. I'm glad we ran into each other at the post office the other day. I also can't wait to see the piece in the magazine."

Fran stood up. "I'm going to try to have it run early next week. That way we get a December fifteenth or so release, and it's still early enough before Christmas and the holidays. It's difficult to get anyone to pick up a magazine once all of that is in full swing."

"Please let me know when it's released," said Dani as Fran led her to the door.

"Well, I really must get going. Armando is waiting." With that, the door closed and Dani walked across the motor court and back to her car. Dani thought about the magazine that Fran had now been a part of for the past few years.

During the spring and summer months, there were stacks of luxury real estate magazines and glossy local periodicals that were available for free in front of shops, restaurants, and businesses throughout the Hamptons. It's a familiar sight. Looking into any of those real estate magazines reveals a hidden world. This world is unseen by tourists who are traveling the main thoroughfares that carry people through each of the respective little villages that comprise the Hamptons region on Long Island's south fork.

One can make the entire trip from Southampton at the end of Sunrise Highway to East Hampton and Montauk at the very end of the island (which is part of the township of East Hampton), without catching a really meaningful look at any of the estates, particularly the waterfront ones featured in those beautiful photographic periodicals that are distributed to anyone interested for free. There was no shortage of beautiful waterfront locations to live in throughout the Hamptons if one had the money. Many people may think immediately of Meadow Lane, or Billionaire Lane as it is often referred to, in Southampton as a premier waterfront Hamptons location to reside in. Others will think of the famous people that they've heard of living along the shores of Georgica Pond in East Hampton. However, there are so many additional beautiful waterfront locations throughout the Hamptons that may be less well known. A few certainly include Mecox Bay, Moriches Bay, Peconic Bay, Wooley Pond, Sagg Pond, Gardiner's Bay, Sam's Creek, Lake Agawam, along the shores of Shelter Island, and of course, along the Atlantic Ocean itself to name just a few. Most individuals visiting the Hamptons will only perhaps catch a glimpse of those homes and places featured in the glossy pages of the free magazines, which enchant even the most casual viewing eye that decides to peruse them.

Dani thought about this seriously as her car emerged from behind the high privet hedge shielding Fran's sumptuous property from the road and the eyes of anyone passing by. It had always amazed her, from the time that she was very young, what splendor, luxury, and glamorous country living actually lay behind some of those hedges of Hampton's privet. She had once more seen a bit of it at Fran's home, but only a small taste.

Fran's magazine may have only been started a few years ago, but it was now being featured alongside all of the other glossy magazines outside of storefronts in the Hamptons during the summer months. It too had glossy, full cover photos, a lot of celebrity coverage, high-priced luxury real estate listings, and content just like any of the others that all offered a brief glimpse into life in the Hamptons.

She liked Fran, but Fran too had secrets that she wouldn't let anyone know. Dani didn't know exactly what business Fran was in that was so lucrative, for starters. The only thing that she revealed publicly was her role with the magazine. She frequently appeared in the various society or splash pages of local publications at this or that event but never revealed exactly what she did. Perhaps Armando was another one of those secrets. The Hamptons itself was a place that held secrets like any other.

Christmas and the bareness of the cold of winter may have enabled some stronger glimpses of that secret world, but it never went beyond the point of limited disclosure. Dani was fully aware of that. The secrets here would never fully be discovered, but the Christmas season did make the world of a bistro owner and a socialite/magazine CEO seem and feel a little bit closer, if only for a moment.

CHAPTER 16

It was December fifteenth. The month was rapidly moving along. Marcos had been out driving around Westhampton Beach all morning and still, there was nothing. He had not found one viable commercial property other than Dani's bistro and the four acres behind it. It was the only piece of real estate that could possibly meet what Sheila and her client were looking for. The village of Westhampton Beach's square mileage only comes in, as far as square mileage is concerned, at a modest three. This was not a lot of area to work with for what the company was asking. It was also making it exceptionally difficult for Marcos to find an appropriate property. However, after the day together on the boat and going through the storm, he couldn't even imagine bringing himself to asking Dani to sell the property. He kept thinking about her determination, drive, and desire to build upon the legacy left to her by her family. He respected her for it. Additionally, he had real feelings for her. She would never want to speak to him again if he dared to mention what he was considering for the property upon which her bistro sat. It was becoming an increasingly difficult and perplexing situation. There didn't seem to be an easy solution.

He thought about asking Sheila if both she and the client would be willing to expand their search to the much larger region of Southampton township as a whole. It was a proposal that could potentially work. Even Westhampton Beach itself was technically part of Southampton Township. Where was the harm in broadening the search just a bit? Would it make a difference in the outcome? Why did Sheila's clients have to be so rigid about their request? Secretly, he even wondered if this was all some kind of setup by Sheila to push him out of the firm. Maybe there was no actual client who needed a retail space to be built in Westhampton Beach. She had pulled off some very devious business maneuverings in the past. Additionally, they certainly weren't on the best terms these days. It was a realistic possibility that more was at work here behind the scenes than Marcos had initially thought. He really didn't want to have to propose the idea to Dani of having her bistro, home, and four acres of vineyards sold and bulldozed so that a commercial development could come in on the property. Broadening the search to all of Southampton would expand the possibilities and potential properties available. Sheila did have moments of sanity. Although fleeting, in those moments she could even be—dare he think it—nice, and if it was a really good day, reasonable. There was a possibility that she would see how difficult this was and get her client, if there even was a client, to bend a little. *Maybe I should call her.*

After arriving back at the house on Dune Road, he went into the living room, sat down, and took out his phone. Sheila was listed under recent past calls. It was then that he had first mentioned Dani's property and now it would be on her radar if he tried to come up with any alternatives. It was a mistake to have said anything about it. *How could I have known at the time?* She knew there was a potential property available right in Westhampton Beach. Sheila would therefore see it as a sign of weakness if he wasn't able to get the owner to commit to a Purchase and Sale Agreement.

He was in an incredibly tight spot. Sheila had him cornered. Marcos almost wished that he had never said anything about it to her in the first place. This was business and he had a job to keep, so what was the alternative? He had to act in good faith and give his boss all of the information about available properties in the area that he had become privy to. This wasn't just about business exclusively anymore either. He had feelings for Dani, and the last thing he wanted to do right now was to hurt her by bringing up a subject that was sure to be volatile and charged with difficult emotions. It would be over; he was sure of that if he said anything about this to her. He had to try to work things out with Sheila first. There had to be options. Surely, she would understand. Marcos highlighted Sheila's number and pressed the call button.

Sheila answered directly, which was unusual. The call was usually first responded to by her administrative assistant and then transferred to Sheila only if she felt like taking the call.

"Yes?" demanded a voice on the other end of the line.

"Hi, Sheila. It's Marcos."

The voice fired back without inquiring into how he was or any of the usual preliminaries that take place in a cordial conversation. "Do you have anything for me?"

"No. That's what I was calling about, actually. There really is nothing in Westhampton Beach. I was wondering if there was any way that we could expand the search a bit to include the entire township of Southampton?"

He could feel the anger boiling on the other end of the line.

"Absolutely not," shouted Sheila. "You told me you already had a property for me there in Westhampton Beach."

He knew that she was going to bring that up and sure enough, she did. The cat was out of the bag. Sheila knew that there was a property that met the firm's needs right there in Westhampton Beach and if Marcos couldn't secure it, well, then that had to be his fault and no one else's.

"It's a potential property," responded Marcos.

"It's a property!" retorted Sheila fiercely.

Marcos tried to stay calm. "Yes, but I don't know if the owner will even sell it."

"It's that property or nothing," demanded Sheila. She was in ultimatum country right now and there would be no turning back from it. "You either get me that Westhampton Beach property or you're out of a job in the new year."

Before Marcos could respond, Sheila had hung up the phone.

So that was it. The final ultimatum. It was Dani's property or nothing. It was starting to snow again outside. Marcos had a nice view from the sofa of the snow coming down and once again coating the lawn, terrace, and beach beyond. It was so relaxing to sit there and watch it fall, especially after yet another tense business conversation with Sheila. He had no idea what he was going to do next. Everyone had their cards on the table now. He knew how Dani felt and he knew what Sheila wanted. He also realized that he was at risk of losing his entire developing relationship with Dani and his job with Sheila. There was not going to be an easy route to take in this scenario.

While he had his phone out, Marcos figured he might as well take a look at what was going on in the Hamptons right now. It would be a distraction and he needed one at this very moment. He had been out here for a few weeks already. In all of that time, he hadn't once checked in online to see what was going on locally. One of the first sites to come up seemed to be a popular local magazine. He had seen the pre-labeled distribution bins in front of storefronts in the village a few days ago. This particular magazine must have had a print edition as well that was freely distributed locally during the warmer spring and summer months.

The site itself was visually appealing. A lot of websites about the Hamptons were. They seemed to come on strong with images of beautiful people, clothes, homes, and celebrities with everyone, in one way or another, just living their best life. It had all of the usual coverage. Namely, there was news about local polo happenings, new boutiques that were opening, the latest pop-up shops, celebrities, cars, fashion trends, and anything else taking place out east. However, when Marcos clicked on "dining," something suddenly caught his eye. This was definitely different.

There was a piece about Dani. Marcos noticed that it was quite a lengthy and in-depth interview as he clicked on it. The magazine had placed a strikingly bold picture of her at the top in her chef's whites. She was wearing the traditional hat called the toque blanche and vest with her name embroidered on it in blue script.

In the interview, Dani had discussed with the magazine why she had chosen Westhampton Beach as the place for having a bistro and working as a chef de cuisine. A few of the technical techniques employed in her work were also mentioned in detail. Marcos read on. Interestingly, in the article, Dani had said that she was indeed single. He had been wondering about that ever since they had met for the first time. It brought him a bit of joy knowing this now. He thought she liked him too judging by the passionate kiss they had shared at the marina.

However, there was no way to know for sure. There was definite chemistry between them. Could it really be something that would work out long-term, though? He would be heading back to New York soon and in a way, it seemed futile to pursue. She had her career in the Hamptons and he had his in the city. They would then be separated by all of that physical distance. How could it work out realistically? The interview continued with several questions. In one of her responses, Dani had said that she would consider Park City, Utah as an alternative location other than Westhampton Beach for being in the restaurant business. She had discussed the beautiful scenery and talked about childhood memories out there. It was an interesting and unexpected bit of information to be included. However, he had known various luxury magazines about the Hamptons to also occasionally discuss related luxury resort destinations such as Miami, Park City, Aspen, etc. in some of their coverage, so it wasn't an unusual question for the magazine to be asking her.

Marcos couldn't help but wonder if Dani had actually entertained the possibility of relocating to somewhere other than Westhampton Beach at some point. If that were the case, it would certainly make his pitch to her about selling the bistro and attached property a lot easier. If she was indeed seriously considering opening a bistro elsewhere, a lucrative financial deal on her existing Westhampton Beach property could be the needed push to make it a reality. Both her and Marcos would then benefit. He'd keep his job and she'd walk away with a nice check and a new start in Utah. *This could make everything a lot easier.*

He then thought about all of her family's history in Westhampton Beach. She had shared that private information with him in trust. Would she really walk away from all of that for the money? Dani didn't seem to be a person who was motivated solely by the almighty dollar. She seemed to judge everything by looking at the whole picture of a situation. When it came to family and the life that she already had in Westhampton Beach, he didn't think she would budge so easily. This seemed especially true if Marcos were to suggest walking away from it all and taking the money that his firm was offering. It didn't feel like money would be enough to motivate her on this one, but who knew until the offer had been made to her. Sometimes people talked a good game about history, family, and connections to a place, but were easily convinced otherwise when the dollar amount being offered was high enough. He had seen this on numerous occasions throughout his work in the commercial real estate industry in the city. Maybe how he imagined Dani would react wasn't so cut and dry.

It had all been a lot. After the conversation with Sheila, playing out all of the potential scenarios in his mind, and with the snow coming down outside, a nice glass of wine didn't feel like a bad idea. Marvin and José had both said before they left that he was welcome to any of the cheaper, local, and newer vintages that they had stored horizontally in a wall rack on the right-hand side of their wine cellar downstairs. Knowing that Dani had entertained ideas of operating her business elsewhere also made him feel slightly better now about having to propose the business idea to her later when he had worked up the courage.

Marcos went down the hall from the great room. He then took the glass and contemporary steel staircase to the lower level of the home. Glass doors led into the temperature and humidity-controlled room at the bottom of the stairs. The bottles were all stacked horizontally and there was a small tasting area with a black modern table. Purple had been used as an accent color throughout the room and the comfortable chairs at the table were also upholstered in it.

Alongside the table and hanging on the wall was a modern painting. It was obviously created by José given the bold corner signature in white ink on the blue backdrop. Marcos looked at the numerous bottles of wine in the space. Much to his surprise, Marvin had kept a bottle of Domaine Leroy Richebourg Grand Cru secreted down here, which was from 1949 and goes for over five thousand dollars. There was even a rare bottle of Penfolds Grange Hermitage, which runs a little shy of forty thousand dollars. Marcos couldn't believe the financial investment in wine alone that was contained in this room.

He walked over to the cheaper, newer, and local wines that Marvin and José had said he was permitted to drink. He found a nice red from a recent north fork vintage that would probably retail for around twenty-five dollars. It wasn't Domaine Leroy Richebourg Grand Cru, but for now, on this cold winter's day in Westhampton Beach, it would have to do.

Marcos selected a glass and took it over to the table with the bottle of wine. *Now, where was the corkscrew?* He looked around the room and quickly found a small container that held a range of bar utensils and implements, which included a corkscrew. Marcos opened the bottle and poured the glass of red wine. He sat there in the tranquility and peace of Marvin's wine cellar with its mood lighting enjoying a lovely glass of wine alone on a cold snowy day.

He thought about Dani's words the other day and how she wanted to share the happy moments in life with someone. He was feeling the same way a bit now sitting alone and drinking the glass of wine in Marvin's wine cellar. It would have been a much more pleasurable experience if he had been able to share it with someone else. Dani was right in what she had said. Marcos had been alone for a long time too and had grown used to doing things and taking part in life's special moments on his own. He thought back to those times when he did have someone special with him. Those were the moments that he remembered the most and those were the ones that had been the most special to him.

He did think it would be nice to share these moments with someone else one day. It would have to be the right person. Dani wasn't the only one who had been burned by others in relationships. He had his fair share of people who had come into his life and taken advantage of his kindness. He knew what Dani meant when she said that she was only going to leave the door of possibility open a crack going forward. He couldn't say that he blamed her.

He too had become much more discerning with the years, as to whom he let come into his life. Who the right person actually was, as far as a potential relationship, he didn't know. Someone like Dani certainly matched what he was ideally looking for in a partner. Marcos suddenly thought that maybe he too should follow the advice that he had given to Dani about keeping the door of possibility open. However, he was going to follow Dani's suggestion as well, which limited that door of possibility to being opened only a crack.

Dani's humor, charm, intelligence, worldliness, and beauty had steadily captivated him. He found himself thinking about her even now down in Marvin's solitude-filled wine cellar. He also realized that this whole Hamptons experience would soon be over along with Christmas. It would in the future hold nothing more than a dreamlike quality of something wonderful that had once happened in his life.

So many of the great experiences in his past now felt that way. They were like mirages that floated through his mind during the lonely hours of the late night or early morning of experiences, people, and moments that were once a part of his reality, but now were no more. They existed only in the dream world but were no longer tangible or a part of his everyday reality. He didn't want to see that happen with his Hamptons experience as well. Of course, once his time in Westhampton Beach was over, it would also mean returning to the realities of life in New York City. He wasn't sure that he was ready to face that prospect positively any longer. Something had changed within him being out in Westhampton Beach. A lot of that change had been a result of the moments and experiences that he had had with Dani. He was becoming someone different. He didn't know exactly who yet, but he felt it somewhere deep within himself.

Those realities of being back in New York City certainly wouldn't include snowy walks through a picturesque little Hamptons village bedecked with Christmas lights, having sparkling conversations with a beautiful, successful, and intelligent chef de cuisine, and then sipping designer hot chocolate beside a Christmas tree on the village green. Of course, this was all then topped off by returning to a modern multimillion-dollar beachside mansion on Dune Road where he would wake up the next morning listening to the sound of the waves crashing on the beach.

It all felt beautiful, surreal, and dreamlike. Marcos didn't want to wake up from it or to ever see it end. The arrival and eventual passing of Christmas day itself felt like the very end and termination of so much in his life. In a way, he wanted the days from today until Christmas to take their time in passing, so that he might savor every moment.

Yes, he worried about the job, Sheila, and finding and securing the commercial property. However, his time out here in the Hamptons had already had a mysterious way of calming him down and changing him for the better. Marcos wasn't even thinking much about trying to close this deal or of getting back to the city before Christmas. He liked it out here, and the company of Dani, a little more with each passing day.

He took a sip of the wine. It was refreshing and the perfect calming choice after driving around fruitlessly all morning and trying once again to find the perfect commercial property. It is said that there are synchronicities in our lives. Marcos' phone suddenly lit up and vibrated on the tasting table. It was Dani, the exact person who had preoccupied so much of his thoughts while he was sitting there in Marvin's wine cellar on a cold, wintry day. The call felt like one of those proverbial synchronicities.

Marcos picked up. "Hi, Dani."

"Hi, Marcos," she responded with her usual enthusiasm. "I was wondering if you'd be interested in having dinner with me at the bistro later this evening? We're closing early in the afternoon today, probably around three p.m. I'm going to be working late and thought it might be nice to share a meal and another evening together after I finish up. If you're busy tonight, I completely understand. I know this is very short notice."

Dani didn't know that Marcos had a completely clear schedule for the remainder of the afternoon and evening. She also didn't know that he had been thinking about her words that suggested the hope of being with someone with whom you could share life's small and often fleeting precious moments. It was actually very ironic that she had called when she did. That being said, the final thing Dani didn't realize was that Marcos was nearly out of a job if he didn't come through with something for Sheila within the next few weeks. Anyway, he'd think about that later. He turned his attention back to the phone conversation.

"I'd like that a lot, Dani," replied Marcos. He paused, thinking for a moment. "Is there anything I can bring?"

"No. I have everything here. Thank you for asking. I'll see you around seven p.m., should we say?"

Marcos leaned back in his chair at the tasting table. "That sounds perfect. I will see you then."

After the conversation had concluded, Marcos finished his glass of wine, turned off the lights in the wine cellar, and headed back upstairs to the main level. He still had some unfinished emails and other work on the computer to finish. This would be as good of a time as any to complete it before driving over to the mainland to meet with Dani for dinner. Marcos spent the rest of the afternoon working on the laptop in the great room and watching the snowfall.

Early evening arrived faster than he expected. Marcos put on a fitted red sweater and khakis under a winter dress coat and headed out to his car. Thankfully, he had left the car parked in the porte-cochere so the windows and car were free of ice and snow. The accumulation had been minimal anyway, and the sun had emerged shortly after all of the snow had concluded. It was just enough to add a hint of winter beauty to the landscape, without creating any kind of obstruction.

Marcos pulled out of the property and headed down Dune Road. He began the short crossing over Moriches Bay back to the mainland. The snow on the Dune Road side and the fringes of the mainland glistened along with the sparkling of the bay after another snowfall. It was a sight that could only be experienced at this time of year, and it was made even more special and unique because it was being experienced by Marcos in a place like this.

He reached Westhampton Beach Village quickly. He felt like this was going to be a good night. He parked the car and hurried into one of the shops. A short while later, he was heading down Main Street again and out to Dani's bistro as evening was setting in.

The light in the Hamptons is something that has often been commented upon by locals and those who experience it for themselves when visiting. Marcos saw what people meant as he drove toward the bistro that evening. There truly was something magical to the light over the water and the acres of pine and open fields.

The sun had now set by the time that he reached Dani's bistro and pulled into the dirt field next to her car. It was the only vehicle now remaining there. Dani had told Marcos to text her when he arrived. Marcos turned off the ignition, picked up his phone, and sent Dani a text to let her know he was there.

About five minutes later, Dani emerged from the bistro and walked out into the snow-dusted parking field. The dress itself that she was wearing was sheath and red. Her long, dark blonde hair was complemented by the dress's cowl neck. She looked stunning.

"How are you, Marcos?" She came over to where he stood beside the car and hugged him. He was glad to see that she looked and felt better.

"Hi, Dani. It's wonderful to see you," he replied.

She motioned toward herself. "I know I'm dressed a little formally this evening, but the bistro was completely reserved for a private party this afternoon that I had to be at. That's why we closed so early." Her effortless elegance made an even greater impression tonight upon Marcos. It went so far as to even supersede the already significant impression that she had made upon him during their first evening together walking in the village of Westhampton Beach.

"You look wonderful," replied Marcos.

Dani ushered him inside. "That's very kind of you to say. Let's get inside. It's freezing out here."

Inside the lobby, Dani grabbed his coat so that it could dry off in the coatroom. As she went to take the coat, Marcos handed her the flower arrangement that he had purchased in the village before arriving at the bistro.

"This is absolutely beautiful!" said Dani. "It's the perfect Christmas arrangement. Thank you for this, Marcos."

He had selected a beautiful Christmas-themed arrangement of flowers for Dani. There were red roses, pine cones, sprigs of green holly with berries, and lilies.

This was only his second time inside the bistro and it still impressed him. Marcos looked around at the now empty main dining room.

"This building certainly has a lot of character."

"It should. It has been standing here since the early 1800s," replied Dani.

Marcos was surprised. "That long?"

Dani nodded. "Absolutely. There have been a lot of different owners, changes, and renovations throughout the years. However, the original soul of the structure is still there." Dani's eyes looked around taking in the entirety of her bistro. "I think you feel it even more at Christmas when everything is so beautifully decorated."

Marcos also looked around at the red cloth-covered tables with their candles and evergreen centerpieces, as well as at all of the wreaths and garlands that festooned the entirety of the building's interior. Undoubtedly, it was a space that had watched over a lot of guests throughout the years.

"What was this building originally?" asked Marcos.

Dani folded one of the napkins on a table that was waiting for tomorrow's guests. "It was an inn and tavern for many years from its inception in the early 1800s."

"So, it's still kind of serving that purpose, right?" asked Marcos.

Dani nodded. "It is. It's still taking in travelers and offering good companionship and refreshment. I mean, it even takes in travelers like you, Marcos." Dani jokingly pushed a hand against him.

He pretended to flinch. "And how in keeping with Christmas is that? You were able to take me in at the inn while I'm fleeing from Herod—or was it Sheila?—who's the head of my company in New York City."

Dani laughed. "This time around, there's always room at the inn. It sounds like a Christmas miracle to me, though. It's a good thing that the wise woman here in Westhampton Beach found you." Dani was still laughing as she led Marcos into the kitchen with her.

There were so many wonderful scents all mixing together and filling the air of the space. Dani walked over to check on a pan where she had something already cooking.

"Is there anything I can do to help?" asked Marcos.

Dani looked around for a moment and then pointed toward the cutting board and something lying beside it. "If you could chop those shallots up very fine that would really be helpful."

Marcos walked over to the cutting board and picked up one of the shallots. "Of course," he replied, beginning to finely dice them.

Dani was now working intensely at the pan. Steam was rising, paired with the crackling of the food being prepared in the oil. She added in the shallots and wine.

"I'm almost done in here, Marcos. You can go sit in the dining room if you'd like. I'll be out in a moment."

Marcos went out to the dining room and sat at the table where Dani had placed the flower arrangement. *It's a different feeling to sit in an empty restaurant. It feels like something is missing in the environment.* Although the sun had now set, the night sky outside still had a luminous quality to it. He watched as a few flurries still came down through the front-facing windows of the bistro. Even the small tables, chairs, and arborvitaes in the outdoor alfresco seating area out front were now covered with a dusting of the snow.

It was so quiet this evening. Everything always seemed quieter and calmer when it snowed. The white lights of the Christmas tree in the dining room paired perfectly with all of the red candles, tablecloths, bows on the high-hanging wreaths, and evergreen that tastefully decorated the entire space. Marcos went over to a nearby server station. It was already cleared and prepared for the following day's service. He found a book of matches and lit the red candle in the center of their table.

About ten minutes later, Dani came out of the kitchen grinning with two plates. She placed one in front of Marcos and the other on her side of the table and said "voilà" with a quick motion of her hand over his plate. The entrée looked amazing. It consisted of fresh bay scallops and shrimp served with lemon and sautéed mushrooms. Dani had also brought over a bottle of wine and made an ample pour into their two crystal glasses. Sitting across from him, Dani looked remarkable in her red dress and long blonde hair against the candlelight of the evergreen centerpiece and the Christmas flower arrangement. At the table and in this unique moment sat a traveler and a successful chef and bistro owner who had inexplicably been drawn together for the brief and magical season that is Christmas.

"Let's toast unexplored paths," said Dani raising her glass.

"I agree completely," replied Marcos, clinking his glass against hers.

"This wine has a nice finish," said Marcos.

Dani leaned back in her chair. "It's a nice one. I purchased it the other day when I drove over to the north fork."

Marcos set his glass down on the table. "I haven't been over there yet."

"There are a lot of wineries there, and at the end of the island, you have Greenport, which is a nice little village right on the water. You can take the ferry from the village to Shelter Island. Of course, over here on the south fork, we have the Hamptons and then Montauk with the lighthouse and park at the end," said Dani.

Marcos took a sip of his wine. "It really is nice. There's no disputing that."

Dani seemed lost in her own thoughts for a moment. She looked serious. "I'd like to have a winery and tasting room at some point, as I told you on the boat the other day. It has always been a dream of mine. Every time I drive over there and I visit someone's vineyard, I think about it."

"Why don't you? You could surely do it here," replied Marcos.

"Unfortunately, the acreage isn't enough for what I have in mind. I also can't weather a few years of operating at a loss right now. Maybe if the bistro continues to grow, I'll be able to do it someday. It's a competitive market to break into in the first place and then to thrive in," said Dani.

Marcos thought about the interview with the magazine that Dani had been featured in. "Have you ever thought of going into business somewhere where the operating costs would be lower and there would be more land available?"

Dani let out a sigh. "I have, but this is home. I can't see myself leaving Westhampton Beach right now. I've built up too much here."

Marcos decided not to press the issue. He would bring up the business proposal at another time. He felt ashamed, in fact, for suggesting in a subtle way that she should consider going into business elsewhere. Tonight was too special to mention anything like that anyway or to bring it into the mix.

Dani took a sip of her wine. "What about you, Marcos? What are your secret goals for the future now that you've told me a little about yourself?"

Marcos thought about the question for a moment. "You know, I've done well in the city. I really have. However, it has been an ordeal at times, like I told you when we talked out on the deck. I made it somehow, and I always liked it in there in the beginning, at least. Now though, it's starting to become too much. I think I'm ready for a change. Who knows, I may even be forced into it by my company."

Dani raised an eyebrow. "Why's that?"

Marcos didn't want to talk about Sheila or the business that he would eventually need to discuss with Dani just yet.

He answered but evaded the question slightly. "They have different expectations about what they want from me and what I want for myself. Being out here in the Hamptons has made me look at my life differently."

"A few weeks and you're already looking at your life differently?" asked Dani, surprised.

Marcos explained. "I guess it has been coming for a long time. I thought I wanted the New York City life. I'm not so sure any longer." He was basically repeating what he had told her on the boat. *It must still be bothering him,* thought Dani to herself.

She nodded in knowing agreement. "I used to spend quite a bit of time there during my childhood. The bistro itself caused me to go back and forth quite a bit as well. I mean, the work and business of so much of what happens on Long Island require dealings in the city. I'm always extremely happy though to get back out east. It's always a great relief to me when my train comes into the Speonk station and I know that I'm home again."

Marcos nodded in complete agreement. "I think I know exactly how you feel now."

Dani began to build upon what Marcos had said. "I need calm and nature in my life at this point too. I don't want to live in the anonymity of New York, just like you don't want to either. I want a place where I know people and the community and they of course know me. I had another long-time guest come in yesterday and actually bring me a Christmas gift. At the end of the day, there's a small-town feel here. It's moments like that which make this a very special place and make me want to stay."

"I agree with you, Dani," said Marcos. "I was walking along Thirty-Fourth Street after coming into Penn Station a few weeks ago. I saw all of these kids that had to be in their early twenties at the most. They were hurrying about, on their phones, texting with each other, and generally excited about everything. They're young and ambitious. I'm still ambitious, but not in the way that the city requires, like I told you already."

Dani took a bite of her food. "They haven't seen as much of life yet as we have."

Marcos nodded. "That's very true. They're chasing that New York City dream that they've seen in the movies. It's the same dream I chased when I decided to leave Kentucky. You and I both know that it can be more of a nightmare at times than a dream. They have the youth and ambition for it, though. Some will succeed, but others will burn out and head home. That city can take a lot out of you quickly. The thing that I realized is that I don't want to chase what they're going after any more in my life. Ultimately, I'd like to be working for myself in some capacity. There's no freedom in having to always be subject to some sort of paymaster and whatever their whims of the moment are," said Marcos.

Dani smiled broadly. "See, that's the wine helping you now, Marcos, to make better decisions and profound observations."

Marcos grinned. "In vino veritas."

Dani laughed. "You're right about that. In wine, there is certainly a veracity that we often try to hide not only from others but also from ourselves."

The good food and wine were starting to loosen both of their inhibitions. Marcos grinned broadly all of a sudden. "So, I know it's none of my business, but I did see that the article mentioned that you are single."

Dani took a bite of the scallops. "Hmm. You saw my article? Well, it has kind of become everyone's business now, I suppose. Fran insisted on asking me that ridiculous question and including it in the article."

"Fran who I met in the post office?" asked Marcos.

Dani nodded. "Exactly. She's the head of the magazine and is involved in various other business interests."

"What are those 'interests?'" joked Marcos.

"You see that's the thing, Marcos. I've known her for several years now and she has never once told me. Fran always says exactly what I said to you whenever anyone asks her about her work. That being said, everyone out here knows her. She's outgoing, cares a lot about the community and the people, and she's almost always featured in some form in the splash pages. In addition to her business interests, she's something of a socialite," said Dani.

Marcos took a sip of his wine. "She sounds fascinating."

Dani nodded. "She is most certainly fascinating and maybe a touch eccentric as well. However, when you're wealthy, people find even being eccentric a fascinating and amusing quality. All of that aside though, she really is very nice."

"Hopefully, I'll have the opportunity to meet her again someday," replied Marcos.

"If you spend any time out here, I'm sure you will," agreed Dani.

Dani ate some of the sautéed mushrooms. "So, now that you know about my singleness, I have to ask you whether the same applies? Honestly, I've been curious. An attractive individual such as yourself wandering around in the Hamptons could raise an eyebrow or two on a fellow single individual," said Dani jokingly.

"Did you just call me attractive?" laughed Marcos.

Dani grinned. "I think I might have actually."

"I'm glad," said Marcos. "The answer to your question though is, yes, I am single and otherwise romantically unattached."

Dani took another sip of her wine. "Good to know. Good to know."

Marcos pretended to scan the room. "I noticed that even with all of these decorations that are in here, you forgot to include any mistletoe."

Dani laughed. "I'm glad you noticed. Did you know that mistletoe is generally a parasite that feeds on a host and as if that wasn't enough, it has poisonous berries?"

Marcos laughed. "You know, Dani, you really have a wonderful way of romanticizing the holiday season."

Dani thought about what she had said for a moment. "Well, to be fair, it was also used by the Greeks and Romans for healing purposes and the Druids viewed it as special because of its capacity for blooming in the midst of winter."

Marcos grinned. "I suppose you did the right thing then, because if it was here, the refutation of a kiss under that parasitic plant would be considered most unfavorable as far as luck goes."

"You see, I knew what I was doing and actually did everyone a favor by omitting it from my décor this year," responded Dani with a hint of friendly sarcasm in her voice.

They finished the scallops and mushrooms. The meal had been delicious.

"Now for the dessert, my favorite part," said Dani mischievously.

Marcos picked up the empty plates. "I completely agree. Let me help you clear the table."

In the kitchen, Dani had prepared two plates that were sitting prominently on the pass. They resembled French toast. Dani saw Marcos eyeing them.

"Let's bring those out to the table. We can take care of these dishes later or tomorrow."

The wine and good food were starting to make both Dani and Marcos a little less motivated and a little more tired as the evening progressed.

"Is this French toast?" asked Marcos as they walked back out to the dining room together with the plates.

Dani grinned. "No, mon ami. This is my version of pain perdu."

Marcos appeared confused. "I will have to ask you, Dani, what pain perdu means?"

Dani smiled. "It is literally 'lost bread.' However, this is the real French toast."

"I expected nothing less in a French bistro where you're in charge," said Marcos jokingly. He paused for a moment thinking. "You know, it's kind of interesting that we're talking about 'lost bread' right now in a way."

"Why's that?" She looked quizzical.

"Well, it's just with everything that we talked about on the boat. I told you how I feel kind of lost still being in New York City after all these years. You were telling me about how you don't know how things are going to fall into place so that you can eventually have your winery and tasting room. Maybe we're both kind of 'lost bread' in a way ourselves."

Dani smiled. She liked how Marcos was always finding the deeper meaning in the things that she said. "I never looked at it that way, but you're right."

They put the plates down on the table and opened another bottle of white wine. Dani took a bite of her dessert. "Perfection!" she exclaimed, holding up her right hand in a state of wonder and amazement at what she had just created.

Marcos took the first bite of his. "Dani, this is incredible. The taste is exceptional."

There was a dusting of sugar, fresh strawberries, and almonds on the bed of brioche bread. It was full of taste despite being relatively simple in its preparation as a dessert.

They continued eating their pain perdu, drinking wine, and talking late into the night. They were two people together now, rather than alone. Each was an independent individual who had somehow found another like-minded soul in a complicated world. Both were now trying to find their way forward in the world separately but also together so that neither might be lost any longer.

The time passed quickly as it always does when two people are enjoying themselves and each other's company. It was now nearly one in the morning. The conversation, food, wine, and spirit of Christmas had permeated the entirety of the evening. Dani and Marcos both felt happier, calmer, and better than either had felt in some time. Maybe it was part of the magic of Christmas. Perhaps it was the enjoyment of two kindred spirits who were previously strangers, now meeting and spending meaningful time together. They took the dishes back to the kitchen, cleaned the table, and reset it for the morning and tomorrow's guests.

"You're welcome to stay over tonight, Marcos, if you'd like. It's already after one in the morning," said Dani as she discarded the remaining crumbs from her dish into the receptacle.

"I certainly don't want to impose upon you," replied Marcos. Dani walked over to the light switch panel to begin shutting down the kitchen for the evening, or early morning now as the case may be. "It's no imposition at all. It would be nice actually."

Marcos looked at her standing by the light switch panel. She still looked as radiant as earlier when they had met out in the snow in front of the bistro. "Thank you, Dani, I'd like that. It's just that I don't think either one of us can drive tonight at this point. Are you sure you don't want me to call a car service for us?"

Dani smiled. "That's not necessary at all. I live a little way behind the bistro beyond the vineyard. We can walk back."

"You continue to surprise me, Dani," replied Marcos. She shut off the lights, and they returned to the coatroom in the front of the bistro to get their jackets before heading out into the snow.

Dani slipped on her dark green coat that was double-breasted along with a warm winter beanie hat. Marcos once again put on his dress coat that had now dried out fully in the coatroom after their all-night conversation together. They walked out through the side door of the kitchen and into the snow and night.

There was a full moon above them, which illuminated the entire landscape brightly in these early hours of the morning. Nighttime at the vineyard looked different than during the day and especially in the snow. The neat rows of cabernet sauvignon vines stretched out over the gently rolling four acres and were completely covered in snow now. Gentle mists of white occasionally rose from the ground. The scrub pine forest all around them in the distance was dusted with snow as well and the green and white at night looked particularly picturesque.

Dani and Marcos started the walk back to her home on a path through one of the snowy rows of vines. Marcos was taking it all in. "It's hard to believe that all of this exists only some seventy-odd miles from New York City on the fringes of the Atlantic."

He knew that he had mentioned this out on the water with Dani, but it continued to impress him that the landscape could differ so widely within such a short distance.

Dani smiled. "It is surprising. You know, since you were so disappointed that I didn't have mistletoe in the restaurant, maybe we should look for it out here tonight." She brushed against him playfully.

"I think it's way too cold for that," said Marcos.

"Well, I agree. There is a type of mistletoe that grows in New York, but it's much more common in other places. I doubt we'd find any," replied Dani. She continued. "However, that doesn't mean that we can't enjoy what it encourages."

Marcos looked at her with a sparkle in his eyes. "I suppose that's very true."

Dani suddenly stopped and looked directly at Marcos. In an instant, they kissed under the bright full moon, in the snowy row of grapevines there in the early morning hours. It seemed as though there was no longer any doubt that both Dani and Marcos had feelings for each other. Both felt relieved with the knowledge that their feelings weren't one-sided. This kiss under the moon out in the snowy vineyard seemed to finally solidify what had been a lingering question for both of them. It had been hanging in the air like a subtle mist that couldn't be seen through since they had taken their first walk together through Westhampton Beach Village. Now, there finally appeared to be resolution, and both of them felt it in that instant tonight.

One moment of affection, as is so often the case, leads on to more. This unexpected and pleasant moment between Dani and Marcos was no exception. That single action had now lit a fire in both of them. It had set into motion a wanting and needing that required only its full completion before both would be satisfied on this cold, snowy morning. They walked now just a bit faster toward the converted red barn that Dani called home on the edge of the snow-dusted scrub pine forest.

It had been building all along. The interest and sexual tension had been there, albeit not to the level it was at now, but at perhaps an emerging stage. It had started from that first moment when they met and Dani explained a French fascination with Viennese pastries to Marcos. Tonight, it wasn't pastries, but rather each other that both were endlessly interested in.

There were no lights on in the converted barn as Dani opened the door. The large great room with its high vaulted ceiling, light wood flooring, beige sofas, and stone fireplace was dark and silent. Only the moonlight and the brightness of the glistening white snow outside streamed in through the large windows. Dani hung their coats in a small room off of the entrance foyer.

She took Marcos by the hand and led him up the black iron spiral staircase adjacent to the foyer that led up to the converted loft of the barn, which was now the master bedroom. There was an air of anticipation and excitement that lay adrift in the air and it felt cast over the entirety of the moment before them.

Upon reaching the landing, they entered the spacious master bedroom. It was a large space for what had once been merely a loft area. There were grayish wood floors and a separate sitting area with two comfortable chairs and an electric fireplace built into the partition wall separating it from the bedroom. Next to the bed with its high upholstered gray-colored headboard was a black modern dresser with silver hardware. Windows throughout the elegant space looked out toward the vines and the winter landscape.

Dani said, "Make yourself at home, Marcos. I'm just going to go into the bathroom to change." Dani walked across the room and went through two double doors leading into the ensuite bathroom. Marcos took off his red sweater, shirt, and khakis. Now in just a pair of blue boxer briefs, he climbed onto the bed and waited for Dani's return. A short while later she came out. They embraced and succumbed to what had been developing between them from that first early meeting at Dani's bistro.

Dani and Marcos had both been on their own for a long time. They were independent, each in their own right, and neither was actively seeking or looking for a "soul mate," "twin flame," "better half," or whatever the popular jargon of the moment consisted of and demanded as necessary for fulfillment. However, they both wanted someone to share the special moments of life with and to quell the loneliness that each of them felt deep down within themselves. Both felt a sense of contentment, relief, and happiness now with the act that had just taken place between them. It was a moment of calm and a release of tension amidst the storms of life.

The following morning arrived sooner than expected and with it the commitments that a new day brings. Marcos had an additional assignment that he had to get back to working on remotely at the Dune Road house while he was still out here in the Hamptons. It consisted of a commercial development project for an environmentally challenged and underused property located just north of the city. Dani had yet another group who had booked out the entire bistro for their holiday party. With the exception of the summer tourist season, this was the second busiest time of the year at the bistro. As a result of the booking, she had a full day of commitments ahead of her.

When they said goodbye the following morning, both had rested a little easier knowing that they wouldn't have to wait very long to see each other again. In a mere two more days, they would be meeting on Saturday morning for their rescheduled walk at Rogers Beach. Neither could wait, and it was that excitement and anticipation which would sustain them through their work projects until the arrival of the weekend.

CHAPTER 17

People from the past can enter into our lives again at unexpected moments. Today, there are a variety of ways in which they can come back to us. A text or call from an unfamiliar number may arrive. A message from a name we once knew somewhere in the past on our journey suddenly comes to us perhaps through social media. Dani thought about this when the phone on her bedside table charger unexpectedly vibrated early on Saturday morning.

It was December the eighteenth. The name on the screen was familiar.

"Hi, Mark," answered Dani as she accepted the unexpected call.

Mark sounded calm and poised. "Hi, Dani. I hope I didn't wake you. I know it's early for a Saturday."

Dani had already been up and working in bed for a few hours. She had been planning out the details for a few of the New Year's Eve bookings at the bistro that had recently come in. "No, not at all, Mark. It's good to hear from you. I know it was a bit awkward how everything ended the other night."

"I should have mentioned that I met someone beforehand while we were still at the bistro and before we went back to your place," replied Mark.

Dani thought for a moment. "Don't worry. We have always been and will continue to be friends. I think with the wine and the surprise of seeing each other after so long, we both forgot ourselves and everything else in our lives for a minute."

Mark agreed. "I think that's part of Christmas. We put off the realities of our own lives for a moment. I'm glad, though, that we're okay."

Dani smiled although Mark couldn't see it. "I'm glad too, Mark."

Mark continued. "I'm calling because I have something important to tell you. I also wanted you to be the first person to know out here on the East End."

"Of course. What is it?" replied Dani, her curiosity now piqued.

Mark cleared his throat audibly. "Remember how I told you about the restaurant that I was supposed to be opening in Montauk this summer?"

Dani couldn't forget. That was how everything had started again between them. "Of course. It sounded like a great idea. I also think you'll be a great competitor of mine in the near future." She let out a brief laugh.

"Well, I won't be your competitor, or anyone else's for that matter, at least in the Hamptons for the foreseeable future," replied Mark. He added, "The money for the project was put up by an angel investor."

Dani interrupted. "I have to ask you again who an angel investor is. I remember hearing about them years ago in business courses, but I'm going to need you to refresh my memory."

"Of course, Dani," replied Mark. He continued. "An angel investor is someone with a lot of money who privately puts money into a startup like our fledgling restaurant project. It gets the thing going and off the ground."

"That sounds like a good thing, Mark. They get a share of the equity in the business and you cut out having to deal with the bureaucracy of banks and other types of loan vehicles," said Dani approvingly.

Mark didn't sound as excited. "That's what I was thinking too, initially. But now the investor has pulled out and the whole project is off."

Dani couldn't believe what she was hearing. "So the restaurant in Montauk isn't happening?"

"No, unfortunately it's not, Dani, and I wanted to tell you first. You've always believed in and supported me since I started out in this field," replied Mark.

"You're an excellent chef and you have a lot of talent. It was easy for me to believe in you," said Dani.

Mark continued. "I also wanted to tell you that I'm going back to Spain. I've talked it over with Mariela. Her family is still there in País Vasco and I'm going to try my hand at the restaurant business again over there. I think it's time. I've devoted a lot of years, time, and energy to trying to make it in New York. When you stop seeing a return on what you've put into something, it's time to go."

Dani thought for a moment. "I agree with you, Mark, you already know that. I'm wishing you the best with everything in Spain. Please let me know if you need anything. I'm always here."

"Thank you, Dani. I appreciate that a lot. I'll keep you updated as I start off on this new journey. It could actually turn out to be exciting," replied Mark.

"Please do, and you're right. A new beginning like that could be very exciting and maybe even a change for the better," replied Dani.

Dani could hear voices in the background and Mark suddenly seemed slightly rushed. "Thank you again, for everything. Let's talk again soon. Un abrazo fuerte, Dani."

"I send the same to you, Mark. You know that, and we will talk soon," responded Dani as they ended the conversation. Dani lay there in bed thinking. Mark was off to a new start in his life. In a way, it seemed destined that things hadn't worked out between them. He was off to Spain now, and Marcos had come into her life almost at the same time that Mark had exited. At times, there did seem to be a synchronicity to things.

Dani looked at the time. It was already nine-thirty. *I've got to get dressed and drive out to Rogers Beach. I'm supposed to meet Marcos at ten.* This realization led her to leap out of bed and head into the bathroom to start getting ready for the day ahead.

Marcos drove along Dune Road on the barrier island. He was heading a bit farther east today. On his left, Moriches and Moneybogue Bay came into view. It was there that he and Dani had sailed through during the nor'easter. He couldn't look at any of it the same way again remembering all they had been through in trying to get back to the marina on that wintry afternoon.

A brief moment later, Marcos reached the point where Beach Lane coming from the mainland hits Dune Road and the entrance to Rogers Beach is situated at its termination. He pulled into the parking lot. Marcos walked from the parking field through the gazebo and down to the beach and the shore of the Atlantic Ocean. He stood there watching the waves come in against the shoreline and then gradually recede and go back out. It was still a few days before the official December start date of winter. Here at the beach, it had already arrived. The dunes and beach grass still had a faint dusting of snow kept within them from the relatively recent snowfall. However, the snow on the beach had now for the most part already melted.

Winter at the beach is not measured solely by the snow on the ground, though. Instead, it is a certain look in the sky, a different sparkling out on the water, and a quickening crispness in the beach air which indicates that one is indeed in the presence of winter at the shore.

Marcos was taking all of this in when Dani came walking through the gazebo and down to the edge of the Atlantic Ocean where he was standing watching the waves. He caught a glimpse of her heading toward him. She wore a cobalt blue coat, cropped dark blue ankle jeans, aviator sunglasses, and ankle boots. The winter sun illuminated her dark blonde hair against the vibrant color of her winter coat and green eyes.

Dani walked down the last stretch of empty shore leading to the water's edge.

"I've missed you, Dani," said Marcos as she approached him.

Dani reached out to hug him. She felt his well-developed biceps and back press against her as she held him close to her. "I've missed you too, Marcos."

All of the feelings between them from the other night rushed back as though no time had passed between them.

"How do you like it here?" asked Dani looking out toward the ocean in front of them.

Marcos continued staring out toward the horizon. "I've always liked the beach and the ocean. You don't have the opportunity to see a lot of it, at least not like this, in the city. It's definitely better being on solid land right now than sailing across Moriches Bay during a nor'easter."

Dani laughed and nodded in agreement. "That's true. Being able to come here whenever I like is something that I enjoy living out here all year. I see all four seasons at the beach. There really is a special element to each one of them."

They began to walk together along the seemingly unending stretch of sandy Atlantic coastline.

Dani looked at Marcos. "I have to ask you something."

Marcos watched a seagull gliding gracefully over the water.

"Of course." Dani continued. "I don't want to see this end. All of this between us made me realize that I never asked you how long you'll be out here in Westhampton Beach."

Marcos didn't want to think about this time concluding either. This was especially true after having met Dani and the many special moments they shared.

He paused, not wanting to answer what suddenly seemed like a very difficult question.

"I go back to the city after Christmas."

Dani's voice dropped a little. "I was afraid of that."

She was thinking to herself for a few minutes while they continued to walk in silence. There was only the sound of the waves crashing on the beach. She pushed her windblown hair back in place. "So many people come out here only for a season. It's difficult to get to know someone when that happens."

Marcos looked down at their footprints in the wet sand along with a few scattered seashells and pieces of driftwood. "I wish it didn't have to be this way. I thought I'd miss the city when I first came out here. I've started to feel differently now. Meeting you has been a large part of that change."

Dani continued walking with her eyes focused on the distant stretch of sand ahead. "That's difficult out here. There are the people who live here all year long who you get to know. That's wonderful, of course—at least for the most part." She laughed a little and then added, "but you do meet many other interesting people who, for example, come out only for the summer season." Dani paused. "You start getting to know them and then all of a sudden, it's Labor Day and they're heading back already to wherever they came from. Maybe you see them again the following year, maybe not. I suppose though that it's part of living in a beach resort-type area like the Hamptons or anywhere similar."

Marcos picked up a seashell and admired its intricate details. "I think that does have to be difficult. It's different from life in the city."

They walked on. Marcos couldn't decide what to do. Something had been weighing on his mind and he was going to have to tell Dani sooner or later. It was inevitable. He decided that this was the moment.

Marcos took a deep breath and exhaled. "I have to tell you why I'm really out here, Dani. As you already know, I work in commercial real estate for a company based in the city."

Dani appeared unfazed. "I know, Marcos," she replied.

Marcos looked at the sandy beach ahead. "I didn't get to tell you the details when we went out on the boat the other day. The principal of the company, Sheila, has an important client at the moment."

Dani turned to look at Marcos. "I don't see what this has to do with me."

Marcos sighed and continued. "This client wants to build a modern commercial development here in Westhampton Beach. This is a big project that they're proposing. They don't want a small existing store in the village or a lease on something. There's even the possibility of a pad site if the project clears zoning."

Dani stared at Marcos. "I don't know if that's going to work here."

Marcos continued. "I've been looking for the past few weeks out here and haven't found any properties that meet Sheila's requirements."

"It's a tough market and available land is limited. You really shouldn't fault yourself," said Dani.

Marcos took a moment to summon the courage for what he had to say next.

"Dani, your bistro and the attached acreage is the only property in the area that meets the requirements for what she is looking for."

Dani's face changed quickly to one of complete shock and then anger. "You want me to sell my family's French bistro to a commercial developer from the city?"

Marcos didn't know how to respond, because that was exactly what he was asking for.

Then he thought back to Dani's interview in the magazine. "Dani, you said that you had considered Park City, Utah as a potential future location for your bistro."

Dani gasped. "Now you're using my own words against me to get what you want?"

Marcos interrupted. "There's more land and maybe more opportunity in Utah, Dani. Who knows? The Hamptons are not the most cost-effective place to be running a bistro, much less dreaming of building a winery and tasting room. Long Island itself is notorious for its high taxes."

"This is home, Marcos!" exclaimed Dani. "I can't believe that after I told you all about my family's history and how hard they worked to build something out here and how long it all took that you would even suggest something like this to me. I shared all of that with you in confidence. You've now completely dismissed it and used the rest of what you've gathered against me to make your case. I can't believe this."

He would not be deterred. "In Park City you can get people coming in to your bistro from all over the country and the world. There's a lot more to do out there than in the Hamptons. You have the mountains, skiing, and a thriving dining and resort scene. You could extend your reach with a French bistro there. It would go far beyond just those with money coming out from New York City. Here they come to be seen, photographed, enjoy a splash in the water, buy some cute outfits at the pop-up shop of the moment, throw a clambake for themselves and their other rich friends on the beach in the middle of the summer, and then head back home for the rest of the year."

Dani was now indignant. "That's an arrogant and unfair generalization. I can't believe you. You talk to me like this after everything we shared together!"

Marcos continued while he still had momentum for making the argument. "Things are changing here, Dani. They're already widening Sunrise Highway going east."

Dani interrupted him. "It's still a pretty drive. I always think about that whenever I cross the Shinnecock Canal and Sunrise Highway takes me into Southampton."

Marcos disregarded the statement and went on with his campaign. Billboards are starting to crop up on what used to be a scenic two-lane road through the Pine Barrens. There are a lot of housing developments too, one after another now, where there used to be farms or open land. The east end is changing fast, Dani."

She now looked increasingly fed up with Marcos. "So you think I should just sell the bistro and land to you and Sheila that has been in my family for years now?"

Marcos was silent.

"Then your commercial development company comes in, bulldozes everything, and puts in another shopping center. This area then becomes characterless and the same as everywhere else. Maybe you even get your pad site. Then you can stick in yet another fast food drive-thru and maybe a bank as well. Hey, if the community is lucky maybe they'll even get one more medical practice building. That's what they really need on Long Island with them already along every damn stretch of road."

Dani took a deep breath and then continued. "Let's just change the whole character of this small town. Hey, as long as you and Sheila are happy, why not? Let's have another unfeeling multinational corporation come in and make a huge profit. Maybe the politicians can even skim a little graft off the top of the deal along the way. They'll probably join right in and support your little project wholeheartedly, the corrupt bastards. It sounds wonderful. I told you about the history of the bistro, both with regard to my family and the town itself. Now, you turn it all against me. You even took what I used in an interview as ammunition for building your case. Money is not the only deciding factor for me, Marcos. Maybe for politicians and a lot of the people who make the big level and highly politicized decisions in this country, but not for me, damn it."

"Dani, think about it," said Marcos in a calm voice.

Dani stopped him. "This conversation is over. Maybe even what happened the other night was only a tactic to make me more amenable to handing over the property to you. Maybe it was all a charade to get me to come around to selling. You wanted to soften me up. That was the plan all along. I can't believe I was stupid enough to fall for it. This is unbelievable, just unbelievable. You know what, just send me the damn Purchase and Sale Agreement so I can see what you're offering. It'll be entertaining for me to see what number and conditions you and Sheila place on family, history, and community. Maybe I'll just send it back and tell you to go fuck yourself."

Dani turned away from Marcos and the shoreline.

"I'm leaving," she said. Dani proceeded to hurry up the beach and then through the gazebo leading back out to the parking field.

Marcos called out, "I do care about you, Dani."

It was too late. In a few minutes, she had disappeared. Marcos now stood alone on the windy beach. He was unsure more than ever about what, if anything, came next during his remaining week in Westhampton Beach.

CHAPTER 18

It was a new day and moving closer toward Christmas. Dani couldn't believe the change in Marcos. He seemed like a different person yesterday. He was so unfeeling and businesslike after everything that they had shared together. Now he wanted her to sell the bistro to a commercial developer and for her to leave Westhampton Beach and start over again somewhere else. How could he even propose such an idea to her after she had told him about how much the community and area meant to her and her family? How could he just disregard the entirety of her family's history and her own desire to build upon the legacy that they had left her with? It had all been so callous and cruel. The words he had uttered on the beach didn't feel like they were coming from the same person she had come to know. Someone who was a complete stranger to her only a few weeks ago was now suggesting that she completely change her life because a company that he worked for desired something that she had and wanted to make a profit off of it.

Dani needed some space and time to think. Fran had called yesterday and left a message while she had been at Rogers Beach with Marcos. She had a copy of the print issue of the magazine that Dani had been featured in and wanted to give it to her. Fran had asked if Dani would be interested in meeting with her for coffee on her way back east to Westhampton Beach the following day.

It seemed like a good idea. Dani had some items that she had to purchase, which weren't available in Westhampton Beach, and ironically enough, necessitated stopping at one of the big-box corporate chain stores further west along Sunrise Highway.

There was a corporate holiday party taking place later that evening at the bistro as well. The staff at the bistro would be more than capable of handling everything until she returned. Dani felt like she needed the diversion anyway today. It wouldn't be a problem to escape for a few hours, see Fran, and then get back in time to Westhampton Beach to play master of ceremonies for all of the corporate people at the bistro. She got into her car, pulled out of the dirt field in front of the bistro, and headed toward Southampton.

The drive went well and before long she passed Shinnecock Hills Golf Club and connected with Sunrise Highway in Southampton. The eastern part of Sunrise highway was pleasant enough with a great deal of green, open land, and the protected Pine Barrens region. However, the green of the eastern areas through which the highway passed soon changed. Before long, the scene on both sides of the road became that of strip mall after strip mall and fields of concrete and gray as it moved further west, steadily advancing toward New York City.

Sunrise Highway was indeed being widened, even out east now. She wasn't oblivious and certainly knew what Marcos had been talking about. He wasn't wrong in what he had said. New signs and housing developments were popping up amidst the green unbroken pine expanses. Moving further west, the open space seemed to dissipate altogether for the most part. There were spots such as the Connetquot River State Park Preserve that offered a little bit of preservation along the way, but that was the exception rather than the rule. The frantic pace of the traffic also picked up. It was during times and drives like these that Dani was glad she lived and worked in a place like Westhampton Beach. She didn't like traffic, congestion, or living with too many people too close together. She needed nature and openness in her life. Dani had thought Marcos felt the same.

They seemed to have so many joint interests and shared feelings. Now, he had turned into someone who wanted to make Westhampton Beach look like a lot of the rest of Long Island. Who was he, really? That wasn't the Marcos who she had come to know who showed up on the beach and argued with her determinedly about why she should sell her bistro and acreage. Dani didn't know if she could ever trust him again after that. At the moment, she didn't want to ever see him again. Well, he'd be gone and back to the city soon, so this would all be just some strange, surreal experience that she could just forget about and move on from.

She had also developed feelings for the Marcos who had walked with her through Westhampton Beach Village and who drank hot chocolate with her on the village green at night in front of the Christmas tree. The Marcos who had been out on the boat with her as well had been so caring and empathetic. They had laughed together and enjoyed each other's company tremendously. This change in him didn't make any sense.

Dani continued driving. The laid-back, community beachside atmosphere and the natural beauty of the area surrounding Westhampton Beach had a calming effect on her. The area that she was seeing from her car right now stressed her out. Marcos had made a point about all of this, which was partially correct. However, he had failed to acknowledge the open land preservation work that was taking place out east. He had also dramatized everything and created a pending sense of urgency instead of the more accurate assessment that everything wasn't going to turn into strip malls, banks, fast food drive-thrus, medical buildings, and concrete overnight.

Dani thought about those free real estate catalogs that she would sometimes pick up and browse when walking through the village. They showed the Hamptons with a lot of forests, open land, and huge properties still available. It didn't appear as though eastern Long Island would be turning into the suburban sprawl and congestion of the island's western end anytime too soon. That didn't mean that open land preservation steps and action weren't important or didn't need to be taken quickly. It certainly did, and Dani knew herself how much the area around Westhampton Beach itself had changed since her childhood there.

Many of the forests, fields, and open areas that she had explored and enjoyed as a child were no longer in existence and that was in a relatively short span of time. Preservation was something that had to be taken seriously out east. However, there was no need to create the sense of panic that Marcos was trying to instill in her in order to get her to sell. Marcos had also said to her about how much he appreciated and enjoyed the open spaces of his childhood in Kentucky. Why would he want her to sell the bistro and land so that it could be built up? Again, none of it made sense. The Marcos who she had talked with on the boat and the beliefs that he had claimed to have did not match the person who had argued with her so vehemently at Rogers Beach.

The traffic moved faster here and Dani almost missed the off-ramp for the exit she needed. She pulled into the shopping center directly off the highway moments later. Dani walked into the national chain bakery where Fran said she would be. The place was already busy with people in line buying pastries, sandwiches, and beverages. Dani couldn't help but think about how different the atmosphere here was in comparison to her French bistro in Westhampton Beach.

She finally found Fran comfortably ensconced in a corner of the dining area with her coffee and pastries already ordered and set before her on the table. She stood up as Dani approached the table. "Dani, I'm so glad you could come out here today to visit for a bit."

Dani smiled. "I'm glad to be here, Fran. I needed a little break myself from all of the busyness at the bistro right now."

Fran reached over for something next to her. She handed Dani a few copies of the print issue of the magazine she'd been featured in.

"Thank you for saving these for me," said Dani flipping through one of them.

Fran smiled. "You are most welcome."

Dani found the article. "I do like the picture of me that you put in here, Fran."

Fran looked over at the photo of Dani and the article that she was now holding in her hands.

"It's a wonderful picture of you, Dani. I would have done the earrings a bit different, but still wonderful nonetheless."

Dani looked again at the photo. *What was wrong with the earrings?* She knew Fran didn't mean any harm by the statement. She was discerning and selective about absolutely everything in her life. That was just her way. She could have easily said something to Fran as well about her deciding to wear "brown in town." Her better judgment won out and she decided against it. Dani chose to change the subject instead.

"What were you up to today? I was surprised to hear that you were all the way out in Nassau. I thought you didn't like to leave the east end any more than was absolutely necessary."

Fran had a grimace on her face. "I don't, Dani. I had an appointment with my financial therapist and that was what necessitated me going into Nassau this morning, unfortunately."

Dani absentmindedly placed a napkin under her hot coffee. "I hope everything went well in there today."

Fran took a bite of her pastry. "It did. It actually went very well. We're working on the relationship between me and money. Things are improving, and I'm having less anxiety. Tell me though, Dani, you said you were meeting with that Marcos yesterday when you called me back. How did all of that go?"

Dani shook her head as though to suggest that it wasn't even worth asking. "It didn't go how I thought it would, Fran. I believed that it was going to be a beautiful morning. It didn't turn out that way at all."

Fran looked disappointed. "Don't worry about it. I have someone I want you to meet. I want you to come to a masked fancy dress ball that I'm having at the new house on Christmas Eve. You can meet him then."

Dani sighed. "I don't know, Fran. Christmas Eve? I probably won't even want to go out anywhere that night. I'll still be recovering from all of the holiday parties that we've been having at the bistro."

Fran thumped her bejeweled hand on the table. "I won't accept no, Dani. You're not doing anything that night. I know that and you know that. Come out, and let me introduce you to someone."

Dani leaned back in her chair. "Fran, I've had two failed romances in a matter of weeks. How much more do you think that I need to be put through at this point?"

Fran was incredulous. "What do you mean two failed romances?"

"Well, there was Mark who used to work for me. He's a lot younger, but I always thought there was something there between us. He gave me a big hug and walked right out of my life. Turns out he has a pretty serious girlfriend and is moving back to Spain now," said Dani.

"Don't worry about that. Look at me and Armando. He's a lot younger, and that is working out brilliantly. In fact, it's going even better than I hoped. I know, though, that me bragging about myself is not encouraging. What I'm trying to say is that there's always another personal trainer, pool boy, or tennis instructor. Believe me, Dani. So who else?" asked Fran.

Dani always appreciated how Fran could infuse a tense situation with humor, bluntness, and somehow make it all seem better. The second one is out here from the city on business over the holidays. He's around the same age and I really thought we had something special together."

Fran scowled after taking a bite of the scone that she had ordered. "So, what's the problem? No good in bed or something like that?"

Dani took a breath. "No, it's not that. He's all about business. He wants me to sell my bistro to the commercial real estate development company that he works for and move to Utah."

Fran was aghast. "You're kidding me? That's absolutely ridiculous. I can't even believe that he suggested that to you. Forget him. Westhampton Beach is your home. Who the hell is he anyway?"

Dani sighed. "I was attracted to him, and we did have some nice moments together."

Fran didn't want to hear it. "Come on. Lose him. I only work with winners and I've got one for you. Come to the ball on Christmas Eve and see what you think. It's a risk-free commitment."

Dani was still non-committal to Fran's continued insistence regardless of her saying that there was no risk involved. "I'll think about it, Fran."

Fran stood up from the table. "Dani, this has been a pleasure as always. Thank you for driving all the way out here to meet me. Let's try not to meet in western Suffolk, though. I don't know how much more of this congestion and people living so close together I can handle. My wealth therapist today told me to be gentle with myself and to not bring unnecessary pressure into my life. I intend to do just that and to follow their advice to the letter. This trip stressed me out today. I hate driving west on Sunrise Highway. In fact, I don't think I'll be leaving the east end again anytime soon. Well, of course, with the exception of seeing my therapist. Maybe I'll hire a car service next time." Fran was drifting off into her own thoughts.

Dani took back the conversation quickly. "You're welcome, Fran. I actually have to stop in at one of the stores in the shopping center before I head back myself," replied Dani.

Fran grabbed her Birkin bag. "Well, in that case, I better get going. I will see you back in Westhampton Beach. I also expect to see you on Christmas Eve." They hugged.

"We'll see, Fran," replied Dani as they both said goodbye.

Dani opened up the engine on the long straightaway of highway back east toward Southampton. The corporate holiday party was already in full swing when she arrived. She could hear the music blaring outside from the moment that she approached the parking field in front of the bistro. Everyone was inside, getting drunk, talking about how things were going at work, and having a generally good time, or at least drowning out the negative memories of what they had to deal with in the year that was almost behind them. The grab bag was in progress, which meant the party probably didn't have too much longer to go. The wait staff would be glad to have everyone out. They were always anxious to clean all of the tables as quickly as possible and to get home early for the night. It was hard being sober and rational when everyone else was blasted out of their minds. The staff at the restaurant had experienced this many times and was always glad when everyone had finally gone home for the night. Dani hurried into the kitchen to check on everything. As she rushed into the kitchen, her phone beeped.

She really didn't have time for this, but it could be important. Dani removed the phone from her pocket and greeted the sous chef who was predominantly handling the party today. There were two missed calls from Marcos. *That has to wait.* Her email also had a small number one next to it. Dani clicked on the message. It was the Purchase and Sale Agreement for her bistro and the acreage sent as an attachment.

CHAPTER 19

It was early morning. José had told Marcos that he often liked to spend quiet time alone in the home's east wing. Marcos hadn't had a chance to get over there yet. He couldn't sleep any longer anyway and felt awful about everything that had transpired between him and Dani. *What was I going to do? I had to at least propose it to her and make it sound logical and convincing. It was my last hope at still having a job in the new year, so what choice was there?* he thought to himself while walking through the empty and spacious Dune Road house.

There was a long, almost processional type hallway with square columns. It led under a series of softened or eyebrow arches to the east wing. Windows along the passageway faced out toward the backyard. The hall finally emptied into a combined media room and home office at the furthest reaches of the house. It was impressive. There was a French oak herringbone floor that had what looked like a chevron pattern imprinted upon it. This side of the house was extremely private, particularly when compared to the rest of the home with its open floor plan and minimal use of separating walls.

He was glad that he had opted to wear comfortable blue sweatpants and a long sleeve white premium quality loungewear shirt before coming over to this side of the house. He wanted to be comfortable, but it was a bit cold over here. The room itself was devoid of any Christmas decorations. This was paired with the piercing and bright December light that poured into the space from the backyard and beach beyond. It had a January feel. The feeling of January can only be described as the sensation that one feels when Christmas has passed and the work of a new year is at hand. January meant going back to the city, long working hours, and all of the stress that his workdays normally involved. Marcos was glad that he at least had a little more time before that would all become his day-to-day reality once again.

Dani hadn't answered any of his calls. He couldn't say that he blamed her. He hadn't expected her to answer him at this point. He knew he might have destroyed any hope of there being a relationship between them. He had also debated about whether or not to send her the Purchase and Sale Agreement. Considering the fact that it had already been brought up and the damage had been done, maybe it was better that she had at least seen the number that Sheila was offering. Marcos himself was no longer sure whether he personally wanted Dani to sell the property or not to his company. The bistro was a special place. He couldn't say that he was too fond of seeing it all bulldozed and turned into yet another huge shopping center. However, he didn't want to lose his job. It was a mixed bag with no easy answers.

Speaking of Sheila, Marcos was suddenly reminded that there was only one thing left to do on that front. He stood up and walked over to José's desk where he had left his phone. Marcos sat down in the contemporary and modern executive office chair. He looked out at the wintry backyard landscape and pressed the call button after selecting Sheila's number from his contacts.

Surprisingly, she answered almost immediately herself. Marcos wanted to ask her if business was slow and that was the reason why she was suddenly taking her own calls these days. He then thought better of making that comment and wisely decided against it.

"Have you got anything for me?" Sheila snarled.

"I have nothing," replied Marcos. He was ready to accept defeat and face the firing squad.

"Nothing," she almost shouted.

"Nothing," answered Marcos. "I gave the Purchase and Sale Agreement to the owner of the bistro and acreage that you were interested in. This is the only property in Westhampton Beach that even has the potential to work out for us. However, being realistic, I don't think she is going to sell. There's really nothing more that I can do on the project."

The line was almost deadly silent for a minute. Sheila returned suddenly. "Then you're fired, Marcos."

She hung up on him immediately. *So that was it.* All the years with that company and all of the loyal service that he had given to Sheila had now just ended in an instant. In a way, he knew that this was coming. There was no possible good that could have come out of not securing the sale for the company. *I might as well enjoy the time that I have left out here at the company's expense,* thought Marcos, resigning himself to what had just taken place.

Not even five minutes had passed when his phone started ringing. This was a more welcome phone call. It was Monique.

"I have some great news for you, Marcos," she said excitedly on the other end of the line.

"I could use some great news today, Monique," replied Marcos.

She continued. "I've worked several years with this one client from Westhampton Beach. She's heavily involved in the real estate industry out there. Anyway, there is going to be a Christmas Eve masquerade ball at her home in Westhampton Beach in a few days."

Marcos wanted to, but he really couldn't get excited about a Christmas party right now. However, he feigned enthusiasm for his friend.

"That's wonderful to hear, Monique."

She continued. "That's not all. I can bring a guest. My husband doesn't want to make the long trek from Park Slope here in Brooklyn out to Westhampton Beach just for a party. So naturally, I thought of my friend and coworker, Marcos."

Marcos was surprised by the invitation, especially at such short notice. The party was only in a few days. He really didn't feel like going to any kind of party or social event right now with everything that had taken place both between him and Dani and then the entirety of the situation with Sheila.

"I'm actually your former coworker now, Monique," said Marcos in a heavy-hearted tone of voice.

Monique was confused by his statement. "What do you mean?"

Marcos paused. "I mean, Sheila fired me. I couldn't get the Westhampton Beach commercial property deal to work out."

Monique couldn't believe it. "I'm so sorry to hear that, Marcos. That's not right. You had no control over whether or not there was a property available in Westhampton Beach. It's a small area. How could she have expected that from you?"

He paused for a moment. "I guess it was all coming sooner or later. It has always been a tense and volatile environment in that office. I hope you'll understand, though, why I'm not really in the mood to go to a Christmas party right now."

The sympathy ended there with Monique. "Well, you get in the mood, Marcos. I need you there as my plus one, and we'll have a great time regardless of that bitch Sheila and the shit show that is that company."

"Let me think about it," replied Marcos.

Monique would not be put off that easily. "There's nothing to think about. Haven't I always come through for you in a big way? Look at that fancy home you're staying in right now. That's all courtesy of me, Monique. So you get yourself in the mood, Marcos. I'll pick you up there on Dune Road on Christmas Eve."

Marcos knew he wasn't going to win this. "Alright, Monique," he replied.

Apparently, he was going to have to go to a Christmas Eve masquerade ball this year whether he felt like it or not. It would be nice if some other Christmas miracle came through as well. *I have to try to tell Dani about all of this.* He began to dial her number once again.

CHAPTER 20

It was early morning and Dani woke up to a new message on her phone. Marcos had left a voicemail. Dani didn't want to listen to it. What was there left to say at this point? He had advocated that she give up her entire life here in Westhampton Beach so a corporation could come in and enrich themselves at her expense. *Maybe I'll just listen to it anyway. I don't have to call him back.* It was more curiosity than anything else. Of course, he was attractive. That never hurt anything, but attractiveness and affairs of the heart would never compensate for what he had said and so selfishly supported and tried to push upon her. She entered her voicemail code to see what he had to say.

"Hi, Dani. I apologize for what happened at Rogers Beach the other morning. I acted out of character. I also acted out of fear of losing my job. That's no longer an issue now. I let a boss and company dictate and persuade me to do something, which I knew wasn't right. I hope you'll give me a second chance."

The message then ended abruptly. *What did he mean by saying that fear of losing his job was no longer an issue?* She was going to have to think about all of this for a while before making any kind of decision. Regardless, things were too busy at the bistro right now with Christmas right around the corner to get involved in any kind of unnecessary personal drama. There was the new year for that, if she even wanted to entertain it.

Dani had worked a sixteen-hour shift yesterday and today until eight at night. She had gone home to get some sleep after feeling completely exhausted and left her sous chef in charge of everything once again. It was already eleven p.m. when something happened that would forever change the destiny of the bistro. There was a holiday party taking place in the dining room and everyone seemed to be fully enjoying themselves.

The guests had enjoyed the dinner. Nicoise salad with its hearty blending of eggs that were hard-boiled, tomatoes, peppers, potatoes, and green beans had been a hit with everyone as a starter. The coq au vin or braised chicken in red wine had been declared exceptional by table number four. Finally, the meal was rounded off by crepes bursting with flavor for dessert. Everyone was satiated long before they arrived on the dance floor after the meal. Outside, it had started snowing once again. It appeared that this was going to be a hard winter on the East Coast.

Behind the scenes, the kitchen had been extremely busy. It was the holiday season and only a few days before Christmas. This made it even busier than usual. Everyone was working together at full capacity to produce quality meals that were delivered to the guests in a timely manner. The rush led the sous chef to accidentally spill some grease on the stove.

This negligence was easily missed given everything that was going on. A short while later another chef was preparing a dish on the same stove. As the heat was turned up, the grease ignited. This happened just as she went over to the pass on the other side of the room to check on some dishes that were about to be brought out to late arrival guests in the main dining area. No one was aware of what was happening on that cooktop, because everyone was preoccupied with their own work and assignments at their respective stations.

Due to the holidays, there had also been a lapse in the cleaning of the oven hoods in the kitchen. This particular hood above the grease spill had an opening that had been reduced to a very narrow passage through which dirty air could escape. That air would normally go up through the passage and into the kitchen's exhaust. The passageway had now become very limited and nearly blocked.

As a result of the solidified grease in the hood and then the inadvertent igniting of the spilled substance on the cooktop, the fire quickly took off. Its speed and rapid development grew even quicker than it would have under normal conditions. Those normal conditions would have meant a situation where the hood was clean and effectively channeled the now poor air from cooking into the building's exhaust without any problem. That was not the case tonight. The fire grew and spread with overwhelming rapidity.

As soon as the first chef saw the flames taking over the kitchen, they demanded everyone in the dining room to evacuate immediately followed by the entirety of the staff. Everyone instantly fled out into the cold wintry night.

Dani was resting peacefully in the master bedroom at her home. She was absolutely exhausted from work. This time of year at the bistro always felt like something that just had to be endured and persevered through. It had all taken its toll, and she needed the rest at this point. All of a sudden, she woke up to the smell of smoke drifting in through her bedroom window. She had left it slightly open even in this cold weather, thinking that the fresh air would help her sleep. *I have to close it. I don't want to get up, but I can't take that smell,* thought Dani half asleep. In a groggy haze, she got out of bed and walked over to the window. There was something bright and orange-colored on the horizon. She wiped her eyes and took a second look. It seemed as though there were flames in the distance. Then she suddenly realized that what she saw in the distance were indeed flames. Those flames were also taking place right on the site of her bistro.

Dani hurried down the spiral staircase from the master bedroom. She frantically grabbed her coat and was out the door and running as fast as she could across the snowy acres of grapevines at night. The air was filled with smoke and she could see the bright flames in the distance. They stood out against the dark and cold winter night, engulfing everything in sight.

She heard cracking and crashing as the bistro collapsed section by section. The water from the fire hoses fiercely hit against the building in an attempt to quell the out-of-control flames. Dani ran to the field and watched in horror.

The flames were everywhere. They had completely taken over the building. Even the vegetable garden and stands of pine out back with the benches where people would sit after dinner had been completely consumed. Charred and broken trees, benches, and land now lay there instead. Where the water had slightly abated the blaze, Dani could only see vestiges of what once was starting to emerge against the night sky.

All of this and right before Christmas, thought Dani in a state of utter shock and horror as she looked at her life's work and that of her family before her destroyed. This was the one thing that symbolized continuity through the generations in her family and meant so much to her. Now, it was all gone.

The snow had quickly turned into blizzard-like conditions and accumulated in deep drifts and embankments. The main road out in front of the bistro was nearly impassable. Subsequently, it took even longer for the blaze to be accessed and quelled. All of the diners stood outside in the snow far from the front of the building, utterly shocked by what they were witnessing. The bistro was entirely engulfed and shortly thereafter, was no more.

CHAPTER 21

The next day, Dani woke up early to head over to what remained of the bistro. The smell of smoke was still heavy in the air. It hung there as though acting as a reminder of what had happened, even though a new day had arrived. It was a smell that was powerfully discernible even from a distance as she crossed the fields of vines on her way to the ruins.

Dani couldn't believe what she saw as she approached the remains of the bistro. There were toppled and black arborvitaes, pots, and all of the alfresco dining furniture. It was all destroyed. Sections of wall had completely blown out and all of the glass was gone from the French doors and windows. There was no longer any separation between the indoors and outside.

She cautiously walked into what remained of the main dining room. It was indistinguishable now from what it once was. This had been a room decorated to the hilt for Christmas. It had been the scene of many parties, celebrations, and events through the years. Charred beams had fallen and lay across what was the floor. Some were pitch black and still hanging down from above. The occasional red bow or fragments from some of the Christmas decorations could be seen, but for the most part, everything was completely scorched and indiscernible.

The dining tables and chairs were all toppled, completely black, broken, and burnt. Inside the kitchen area, the remains of the stainless steel appliances were nearly blackened beyond recognition. They too had become nothing more than charred physical objects. The roof of the bistro itself was gone and Dani looked up at the blue winter sky above her. The smell was overwhelming. She had to get out of here. Dani walked over some of the toppled and burnt chairs and tables. Her boots crunched on some broken glass from the shattered and signed celebrity portraits that had once hung on the hallway leading to the kitchen.

Dani walked out toward the scorched back garden area. The broken and burnt scrub pines and scorched plots of vegetables sat forlornly before her. This didn't even look like a project where there could be only a partial demolition. It was all destroyed, and the entirety of the site was going to have to be cleared. A building with so much history and heritage for the community and her family was now gone.

Then the reality hit her of the cost that would be involved in the rebuilding. She didn't even want to think about that right now. Yes, there would be the insurance money, but that would in all likelihood not cover the entire rebuild. It had all been too much—the fire, and then everything that had gone on previously with Mark and Marcos.

She thought about Mark and Marcos and the moments that she had recently shared with both of them. It had been special. It had also been a reprieve from the day-to-day grind of running a bistro. It was a pleasant diversion and those don't always come along so frequently. She felt bad that things had to go the way that they had. However, it wasn't her fault. The way that Marcos had confronted her and tried to convince her to sell something that was so important to her and the community was appalling. It didn't even seem like him that day. It was as though he was someone else. Maybe there was something else on his mind that day that was leading him to act that way. Of course, maybe there wasn't. Maybe that was the real Marcos, not the romantic and charismatic person who she had spent that wonderful evening and day out on the boat with previously. He had said something in the phone message about the job being no more, but what exactly did that mean? Was he out of a job? Had he acted that way to her because of his job and whatever pressure it was putting him under? She really didn't know.

In a way, she wished that there could be another chance and another opportunity to try again with him. They shared a lot of commonalities, which had made the developing relationship even more special and unique. However, there couldn't be a second chance if he was going to continue acting the way that he had.

The other issue that continued to trouble her was the thought of having to attend Fran's Christmas Eve masquerade ball. It sounded like a beautiful party. Fran was a friend who she had known for years. If she didn't go, it would surely be seen by her as an offense. However, after everything that had just happened in a mere few days, how could she go to a party and act as though nothing at all was wrong in her life? Everyone would be asking questions and wanting to know about the fire—why it happened, whether or not she was going to rebuild, and who knew what else. Dani didn't have any answers. She couldn't even tell herself what was going to happen next, much less anyone else at this point.

Dani looked out at the charred remains all around her across the wintry landscape. The scrub pine in the distance was still green and hadn't been burnt by the fire, thankfully. It felt like life and rebirth, seeing that vibrancy far away at the edge of the snow-covered fields and especially in comparison to the destruction in front of her. Dani hoped that there would be a rebirth this Christmas in her own life as well.

CHAPTER 22

Christmas Eve was tomorrow. Dani wasn't taking his calls, he had lost his job, and the commercial property deal in Westhampton Beach wasn't going to happen. It felt like Christmas wasn't going to be especially "merry" this year. Marcos had already decided that given everything that had taken place, he was now going to head back to the city on Christmas Day. The traffic might be less that day heading west toward New York because it was a holiday. It therefore might be a good day to leave the Hamptons behind and see if there was anything still left of his life in the city that could be salvaged.

Right now, he would go for one last run on the beach. He had gotten used to these refreshing morning runs on the shoreline. He loved hearing the waves crash against the beach while he ran and watching the sunrise each day over the vast Atlantic Ocean. He was going to miss being able to do this each day when he returned to New York. There wouldn't be time tomorrow for his run with all that he had to accomplish, and then there was the masquerade ball in the evening. Today would have to be the last day of this wonderful morning routine that he had become accustomed to.

It had been beautiful out here in Westhampton Beach. It was the change of pace and lifestyle that he sorely needed. However, nothing was waiting for him out here any longer. It had become just another beautiful place that he had visited in his life, but not somewhere to which he had formed any attachments that would in any way suggest a need to stay. He and Dani weren't going to develop something meaningful together. That appeared to be over now as well. At least he still had a few friends in the city. Given everything that had happened with Sheila, Marcos didn't really feel any positive connection or feelings for the city either. New York felt stressful and anxiety-producing after having been out here. It was going to be difficult adapting to the lifestyle in there once more. The end result of it all was that he felt cast adrift and had a persistent feeling of not belonging anymore to either place.

He had spoken on the phone last night to Marvin and José. They had gone over to Spain for a few weeks and initially intended to pass the entire holiday season there. The weather had been wonderful along with the food and seeing José's family. Marbella was near paradise compared to the harsh winter of New York at this time of year. An emergency business situation in New York had unexpectedly arisen, changed their plans, and resulted in them coming back only a few days ago. It hadn't been a choice that either José or Marvin wanted to make. They were staying at José's loft in Manhattan at the moment. Marvin had said to José that he should continue to spend the holidays in Marbella with his family and then come and join him in New York after they were over. José had instead graciously insisted on staying with Marvin and coming back to New York as well.

Interestingly enough, they were also friends with Fran. *She really did seem to know everyone.* José and Marvin were even attending her Christmas Eve masquerade ball tomorrow. Marcos had told them that they should come back to the house in Westhampton Beach, rather than making the long drive back to the city after the party. He was going to be leaving anyway on

Christmas Day so they were welcome to take over at their home again. They both accepted the invitation and were happy to be coming back to Westhampton Beach after being in the city.

So, it was all done. There would be nothing with Dani, he'd drive back home to New York City on Christmas Day, Marvin and José would come back to their house, and the whole time that Marcos spent out here in Westhampton Beach could be chalked up as a failure and a complete waste of time. He didn't know what was next but didn't want to think about it either right now.

After the run, he'd clean up and go for one last walk by himself in Westhampton Beach Village. He wanted to enjoy it one final time while it was still decorated for the holidays. It wouldn't be the same without Dani. He also knew that nowhere is the same after Christmas. The decorations don't have the same impact or create the same sense of anticipation and excitement that they do in the days leading up to the holidays. He wanted to feel that one more time, even if he had to feel it by himself. Today and tomorrow were his last two days out here and he wanted to remember them in a positive way. It was going to be hard to feel the Christmas spirit or be in a celebratory mood without Dani. He wouldn't even be going to the ball tomorrow if it wasn't for Monique forcibly persuading him to attend.

Marcos put on his sneakers. The weather outside looked sunny, cold, and refreshing. Before heading out on his run, he walked over to the Christmas tree that he had set up in the great room. There was the decoration from Dani, the ship's wheel with the compass, sitting near the top of the tree. He hadn't followed what he personally felt was right and had paid dearly for it. This would be his one significant souvenir from Westhampton Beach. *Hopefully, it will remind me to follow my heart and what I know is right in the future.* He took the ornament off of the tree and went back upstairs. Marcos packed the ornament carefully in his suitcase. After tomorrow, all of this would be a memory. The ornament would travel with him back to New York City and maybe in the years to come, he'd still look at it and remember Dani. She would always be someone he had met at a unique moment in his life. That would be his fondest memory of the time that he spent in Westhampton Beach, New York.

Marcos went down the stairs and out through the doors of the great room to the backyard and beach beyond. Taking a deep breath, he set off on his final Hamptons beach run.

CHAPTER 23

New York City

Sheila and Bernard walked briskly along Fifth Avenue. Winter had come to New York and the cold this morning felt brutal. The Guggenheim Museum came into full view as they reached East 89th. It was a quiet morning in this part of Manhattan and she had decided to bring her boyfriend with her to take in some art. Sheila was anxious to get inside and to ascend the ramp that spiraled upwards through the various and frequently changing exhibits. However, Bernard had other things on his mind besides art.

He looked at Sheila as they walked in through the front doors of the museum. "My daughter still needs a job, Sheila. Is there any chance—"

"How many times are you going to remind me, Bernard? You're really starting to get on my nerves. We've been seeing each other for a year now, and I feel like you've been asking me that same stupid question over and over again since the start of our relationship."

Bernard interrupted. "It's not such a stupid question for her, what with not having a job to go to every day."

He decided to change his tone rather than pissing off the woman who held the key to his daughter's success in New York.

Bernard looked upwards at the modernist circular interior of the building. "Sheila, come on. You know how hard it is for young people. They finish with a worthless college degree that some high school teacher or guidance counselor tells them is the key to success, all the while filling their heads with fake numbers of how much money they'll make after they get it. Then they're deep in student loan debt, and you and I both know that without any connections, they're finished. Who's going to hire them, other than some civil service job if they're lucky enough to get picked on the list or have the right connections?"

Sheila looked directly at Bernard. "I'm not stupid, you know. You really think I don't know that, Bernard? I know how things work around here, probably better than you. However, I'm not some kind of charity or vending machine that just hands out jobs at will to the people who need them."

They were both starting to get stressed again after what should have been the start to a pleasurable morning.

"But you could actually make it happen, Sheila," Bernard persisted. "The kid doesn't know anyone who's influential or connected in the city. I told her to stay with her mother and work in the small town where she grew up. In a lot of ways, there is more opportunity there than in this big mess here. You know these young people, Sheila. They're influenced by all of the lies and crap that they see in the media and on television and think for whatever reason that New York is where it's all at and that they're going to strike gold there."

Sheila wanted a cigarette but couldn't smoke inside the building. She took a deep breath. "This city is a shithole. I don't know why anyone would want to come here anyway." There was a moment of silence in the room.

"You're living pretty damn good, though. Let's be honest," replied Bernard.

Sheila fired right back at his sarcastic comment. "That's because I'm the fucking boss. What the hell do I care about some little twenty-two-year-old shit who is right out of college and just getting started in the nightmare that is this city? She'll learn fast enough on her own, with or without me, how shitty the process of getting ahead anywhere or with anything can be."

Bernard gave her an imploring look. "I'm just asking you as a personal favor, Sheila, please."

Sheila paid for the entrance tickets at the counter. "I'll see what I can do."

Bernard smirked and leaned in to kiss her. *Maybe things would work out after all for his daughter in New York*, he thought feeling satisfied.

The end of the workday had arrived at long last. Monique was going to take the subway back to Brooklyn. However, an important client meeting at the office in Rockefeller Center had consumed the entirety of her lunch break. She needed to get something to eat before heading home for the night. Monique walked a few blocks to get away from the beehive of Christmas tourist activity taking place in and around Rockefeller Center.

It would have been difficult to find anywhere to actually sit down and eat, anyway. This was partly because the tourists generally stayed on a pretty typical and well-worn trail through the area, and in doing so, flooded any restaurants placed along it.

Monique thought back to a comical incident she had once witnessed here in Midtown. Two individuals had emerged into the light on the street out in front of Penn Station and Madison Square Garden. Their train from out of state must have arrived at the station in the bowels of the earth below them, and they were now having their first look around the city for the day. The two individuals were obviously from out of town, but from what Monique could gather, one had at one point or another been to New York City previously.

To convince her friend that she was indeed the more experienced, knowledgeable, and street-seasoned New Yorker, the one individual put her hand hard on her friend's shoulder. She cast a suspicious and roving glance at everyone and everything around her there on the busy sidewalk.

In a knowing voice she whispered audibly to her friend, "You know, this isn't one of the safest areas of New York." With that, they hurried off rapidly down the block along with the other throngs of tourists. Monique was taken aback by their statement and a little amused at the same time. She had never heard the heart of New York City, midtown itself, being described this way.

Monique continued her walk. A short while later, she went into a small diner a short distance away from Rockefeller Center and down one of the nearby side streets. She was quickly shown to a booth and sat down. Suddenly, she heard a very familiar voice giving explicit instructions to the waitress. *Oh shit, it's Sheila.* It was bad enough that she had to spend every day in the office with Sheila. She certainly didn't want to have to try to make polite conversation with her now during her free time. A man was walking with her to the table as well. Monique averted her eyes from them, slid over into the far corner of the booth, and tried to look busy studying the menu.

Fortunately, Sheila and her guest were completely preoccupied with their chat and with choosing the right table to sit at. Interestingly, the waitress ended up seating them in the booth directly behind Monique. Even though this was too close for comfort, Monique was relieved that Sheila hadn't noticed her.

Monique placed her order with the waitress and then took a sip of the water that had already been brought over to her table. Sheila was talking as loudly and incessantly as ever in the booth behind Monique with whoever the man accompanying her was.

"Tell your daughter to make an appointment and come see me directly on Monday. My secretary will be expecting her call and knows what to do," said Sheila.

"So you have something for her, Sheila?" asked the man.

"I do. I've been working on it for a while now. You kept thinking that I wasn't doing anything, but I had a plan in place behind the scenes. I finally got around to firing someone in our office who I've clashed with for a long time now. It took me time to figure out a way to get rid of him, but in a manner that would appear reasonable, fair, and go unquestioned by everyone in the office. I have to keep my employees believing in a certain degree of security at the firm. They have to at least think that their jobs are safe as long as they perform and that they wouldn't be let go without just cause. If I didn't create those types of illusions when I wanted to get rid of someone, they wouldn't have any incentive to work hard or to be effective for the company and its needs."

Bernard, as Monique would discover the man's name to be, was in awe of her skill. "You really are brilliant, Sheila. You don't have to tell me of course, but I'd love to know how you ended up pulling it off?"

Monique was confused. What had they been trying to pull off? This was going to be interesting.

Sheila grinned while Monique sat alert in the booth behind her taking in every word. Sheila proceeded to tell him how she did whatever, "it" was. "Well, I can't tell you everything, of course. Let's just say that it had to do with a proposed commercial property development project in Westhampton Beach."

"I've been out there a few times. It's a nice place," interjected Bernard.

Sheila dismissed his comment and continued as though he had said nothing. "I knew from the very beginning that it couldn't possibly happen. I set the whole thing up in a way that would appear reasonable and fair to all my other employees in the office. It all came across to them as merely an employee who just couldn't carry out their responsibilities. Therefore, this particular employee being subsequently let go appeared very reasonable and otherwise justifiable in their eyes."

Monique gasped out loud in the booth behind Sheila. *Shit, I hope she didn't hear me.* Apparently, Sheila hadn't because the conversation behind her continued breezily and without any noticeable breaks.

Bernard was speaking now. "Thanks so much, Sheila, for making all of this happen. I know my daughter will be excited and grateful."

Sheila leaned back in the booth. "Well, hopefully, she'll be a better employee and more trainable than the one I just let go."

Bernard took a bite of his chicken cutlet. "I know she'll work hard for you, Sheila, and she'll be happy to finally have a job."

Sheila grinned deviously. "Is she still looking or did you tell her you were working on something with me for her?"

Bernard paused and took a sip of his water. "It has been almost a year and she's still looking. The college and their so-called 'career center' did shit for her after she finished. They just told her to keep rewriting her resume and cover letter, because that was the ticket to success and gave her the password for a worthless job database through the college after she finished. Only a few of her friends who were lucky enough to find government and civil service jobs somehow found work that could pay the bills. That being said, there weren't very many of them from her graduating class who lucked out in that way either. I didn't say anything to her yet about what we've been working on together."

Sheila took a large sip of her pink gin. "Refreshing," she said aloud, licking her lips loudly. "I'm glad you kept quiet about it. The fewer people who know how business is really conducted in this world, the better."

Monique couldn't believe what she was hearing as Sheila and Bernard now began to move on to other conversation topics. *I have to make a call.*

Marcos had just come out of the shower upstairs when he heard his phone ringing downstairs. He hurried down the stairs to see who was calling. On the screen, it said "Monique." He picked up and Monique's voice instantly sounded urgent.

"I have something important that I need to tell you." There was a pause on the line.

"Of course. Anything, Monique," he replied.

Monique hesitated and then continued. "Well, I was in a diner today after work. Sheila and some guy came in and sat down in the booth behind me."

"Okay," said Marcos, anxious to hear where this was all going.

"They were talking, and I think, but I'm not sure, that the guy's daughter needed a job after college. Anyway. . ."

"You can tell me, seriously," interrupted Marcos.

"Anyway," repeated Monique, "there never was any client with the firm who wanted to build a retail space in Westhampton Beach."

Marcos was in shock at what he had just heard. "You're kidding me, right? This is all some kind of joke?"

"I'm not kidding you, Marcos. I'm for real right now. Sheila set you up."

Marcos couldn't believe this. Monique continued speaking.

"She didn't like you and wanted you out so she could give your job to his daughter. I think she had been planning it for a while from what I could hear."

Marcos went silent. It just felt so shocking and unthinkable. He knew Sheila was dangerous, sneaky, and a shark in many ways. However, he never imagined her doing something like this.

"I don't even know what to say."

"You don't have to say anything. It's all awful, the whole thing."

Marcos paused. "Thank you for calling me, Monique, and for telling me all of this."

"I had to," she replied.

Neither one of them knew what more there was to say at that point. Monique attempted to change the subject. "We have Fran's Christmas masquerade ball at least, right?"

Marcos tried to appear otherwise unaffected by the news Monique had given him prior to the subject being changed. "That's right. It'll be a nice night. You're coming out here to meet me before we drive over together to the party, right?"

"Exactly," responded Monique. She paused and seemed to be searching for something positive to say. "Don't worry about this, Marcos. Everything will work out for the best, and we'll have a great time together at the party."

"I know we will, Monique," replied Marcos as he tried to sound optimistic and cheerful.

After the call ended, Marcos sat alone on the sofa thinking about all that had happened during the relatively short time since he had come out to Westhampton Beach. None of it felt real any longer. The good and the bad all felt unimaginable. He never could have envisioned any of this coming his way. *Where do I even go from here?* he thought to himself as he closed his eyes. Minutes later, he was asleep on the sofa in Marvin's great room. He would have a bit more time before he would need to face whatever came next.

CHAPTER 24

Christmas Eve had arrived and with it the last evening that Marcos planned to spend in Westhampton Beach before returning to the city. He was putting the finishing touches on his evening outfit. He was going to wear a crisp white Oxford shirt, sans tie, with a black blazer and slim-fitting black pants. He looked in the mirror, making sure that his hair was just right. A dark blue and orange mask sat on the bathroom vanity beside him. All of a sudden, a text message popped up on his phone. Monique had arrived and was waiting at the gate. He opened the gates by pressing the necessary button through the app on his phone in the master bedroom and then hurried downstairs to greet Monique after her long drive out from Brooklyn.

Marcos walked out of the house and toward Monique's approaching car. After parking, she stepped out of the car wearing high heels and smiled when she saw Marcos.

"Wow, don't you look stylish, Mr. Marcos."

"You don't look so bad yourself, Ms. Monique," he replied mischievously. Monique had on a stunning emerald green dress and gold jewelry, which made even more of an impression tonight against the snowy landscape around them.

"Would you like a tour of the mansion first?" inquired Marcos.

"Not tonight. I've actually seen it a number of times. Marvin and José are old friends. I even came out here and saw it when Marvin was first starting to build it on spec," replied Monique. She looked at the delicate and expensive watch on her left wrist. "We had better get going or we're going to be late."

With that, Marcos got into the car and they drove off down Dune Road heading toward the mainland and Fran's home in Westhampton Beach. It was a beautiful evening. The view of Moriches Bay was spectacular as they crossed over to the mainland. There was always something about the sunset out here and especially over the water, which made it extra special.

Monique and Marcos approached Fran's estate shortly thereafter. It was a magnificent shingled, very classic-looking Hamptons home situated a significant distance back from the road. The snow on the vast front lawn made the drive up even more dramatic. The home stood silhouetted against the evening sky and snow on the ground with all of the warm interior lights on inside, which cast a glow out over the motor court. There were already a number of cars that had arrived and one was turning in immediately behind Monique and Marcos.

Valets took each car as they arrived at the porte-cochere and parked them a short distance away from the house. Monique and Marcos climbed up the wide stone front steps and were greeted warmly at the front door by Fran's staff. They took their coats and then guided them through the entry foyer and along the central passage which ran through the house from front to back. They then made a left through two large floor-to-ceiling paneled doors that entered into the ballroom.

It was a magnificent space and already filled with well-dressed people milling about, socializing, and indulging in light appetizers. The "great and the good" of Hamptons society in the winter had all gathered at Fran's home for her Christmas Eve masquerade ball. The theme of the décor appeared to be that of a sparkling winter storm, which had elegantly taken over the entirety of the room. There were white, silver, and gold winter-themed decorations everywhere. Flower arrangements, two ice sculptures, white tablecloths, white birch potted flower arrangements, and an assortment of winter décor filled the space with elegant splendor.

Marcos looked around the room in his dark blue and orange mask, taking it all in. Waiters hurried around with glasses of bubbling champagne and canapés. Everyone was resplendent in their finest evening wear and masks. A full orchestra played a wide selection of Christmas music in the impromptu bandshell that had been set up for them in Fran's spacious ballroom.

Monique went over to hug Fran. "So glad you could come tonight, Monique," said Fran.

At that moment, a waitress appeared bearing a silver tray. Monique laughed. "I feel like you always have champagne waiting for me every time that I come out here."

Fran waved her hand, dismissing the compliment. "Monique, there's never a bad time to drink champagne. This is the real thing too, direct from France. On a night like this, I wouldn't let my guests settle for anything less or a domestic sort that is masquerading itself as champagne."

Monique nodded, taking a sip of her drink. "Well, you and I both know, Fran, that real champagne and the right to correctly call itself that can only come from the actual region of Champagne in France."

"You're quite right, dear girl. Most people don't realize that," replied Fran approvingly.

It was rather interesting to see that more than a few local and state politicians had shown up for the occasion. Dani had arrived at the party early, and upon seeing them whoring themselves out once again she couldn't help but remember all of the times that they hadn't answered or responded to her when she needed assistance with something. Only at election time were they amendable. In fact, they were so amendable at that time of the year that they would stop and wave to you, talk with you, and respond to absolutely anything you asked, even if what they told or promised you was bullshit anyway.

Dani remembered seeing these same individuals in the room tonight on television and in ads when they were running for office. During those times, they pretended to be all about helping the common, everyday, and downtrodden individual. Yet, here they all were tonight living the high life in their personal lives.

Fran certainly hadn't forgotten the mistletoe in her décor for the evening. It hung prominently over each entrance and exit to the ballroom. It felt just a bit ironic to Dani to have parasitic plants and politicians all together in the same room at Christmastime tonight. *Hypocrites to the highest degree*, she thought, turning away in revulsion from one who was entering a little too close into her orbit.

Fran had promised to introduce Dani to someone who she approved of at the ball that night. She was a person who always followed through and never forgot a promise. Early in the evening, Fran came over to Dani with a handsome, shaggy brown-haired, and very fit guy by her side. She tapped Dani on the shoulder while she was talking with another guest at the party.

"Dani, this is Sven. This is the one I told you about during our little chat at the bakery." It suddenly came back to Dani.

"Sven is a professional tennis instructor," continued Fran.

"It's very nice to meet you, Sven," said Dani, extending her hand. She secretly wondered why all of the men in Fran's life were young, fit, and somehow personal trainers, tennis instructors, pool boys, or some other occupation associated with keeping oneself in a continuous state of fitness, youth, and top form.

He shook Dani's hand. "We'll all have to play mixed doubles together one of these days," added Fran.

"That would be nice," replied Dani.

Sven's mobile phone suddenly started ringing. "Please excuse me, Fran. This is a call that I have to take."

Sven disappeared to somewhere outside the ballroom. Fran took a long look at him from behind as he hurried out of the room.

"So, what do you think?" said Fran, grinning deviously at Dani.

"He's wonderful to look at, of course," replied Dani. She continued. "It's just that I'm not in a good place right now. The bistro and my entire livelihood are gone. Then I have this situation with Marcos. I don't know whether there is something there or not."

Fran broke in to what Dani was saying. "Don't worry about Marcos, Dani. Remember, he wanted you to give up everything here and go to Utah."

Dani nodded. "I think there was more to it than that."

Fran pretended to throw her hands up as though she were now giving up for good on Dani. "As you wish," she said. "I just think you're missing out on a good thing with Sven by being so focused on this Marcos."

"Maybe, Fran," replied Dani.

"Well, I have to go check on everyone and everything. This is my ball after all," said Fran, already scanning the room for what she needed to do next.

"I understand, and we'll talk more later," replied Dani. Fran headed off, stopping along the way to chat with the various small groups of people milling about her ballroom.

Marcos suddenly saw Dani lightly disguised across the room in her gold and silver masquerade mask. *What was she doing here?* he thought, while at the same time being extremely happy that she was here at the party.

"Ambassador, it's lovely to see you again," said Dani suddenly in her gold and silver masquerade mask to an elderly gentleman on the other side of the room from where Marcos was standing in disguise in his mask. Dani and the ambassador began a convivial conversation. A few minutes later, she continued circulating about the room.

Marcos walked over to her. He slid off his mask. "Hi, Dani. I want to apologize about the other day."

Dani stopped him. "How did you get invited to this event?"

Marcos knew she was still obviously upset with him. "I have a friend who knows Fran."

"Fran usually picks better friends. Usually, she only associates with people who don't sell her out. I'm just a little surprised, honestly," replied Dani.

Marcos stood there not knowing what to say at this point.

Marcos took a deep breath. "First, I want to say how awful I feel about what happened at the bistro. I saw it online. It was the top headline of the day, and I was in shock when I found out. I never wanted to see something so horrible happen to such a beautiful and special place."

Dani stood there silently thinking. She then responded, "You were going to have the whole place bulldozed and turned into another shopping center. How can you say that you feel sorry about what happened?"

Marcos didn't know what to say. "I lost my job, Dani. The only reason I even pitched the idea to you so strongly was because I was forced into it."

Dani stood there expressionless. "Well, I digitally signed your Purchase and Sale Agreement. You win. You have what you wanted from me. I have nothing left now after the fire. There's really no reason for me not to move at this point. I can't possibly afford to rebuild here anyway. Incidentally, did you get the agreement?"

Marcos hadn't checked his email all day. He opened up a browser window on his phone and logged in. There in his inbox was a new message in black. It was the signed Purchase and Sale Agreement from Dani.

"I have it," said Marcos.

"Good," replied Dani. She continued. "Send me the check and then I'll be out of Westhampton Beach and your life as well. Permanently."

Marcos looked again at the signed agreement on his screen. "I don't want you out of my life or out of Westhampton Beach, Dani."

With that, he highlighted the email from Dani and pressed delete with the phone in front of her so she could see.

"Really?" said Dani in complete disbelief at what Marcos had done. He was deleting the very thing that he had been almost pleading her for.

"Really," answered Marcos. He continued. "I want you in my life, Dani. Westhampton Beach is your home and your community. We all need you to rebuild the bistro and succeed again, right here."

A few moments later, José and Marvin came walking over and greeted Marcos and Dani warmly. Spain had been wonderful and they were disappointed to have to return to New York so soon. However, it would be good to be back by the sea and out in the Hamptons again. It wasn't the worst place, after all, to spend the winter now that Marcos would be vacating their home on Christmas Day and heading back to the city. The music continued to play. There was dancing and chatting. Dani predominantly avoided Marcos. She didn't know what to say to him even with his apology. Deep down, she wanted to give it another try, as did he. How could she know that this time would be any different from the last? Suddenly, the notes of a xylophone filled the air as everyone was summoned to dinner. The various groups of people processed with their significant others into the adjacent dining room. All of the tables were beautifully decorated and had place cards demarcating where each party was to be seated.

In an ironic twist of fate, Fran had seated Dani and Marcos next to each other at her table. The table in its entirety consisted of Dani, Marcos, José, Marvin, and Monique. They were all a part of Fran's VIP head table this evening, over which she presided. The appetizers arrived within minutes of everyone being seated. Before anything could begin, Fran cleared her throat audibly. "Excuse me, everyone. Excuse me. I have something I'd like to say to all of you this evening."

Everyone gradually ceased their private conversations and turned to face Fran at the head of the table. "I know I've told some of you through the years that I am involved in various business interests in addition to the magazine, which you are all of course familiar with. One of those interests is that I am a licensed real estate broker and do a little work as an angel investor with new businesses that I truly believe in." This hardly seemed like typical dinner conversation. Everyone was confused and intrigued by the bizarre start that the dinner had gotten off to this evening with these odd statements from Fran.

They were all poised, incredibly curious, and eager to hear whatever she had to say. No one had any idea what Fran could be building up to. "Anyway, most of you know the Basington Farm and farm stand," continued Fran. Everyone nodded in agreement. That was the farm stand down the road from where Dani's bistro had been located. It was a popular spot for both tourists and locals. In the summer, they sold fresh fruits and vegetables. In the fall, there were hayrides, pumpkin and apple picking, festivals, and some of the most delicious cider served on Long Island's east end. Fran paused for a moment. She apparently had something important and significant to tell everyone.

"The family is moving to Florida after having been here in Westhampton Beach for generations. It was a difficult decision but in the end, the one that made the most sense for them."

There were suddenly hushed whispers throughout the room. This was huge news given how long that particular family had been a part of the community.

Dani whispered to Marcos, "I had no idea they were moving and selling."

"Me neither," replied Marcos. At that moment, it felt like the ice had suddenly been inadvertently broken between Dani and Marcos. *Maybe there was a chance to make things right again with Dani.*

Fran continued speaking. "I know we've all had a challenging year, especially Dani with what has just happened. I think all of our hearts go out to her and right before Christmas, no less."

Numerous eyes turned toward Dani along with the sympathetic countenances of various people in the room from the community who knew and loved her.

"The Basington family also had a lot of challenges, and that was in part what led them to sell their farm after all these years," said Fran.

Marvin spoke up. "I didn't think they would ever leave Westhampton Beach. They've been a part of this community forever. How did you find out that they're selling, Fran?"

Fran gathered her thoughts for a second. "As a broker and friend of the family, they came to me first when they decided. They didn't want to see the property put up on the multiple listing service or publicly advertised as being for sale. Most of us know how there are always developers and builders driving around out here looking for vacant land to put another house, building, or subdivision on. The family didn't want to be inundated with all of that. They also didn't want their land going to a developer. As a result, I agreed to take the property on as one of my own exclusive pocket listings."

"I told you it was Fran who really pulled the strings out here," whispered José to Marvin.

Fran continued. "I'd like to offer the sale of the property and the surrounding farmland to Dani first if she's interested. It would be more than enough land for her to rebuild the bistro and to have enough acreage for her dream of a working winery and tasting room in our community."

Dani was completely taken by surprise. "How did you know about my winery and tasting room dream?" asked Dani.

Fran grinned knowingly. "It's a small town, Dani. People talk and know more than you think about each other. So, does that sound like something you would be interested in?"

Dani didn't know what to say. This had been such a surprise coming from Fran. Dani stammered, "Fran, I would love that. I mean, that would be a dream come true for me. I don't know how much I'll get from the insurance yet to rebuild, much less operating at a loss for a few years while trying to build a winery. I don't see how financially . . ."

Fran interrupted. "Dani, as you now know, I'm also an angel investor. I don't invest in a lot of new businesses, but the ones that I do, I believe in wholeheartedly. I want you to know that I have a lot of belief in yours. I'm also willing to put up the necessary capital to get you up and running."

Tears started streaming down Dani's face. She couldn't believe Fran's incredible generosity toward her. "Fran, I would . . ." Dani couldn't even get the words out. "I would love that. Thank you."

Fran was smiling and lifted her glass. "You are most welcome. Now, that's quite enough with all the talk. Our food is going to get cold. Before we begin though, I'd like to propose a toast." Everyone at the table raised their glasses. "To Dani," said Fran in a loud and celebratory voice. "To Dani," cried out everyone at the table. With that, everyone eagerly dug into their appetizers and began chatting with one another while the orchestra played Christmas music.

Fran had revealed one of her secrets that now enabled Dani to fulfill a lifelong dream. Secrets at Christmas weren't limited to New York City or hidden rooftop gardens. There were powerful ones even out here, such as this surprise revealed by Fran.

The party went on until late into the night. José and Marvin had engaged in a show-stopping dance in the center of the ballroom that had everyone on their feet in wild applause. A professional opera singer from the area had come in and performed a wonderful rendition of "Oh Holy Night," and there was even a jazz musician who gave the crowd a smooth rendition of "Jingle Bells." After midnight, Marcos saw Dani standing by the window in the ballroom alone. He walked over.

She was looking out at the snow on Fran's vast front lawn. Dani looked radiant and was wearing a different but even more spectacular red dress than she had worn during their dinner together at the bistro. Marcos suddenly noticed that she was also wearing the sparkling silver snowflake necklace that he had given her on the day they went out on the boat.

"Hi, Dani," said Marcos nervously.

"Hi, Marcos," she replied, quietly turning around to face him.

"It looks like everything is going to work out after all. In no time, you'll have one of the most successful wineries out here on the east end. I guess I'll have to come out more frequently to visit now," said Marcos.

"You're leaving?" said Dani, surprised.

"I'm heading back to New York City tomorrow, Dani. There's nothing out here for me at this point. Of course, there's nothing there either now."

Dani looked piercingly at Marcos. "I don't think you should go. You know, I do need someone to be my head winemaker."

Marcos shook his head doubtfully. "Dani, I don't know the first thing about winemaking."

She stopped him. "You told me you wanted to be independent and not have to answer to a company ever again. You also said how much happier you felt out here compared to living in the city. You could have all of that if you stayed here. Isn't that what Christmas and the new year is all about, new beginnings and starting off on a path you haven't yet explored or taken, but always wanted to?"

It seemed as though she had forgiven him. Marcos smiled with a feeling of contentment that he hadn't felt in a long time.

Her green eyes sparkled as she gazed deep into Marcos' eyes.

"I suppose it is, Dani." Marcos gazed into her eyes. "It looks like everything is going to be okay now after all. You're going to be able to carry on the legacy of your grandparents. You'll also be the one in your family who finally realizes their lifelong dream of having a winery out here."

Dani seemed to be looking right into his soul and seeing the real Marcos, the one who had made such a deep impression upon her this holiday season. "That's very true. I sometimes doubted whether it would ever come to pass. In a way, as devastating as the bistro burning down was, it brought something even bigger and better into my life for the future."

"I think that's true looking at it that way," agreed Marcos.

Dani smiled. "And you won't have to answer to a paymaster any longer. I mean, you will, but it will be to someone who you care about."

"Thank you for that," replied Marcos.

Dani continued. "You won't be a number now or considered replaceable by an impersonal boss or company. We will all need you and want you here. Another bonus is you won't have to return to New York City any longer."

"Now, that's another great Christmas gift that you just gave me, Dani," said Marcos, laughing.

Dani smiled. "You may have now found the happy medium that you've been looking to find in your life for so long."

"I don't understand," interrupted Marcos.

Dani added, "What I mean is you've found a new place and a home somewhere between what New York City and Kentucky have both been and meant to you for all these years. You're going to have the best aspects of both those worlds in your life now going forward."

Marcos looked out at the snow on the lawn thinking. "You're right, Dani. I think this is the place I've been looking for all along."

Dani smiled, "I think it might be too, Marcos."

He looked deep into her eyes. "Most importantly, I think I've finally found the person that my heart has been seeking for all these years as well."

Marcos looked at the snowflake necklace that she was wearing that he had given her. "Someone once told me that 'a snowflake never falls in the wrong place,'" he said to Dani in a soft voice.

"It never does, Marcos. It never does."

With that, they kissed next to the red and green lights of Fran's ballroom Christmas tree.

"Merry Christmas, Dani," said Marcos.

"Merry Christmas, Marcos," she replied.

Neither one of them realized that both Marvin and José were now standing nearby. Marvin, after seeing what was going on, called out boisterously, "Now that's what I call winning at life, kids!"

Thank you so much for reading *A Westhampton Beach Christmas*. If you've enjoyed the book, we would be grateful if you would post a review on the bookseller's website. Just a few words is all it takes! ♥

Discussion Questions

Why are the holidays a unique time of year on Long Island's East End? Why are they unique in your community?

How does New York City and the community of Westhampton Beach influence Dani and Marcos? Have you ever visited or moved to a place that changed or influenced you?

How does the holiday season influence Dani's personal life and work at the bistro? How does it influence your own personal and work life?

Dani's relationship with Mark was a previously unexplored path that she finally decided to consider entertaining over the holiday season. What unexplored paths have you been curious about pursuing in your own life?

What is the family legacy that Dani wants to expand upon and why? Have you ever wanted to expand upon a personal or family-related goal in your own life?

What is the change that Marcos needs to make in his own life and why does he put it off? Are there any changes you need to make but have delayed acting upon?

What gifts do Dani and Marcos give to each other and why? Have you ever received a gift that had some sort of deeper meaning or personal significance?

How do people respond to Dani's goal of expanding into winemaking? Have you ever been known for one thing, but then moved into being recognized for something else? How have people responded when you've gone after a new and different life goal?

Why does Marcos go against his own feelings and beliefs in talking to Dani at Rogers Beach? Have you ever been in a similar situation?

How do Marvin and José influence and complement each other? Have you ever experienced a situation where one person complements another either in your own life or with someone who you know?

How does the theme of "secrets" influence the story?

Research Sources

Andrews, E. "Why Do We Kiss Under the Mistletoe?" *History*,
    https://www.history.com/news/why-do-we-kiss-under-the-mistletoe
"A Quote by Zen and the Art of Happiness." *Goodreads*,
    https://www.goodreads.com/quotes/574102-no-snowflake-ever-falls-
    in-the-wrong-place.
Britannica, T. Editors of Encyclopaedia. "mistletoe." *Encyclopedia
    Britannica*, https://www.britannica.com/plant/mistletoe.
Dr. Vinny. "How many bottles of wine are made from 1 acre of vineyard?"
    Wine Spectator. Online: https://www.winespectator.com/articles/how-
    many-bottles-of-wine-are-made-from-1-acre-of-vineyard-5350.
McEvoy, M. "Organic 101: Organic Wine." *US Department of Agriculture
    Blog*,
    https://www.usda.gov/media/blog/2013/01/08/organic-101-organic-
    wine.
McIntyre, M. "The 20 Most Expensive Wines In the World." *Wealthy
    Gorilla, Online:*
    https://wealthygorilla.com/most-expensive-wines/
Wikipedia contributors. "Westhampton Beach, New York.." *Wikipedia,
    The Free Enyclopedia*,
    https://en.wikipedia.org/wiki/Westhampton_Beach,_New_York.
Wikipedia contributors. "United States Post Office (Westhampton Beach,
    New York)." *Wikipedia, The Free Encyclopedia*,
    https://en.wikipedia.org/wiki/United_States_Post_Office_(Westhampt
    on_Beach,_New_York).